William G. Thorpe

The Still Life of the Middle Temple

with some of its table talk

William G. Thorpe

The Still Life of the Middle Temple
with some of its table talk

ISBN/EAN: 9783337332402

Printed in Europe, USA, Canada, Australia, Japan

Cover: Foto ©Andreas Hilbeck / pixelio.de

More available books at **www.hansebooks.com**

THE STILL LIFE

OF

THE MIDDLE TEMPLE

WITH SOME OF ITS

TABLE TALK

PRECEDED BY FIFTY YEARS' REMINISCENCES

BY

W. G. THORPE, F.S.A.

A BARRISTER OF THE SOCIETY

"Forsan et hæc olim meminisse juvabit"

LONDON

RICHARD BENTLEY AND SON

Publishers in Ordinary to Her Majesty the Queen

1892

TO

THE OLD MEMBERS OF OUR MESS

SCATTERED ALL THE WORLD OVER,

FROM THE GOLDEN GATE TO THE BAY OF ISLANDS,

IN COMPLIANCE WITH REQUESTS

MANY TIMES REPEATED,

AND IN MEMORY OF BYGONE GOOD-FELLOWSHIP

WITHOUT ALLOY.

FOREWORD.

DURING a long membership of the Middle Temple, I have been repeatedly asked to write ' A Book on the Inn' from its social point of view, a task apparently never before attempted. I had just this one qualification, that entering after many years passed in other pursuits, I at once grasped a certain continuity of Middle Temple life with old Cambridge days, and was able to realize to some extent college times over again. A regular attendant at hall and church, many points therefore presented themselves to me as having a special interconnection and mutual self-dependence, which I have attempted to bring out in the following pages.

But all the good stories heard in a long and active life could not be brought under legal headings, and hence the framework of a prefixed autobiography suggested itself for their introduction. If their perusal gives the reader as much pleasure as their compilation has afforded to me, my labour will not have been spent in vain.

W. G. THORPE.

GLOUCESTER HOUSE,
  LARK HALL RISE, S.W.
   March 26, 1892.

CONTENTS

CHAPTER I.

EARLY LIFE AND SCHOOL DAYS.

CHAPTER II.

COLLEGE DAYS.

CHAPTER III.

CEYLON.

CHAPTER IV.

INDIA.

CHAPTER V.

MERCHANT LIFE IN LONDON.

CHAPTER VI.

SOCIAL LIFE.

CHAPTER VII.

SOCIAL REMINISCENCES.

CHAPTER THE LAST.

THE MIDDLE TEMPLE, WITH ITS TABLE-TALK.

THE STILL LIFE OF THE MIDDLE TEMPLE

CHAPTER I.

EARLY LIFE AND SCHOOL DAYS.

Is a Good Memory an Advantage?—Englishmen's Shyness at telling Ages and Names—Puns upon Names—Parentage—Sir William Thorpe—His Son, the Lollard—The Minister and his Button—The Veteran of Badajoz and St. Sebastian—Theatres Fifty Years ago—City Gourmands—Prince Metternich—The Queen's Remembrancer—Brompton Schoolfellows : Kingsley, the Gunters—Sheffield Schoolfellows—The 'D——d Cheap' Pension—Veteran of the Moscow Retreat—The Repulse of the Old Guard—Wanstead Tutor's—De Kantzow—Fasken at Sobraon—A Judge's Canine Tooth Mark.

ONE of our best, and shortest, Temple Church preachers lately maintained that a really good memory is a really great nuisance to its owner, as perpetually recalling his mishaps and *miss*-chances in this terrible muddle which we call Life. But the preacher, like the rest of us, went too much on his own grievances. Custodian of a great church, for centuries the prey of the spoiler, and hardly less so now, though the process is called 'restoration,' every sympathy for art and antiquity has been ruthlessly tortured on Lord Grimthorpe's gridiron, so as to qualify him for a second 'Saint' Lawrence. He has had no interval even, in which to call to mind that there is an end to all things, even to Upper Wimpole Street, as Theodore Hook said on his deathbed. Had he been able thus to comfort himself, he would have realized that with Time the Healer comes also mental dialysis. The sweets come to the top, the bitters sink to the bottom; and a man may do much for himself in both regards. 'Take short views of life,' and 'keep the jammy side up,' are pearls from the practical philosophy of Mr. James Payn, and in the wake of that genial man of the world and cheery *raconteur— magno intervallo*, indeed—I shall shape my own course.

Reticence as to his age is one of the Englishman's most awkward shynesses. It is congenital to the soil: for a Frenchman boldly announces it; with a Chinaman it opens the conversation in place of the weather; and our American cousins do the same. In a railway or tramcar the occupants still are loudly informed, 'My name is Colonel Hiram B. Tunks. I kim from Martha's Vineyard. I am sixty-five years of age, and I cyant help it.' And in Scotland similar frankness has brought its author to grief. When a brother rhymester wearied the fine ear of Bobby Burns by attempting a jingle on his own birth-year, 1739, the bibulous poet made it up for him thus :

> 'In se'enteen hunder thretty-nine
> The De'il gat stuff to mak' a swine,
> 　And pat it in a corner ;
> But after that he changed his plan,
> And made it something like a man,
> 　And ca'd it Davie Horner '—

his victim's appellation.

There are few names to which a jingle or a joke cannot be fitted—witness, Twining, banker and tea-dealer :

> 'Twining would be whining
> Were't not for his tea ;'

and the ex-Lord Mayor, Sir John Key, where the inherent rhyme to 'donkey' verjuiced the baronetcy.

My own name, however, does not lie open to

this; suffice it to say that I was born the last male of an old family hardly above yeoman rank, but domiciled for some five hundred years at a small village on the borders of Derbyshire and Yorkshire, called Norton Lees. The place possesses a fine old half-timbered house, formerly occupied by the family of Blythe, who have a mortuary-chapel all to themselves in Norton parish church, and who suffered heavily for Charles I. I have still the old oak chair—inscribed 'I. B. 1660'; it came to us from him in 1677—which old John Blythe had made to commemorate the Restoration, and in which the iniquities of my kinsman, Francis Thorpe, member of the High Court of Justice, must often have been conned over, with just a little regret that he so narrowly escaped exclusion from the General Indemnity of 1660. My people had fallen from their once high estate, and had migrated from Gleadless, four miles off, upon the disgrace of Sir William Thorpe, Lord Chief Justice in 1350, and the sentence of death, afterwards commuted for a fine, which beggared him.

Lord Campbell is pleased to be very severe upon my ancestor, though he admits that judges

were paid in those days by fees from suitors;
that the Chief Justiciar in 1289, De Hengham,
and all his colleagues but two, had been fined
enormously on a similar charge; and that Shares-
hall, Sir William's successor, had, in 1349, when
a puisne judge, been confined in Caerphilly
Castle for the same thing. But while these
charges might arise from things getting mixed
in those days, an itching palm has ruined in later
times many greater names. Lord Campbell overlooked the illustrious Bacon—'wisest, brightest,
meanest of mankind'; and Lord Macclesfield, im-
peached and convicted in 1725.

Some of the old judges were even reinstated,
like De Hengham, who absolutely died in his
old high office in 1308, from which he had
been dismissed nine years before; and if the
Sir William de Thorpe, Commissioner to open
Parliament, and to assay the French King's
ransom money of 100,000 crowns in 1361, be
not my ancestor, there must have been two men
bearing the same unusual name, of what we should
call Cabinet rank, within ten years of each other,
which is hardly likely. They could not be father
and son, as we shall see below. However, Sir

William became an ancestor and a tradition ; and we were all Williams after him, just as Lord Fitzwilliam's sons are all Williams, all his daughters Maries—since the Revolution.

Our forefather's eldest son, William, was a priest, but an active follower of Wickliffe ; his accusation before Archbishop Arundel, in 1407, is in the State Trials, and also in Foxe's 'Martyrs,' though neither mention his end, which is contained in his own little book, of which I have a copy, the only other existing being in the Grenville Library, British Museum, and bearing Mr. Grenville's note, 'This most rare little book.' From the 'will of William Thorpe,' appended hereto, it seems that he died a prisoner forty years later in Saltwood Castle, that seat of the Archbishop to which the murderers of Becket retired when they had done the deed.

The book itself was a trumpet-call to the Lollards, with its epigraph, 'Be ye no more ashamed to hear it, than ye are and be to do' it.' My copy was printed by the martyr Tyndale, A.D. 1530, and brought over by the martyr Bayfield, who was burned red-handed for bringing it, it being proscribed by an Order in Council, to which its great rarity is doubtless due.

One of us, Godfrey Thorpe (evidently an university man, as he has written Greek in the family Bible), remembered the Highlanders passing south to Derby in the 'Forty-five.   He told the story to an uncle, who told me in 1833, so that three lives cover nearly 150 years.

Our parish was a quiet one, its only celebrity being Sir Francis Chantrey,* who was born and buried in it.   Tradition says that one of the principal residents, Mr. Holy, was given to great hospitality to the Wesleyan ministers, and as one of them was walking through Sheffield after one of his dinners, a button flew off his waistcoat, and knocked down a little boy.

One of our nearest neighbours was a clergyman, who fancied his own knowledge of horse-flesh, and thought much of a butcher's cob which brought out the meat-supply from Sheffield.   A purchase was arranged with the owner for a reasonable price, and the parson rode his new mount to his daily duty as master in the Grammar School ; but the animal had lost all its fire, neither

* Born 1781 ; died 1841.

whip nor spur would get it out of a shuffle, while jibbing and buck-jumping brought about one or two spills.   The butcher was appealed to, and he in turn called his boy and asked him what it all meant.

'He's all right, sir, if you'll only carry the basket.'

A journey in 1837 through Devon and Cornwall brought me into the company of an old Peninsular veteran, who told me of the assault of Badajoz: how he had seen the sword-blades fixed in the breach, the fire-balls thrown to light the French as they drove their muskets into the helpless crowd unable to either advance or retreat, and remembered the enemy's taunt, 'Why don't you come into Badajoz?'   And he told me also of the final assault of St. Sebastian—fifty guns playing over our soldiers' heads for a terrible half-hour, during which the Light Division were coolly making a lodgement on the breach itself.

Of theatrical reminiscences I have but few— Braham singing the 'Bay of Biscay,' Macready as Shylock, sharpening the knife, till, fairly frightened, I whispered to my father, 'Will they let him do it?' and, lastly, a pretty and engaging

Columbine in the Covent Garden pantomime of 'Peeping Tom,' Miss Fairbrother, afterwards to become Mrs. Fitz-George.

My first public school was the Brompton Grammar School, then under Dr. Mortimer, afterwards of the City of London School, a man of amusing parsimony, necessitated, perhaps, by his large family. The story that he chose his wife's and daughters' dresses was probably true ; that he sat by while they were being cut out to prevent cabbaging, is probably an ingenious addition.

In 1841 an uncle by marriage was a Sheriff of London, and I thus attended the laying of the first stone of the Royal Exchange by the Queen. Those were the days of City gormandizing, and some good stories in this line were attributed to the late Alderman Humphrey. He had consumed seven plates of turtle at Birch's, costing five shillings each, and on leaving was accosted by a poor woman. 'Please, sir, I'm so hungry.' Hungry ! —the word fetched him. 'Hungry, my good woman ! there's tuppence for you ; I wish to goodness I was !'

At a great City feed he was placed next to Prince Metternich, who did not do it justice. The

Alderman noticed this, and gave the diplomatist a nudge, pointing with his knife, 'Have some o' that.' The Prince smilingly declined, only to be again similarly attacked over the turtle - fins. Then the Prince demurred verbally, 'I can't eat any more.' This was too much; the Alderman was aghast, and turned to his neighbour. 'What! can't eat no more! Humbug! *try a cold chair.*'

The Alderman was credited with the now lost art of eating two dinners, one on the top of the other; the process, which was of classic origin, must be withheld. But the science of gluttony remained in full force till within twenty years, if, indeed, it has died out even now.

I once dined at the Haberdashers', next to a Queen's Remembrancer, who consumed several plates of turtle. He pleasantly recommended me to do justice to the dinner, and on my advancing Prince Metternich's reason, went on, 'Ah, you should train for these things; eat nothing the day before and the day after.' Justice was justified of her children, for he worked steadily through the *menu*, from Pilgrim Fathers to Benjamin Harrison, as a Yankee would say.

City stories of this kind are legion; they had

rarely a joke in them, such as when Lord Mayor Cowan, at the end of his term of office, removed across the street to his wax‑chandler's shop opposite. Then they put on the Mansion House door—'Gone back over the way.'

My schoolfellows at Brompton were not conspicuous in after‑life. The two Kingsleys, Charles and Henry, were there—the former the same shy, awkward creature he was in after-years, with the effort to throw it off always visible—and two Gunters, of bride-cake fame, whose father's heavy land investments close by were to raise his children to affluence—not to be enjoyed, however, without many a rub. Robert, the eldest, was to be the victim of one of the savagest sarcasms ever made.

When hunting, one day, he reined up near the Master, Lord Feversham, and remarked, 'My horse is very warm.'

'Ice him, Gunter ; ice him.'

My subsequent school life at Sheffield Collegiate School was equally uneventful.

The head-master was Dr. Jacob, afterwards, by the clever canvassing of his friend, Dr. Mortimer, to become head-master of Christ's Hospital.

After a time he retired upon a pension, and when it was told the Royal President, ' Dr. Jacob has retired, sir, on a pension of £500 a year,' H.R.H. replied, ' And d——d cheap, too !' The Field-Marshal may, however, be in error here, as the Doctor is over eighty, and pretty lively at that.

And yet at Sheffield I met two men whose experiences were worth listening to. One was the French master, M. Plisson, a tall, gray, soldierly-looking man, very quiet and reserved. At his own house he would unbend, and tell us the story of his sufferings in the Moscow retreat ; and how, on waking in the morning, the circle round the embers would comprise three or four corpses frozen stiff. This, of course, was from bad management, as ˙ Kennan, in his delightful work on Siberia, records cases of bivouacs at $-40°$ C. But the conditions of the two bivouacs were not identical. Kennan's party were warmly clothed, well fed, and had with them Cossacks, ˙ who kept the fire going.

Mr. Kennan was surveying for a telegraph-cable across Behring's Straits, with land continuations. His party had no fear their bread would fail, or that they might come to see DEATH, while the Frenchmen, with little food and less fuel, knew that behind them was the avenger, the Russian peasant, whom they had cruelly plundered in every way on the outward march, as was the wont of the Grande Armée, whose own turn had now come. If the Moujik refrained, or when he did refrain, from killing his prisoner and stripping his corpse, he unfailingly stripped the living body naked, clothing his own lean form with the furs and woollens with which the man from the sunny South had sought to protect himself from the bitter cold. The victims soon succumbed, of course, to the actual freezing ; but they suffered previously by anticipation. One battalion so stripped to the buff, plunged, naked as they were, into a quarry to huddle together for warmth, and when the winter was over the spring flowers grew up through a mass of disarticulated skeletons.

My friend lived to see Napoleonism again in France. He had worked and striven for it under the Bourbon restoration, and had had to cross the Channel in an open boat to escape the fate of a conspirator against the powers that were.

The other remarkable man I met at Sheffield

was Samuel Wilson, bombardier in the Royal Artillery, who told in his rough way how, at Waterloo, he had taken the wheel off his gun into the square, till the French cavalry had retired, then hurried back to his piece and sent a ' blessing ' after them ; how they brought ropes and tried to carry off the guns, until the fire of the square shot down the horses ; how this went on for hours, until the guns of some eight or ten batteries were all drawn up in a kind of wedge facing inwards, ' when they seed the French bear-skins a-coming, and then they did nothing but fire grape into 'em ; and it was nothing else but sponge, load, ram, fire. It was a great sight ; they nivver took their muskets from their shoulders, but marched straight on when we was a-firing into 'em forty yards off. Whole ranks of 'em was swept away, but they still went on ; just as they passed me, I seed a officer a-leading 'em, his coat all ablaze with goold ; he was a tall man, bareheaded ; he was like a madman. We was the second battery as they passed, and they still went onnards, we a-mowing 'em down all the time ; they only fired once, and that in a weak kind o' way, when all of a sudden they broke and rolled past us, and we had to cease fire, 'cause our own guards was a-driving 'em back.'

The old man had seen the charge of the Imperial Guard, and Ney at their head vainly seeking the death which was to come to him from the muskets of his own countrymen in a few weeks' time.

My uncle's sheriffship was held at a house of Lord Ingestre's, Brompton Park, now part of the South Kensington Museum. The expense of it, some £3,000, and the failure of speculations, made him draw heavily on my father's purse, and with a view to qualify for an Indian civil appointment (eventually diverted to his own son), I was sent to a tutor's at Wanstead, preparatory for Haileybury. At that time there was living there Lord Mornington, the once celebrated Long Tilney Wellesley Long Pole, whose extravagance had ruined the large estate he got with his wife, and broken his wife's heart. The stories about him are not to edification ; he was at that time a miserable gouty wreck.

During my two years at Wanstead I had but few distinguished associates. One of them, De Kantzow, however, headed some really dashing raids in the Mutiny, but did not thereby gain promotion in a strictly seniority army, so left the service in disgust, having perhaps in him the making of another Lord Clive, equally deficient in self-control where he thought himself neglected.

Of another, Fasken, however, a gallant story was to be told. It was at Sobraon, where our men were set to storm regularly built ramparts, on which guns were mounted. His regiment, a native one, was repeatedly repulsed; the officers fell in leading their men, and at last Fasken, second of the lieutenants, was in command. He took the colours, and led them on once more, and as he passed the General, Sir Walter Raleigh Gilbert, the Cornishman shouted: 'Well done, Fasken! what would your father give to see you?' The regiment shouted in return, screwed their bayonets into the face of the work, mounted on them, carried their young leader over the parapet, and when he came to himself he was lying on a heap of loose powder, surrounded by . dead Sikhs, and with the colours still in his hand.

My solitary memorial of Wanstead is a scar on the lower joint of a right-hand finger, left there by the canine tooth of Mr. Justice Holloway, formerly of the Madras High Court,* as the result of a difference of opinion, settled in the way usual half a century back. The judge was bigger and stronger than I, and would have thrashed me if he could have seen to do it ; but his daylights had been darkened, so the battle was drawn, resulting, as such turn-ups often did, in friendship and mutual esteem.

* His name is a household word in Madras to this day.

CHAPTER II.

COLLEGE DAYS.

Entered of St. John's College, Cambridge—Dr. Hymers—Acted as his own Solicitor—Revenge of Themis—Pontius Pilate—The Iniquity in the Chapel—'What's Trumps?'—Adams, the Shy Astronomer—'Billy Whistle'—Porson, 'O Lor!'—The Senior Dean and the Coal-sack—Practical Jokes : The Dirty Sizar and his Clean Collar—Jack Clarke and the Proctor : The Chase, the Collision with the Bursar, the Swim through the Mill pond, the Break into Trinity, the Plunge into the Cam, the Discovery and Expulsion—Prime Minister's College—Lord Palmerston : The Art of putting Things—Leave St. John's—Migration to Queen's—My Rooms in Queen's—Dr. King, the President : His Saddle for crossing Glass-topped Walls—The Charterhouse Man and the Bargee's Tears—The Willesden Coal-siding and the Barbary Ape—Shelford and the Vicarage Cat—Exeter College, Oxford—The Alarming Change in the Bishop's Son— The Young Lady and the Rector—Capture of the Whole University—The Dinner—The Catastrophe—The World, the Flesh, and the Devil—The Isle of Man—Escape from a Rape *by* the Sabines—Keble, of the 'Christian Year,' and his Wife —The Packed Cards—William IV. and 'K.H.'-ing—The O'Haras and their Ark in the Deluge—Setting the Watch in Paris for the First Time in 1805—The German Occupation of Paris in 1871—Laurel-branches from the Tuileries Garden— The Lonely Château—The Revenge for Jena—The Capture of Orleans—The German Head-waiter and his Master.

No Indian civil appointment being procurable, I was entered of St. John's College, Cambridge.

My tutor was Dr. John Hymers, a typical Johnian Don in every way. Son of a butcher at Beverley, he came up from the school there to John's as a sizar. A man of splendid physical strength, but by no means a brilliant man, he took a high degree by simple sheer plodding, and followed the stereotyped course until the big college living of Brandesburton fell in. When Hymers accepted it, he was naturally not a success parochially, and his most welcome ministrations were gifts of tea and sugar to the old women. The population being seven hundred, the income £1,000, and Hymers unmarried, he saved largely, and invested his savings in land, so that he died worth between £100,000 and £200,000. He practised however, one dangerous economy; he was his own conveyancer. He went, indeed, further, and made his own will, and there affronted Themis had him. For excluding his own relations, who had remained pretty much where he left them, he bequeathed the whole of his freehold land to the Corporation of Hull, to found a magnificent Hymers College, forgetting that the Mortmain Acts existed, and the will was therefore bad. Of course, the next of kin sought that aid which is always available when money is in question—the respectable solicitor — and after the needful amount of litigation, a compromise was approved by the court; the Hymers family were made wealthy for life, much against the will of the pious founder, and Hull got its college, though with clipped wings.

The assistant tutor was Dr. Spicer Wood. The person concerned is usually the last to hear anything about himself, but should he see these pages, he may hear for the first time that his college name was ' Pontius Pilate '—not, however, for any misdoing. He was one of the two morning service readers in chapel, and while Wood rattled it through quickly, his colleague droned along as slow as Wood was fast. The story went that, in the Fellows' or Combination Room, Wood had offered to give the other a start up to Pontius Pilate, and catch him up before the end of the Litany, chancing the length of the lessons and the pace of the scholar who read them.

John's Chapel was the old one, and had, at its south-east corner, Bishop Fisher's Chantry, fitted with benches, and occupied during service. Being round a kind of corner, and out of view of all but two or three dons, most of them purblind, it was resorted to for reading books and other diversion, and hence it was called the Iniquity. Great was the astonishment of a senior dean, when, in the hush while the reader was looking up the first lesson, there came from within the Iniquity, 'What's trumps?' He was a most amiable man, somewhat unkempt, and very short-sighted, whose plaintive lament, ' I am become like a pelican in the wilderness,' caused that name to be applied to him.

One of our Johnian lions was the astronomer Adams, styled in books co - discoverer with Leverrier of the planet Neptune. As a matter of fact, the honour belonged to Adams alone, but his paper announcing the discovery, which he left with the Astronomer Royal at Greenwich Observatory some nine months before Leverrier began his calculations, was shelved. Adams' excessive shyness prevented his making it known otherwise, and the nimble Frenchman stepped in level with him. Had he been wisely prudent like Mr. Norman Lockyer, and written off at once to the *Times* and the Royal Society, he

who deserved it would have borne the palm.
Adams' shyness was congenital and amusing.
He would lie by and dodge round corners to
avoid being 'capped,' and, of course, some mis-
chievous men lay by in the same spot for that
very purpose.   Of different metal was 'Billy
Whistle' Whewell, Master of Trinity, and Vice-
Chancellor, who much affected the Madingley
Road for his constitutional.   It was the road on
which Porson was walking with a friend, when
they came to the sign of the 'Swan.'   'Ecce
cygnum,' said the friend.   'O Lor'!' said Porson.
For the information of those rusty in their
humanities, it may be explained that 'cygn*um*' after
'ecce' is a shocking mistake.   'Olor' means the same
as 'cygnus,' viz., swan, and 'signum' means sign.
Whewell liked stopping Johnians on that highway, and requesting them to 'cap' him, sometimes
being told in return, 'You're not master of my
college, sir.'   Such, in fact, was the answer of one
Jack Clarke, on whom he took a terrible revenge,
as will be seen later on.

It is now nearly thirty years since I entered at
my old college a relation who had given his
friends much trouble, but was supposed to have

blown off his waste steam at sea. I took every possible precaution, even to finding him rooms opposite to those of a tutor of a different 'side,' hence, presumably, a greater check upon other men's pupils than on his own. The weak point, however, was, that the tutor aforesaid was always absent from Saturday till Monday, and a door was thus opened for the catastrophe. For the experiment was a disastrous failure, like Davie Gellatly's comment upon the reformation of a drunken laird by matrimony : ' O whilk vanities, he'll mend, Mr. Sanderson, he'll mend, like sour ale in simmer.' A private note from his tutor had apprised me that the college preferred his chambers to his company, but it took some cross-examination to find out the reason why. It came out that the Senior Dean was a great pedestrian, and liked taking duty some seven or eight miles off, going and returning at four miles an hour. On this fateful Sunday, on his return from Landbeach, he entered college by the new court, the centre building of which has a well staircase, down which staircase came a song with a chorus anything but suitable for Sunday, or, for the matter of that, any other day. The Dean captured a gyp (college servant, to wit).

'Go and see whose rooms that song comes from.'

'Mr. Bakingpear's rooms, sir; they're a-practising hymnses before they goes to Mr. Carus's prayer-meeting after chapel.'

'Tell Mr. B. to come to me.'

On his return—'It's all right, sir; they're just a-leaving off of their dewotions.'

'Now, Jackson, you're lying; I insist on knowing what Mr. Bakingpear did say.'

After much badgering the answer came.

'Well, sir, if you must have it, he said as how you warn't his Dean, and I was to give you the Duke of Wellington's answer to the gent which wanted him to buy the hinwisible shell: "Tell him to be d——d in civil French."'

'Go and tell Mr. Bakingpear to come to me directly.'

Here the rusticated one must take up his parable. 'Well, you see, I had to put some gown on, and they gave me a Caius one (bright blue in place of Johnian black), and when I got down he was main waxy; but I kidded and buttered him up a bit, and he was just winding up a jaw about Sunday afternoons, when, hang me! if they didn't send down a lot of coals on top of the pair of us, and some of 'em hit him, so I had to begin over again ; and just as he was cooling they sent down the sack and more coals in it, which broke his cap. After that, he broke out regular mad-like, went up to my rooms, broomed all the men out, had 'em seen out of college, and gated me till I had seen the Master, who told me to take my name off.'

One of our Johnians at that time was son of the Trinity cook, and the beer in his rooms was a thing to be remembered. Our tap at Queen's, though much vaunted, was as swipes in comparison.

We had our usual share of the stupid practical jokes of the day—screwing up doors, painting out names, and so forth. A plan was even discussed for improving Trinity Great Court by blowing up the fountain, and waking up 'Billy Whistle,' obnoxious to Johnians and everyone else. But a very harmless trick, really clever, and planned to suit the characters of both its victims, succeeded marvellously. One of its victims was the Junior

Dean, Dr. Griffin, a most amiable man, of whose personal kindness I, and many others, have a pleasant memory; but an apparent child in worldly ways, and about as unsuspicious of a joke.

The other was a scholar and sizar, parsimonious in clean linen to the extent of reading the lessons in chapel in a collar worthy of a coal-heaver. This state of things had to be put right, the primal difficulty being to get the Dean's missive delivered to the other party, such things being handed over by the marker when the men were dining in hall. That functionary was not to be got over; but he had a son who sometimes took his place, and a daughter who attended to his stationer's shop close by. There is courage of all kinds—a devoted heroic spirit volunteered to 'spoon' the damsel, a nice girl in her way; and it took a week or so of parading her about to get her to induce her innocent brother to deliver the note on paper 'sneaked' from the Dean's table. One Saturday the following note was handed to the victim :

'The Junior Dean presents his compliments to Mr. ——, and has remarked with pain that, when reading lessons in chapel, he does not quite act up to the college unwritten laws. As Mr. ——'s turn will commence again to-morrow, Mr. Griffin begs to enclose a clean collar, which can be returned next Saturday evening after chapel.'

The bait took, the collar was duly worn, and its darkening hue throughout the week recorded. Never were there so few fines for missing chapel ; the place was full of ordinarily noisy men, and the bets in the Iniquity, 'five to one he doesn't,' reached the wondering ears of Collison, the Senior Dean, the reverse of his colleague in every way except where a joke came in. On that last Saturday the Junior Dean's staircase was mobbed, his outer room filled ; but when 'dirty Jonathan' appeared the crowd made way, and there was a death-like hush as he entered the private room. It took some five minutes to convince the victim that there was some mistake, but when the Dean appeared, bowing him out, the screams of laughter told the story. Griffin looked terribly severe, and got out, ' Mr. Thorpe, I'm ashamed of you,' when the joke reached at last his nervous centre, and he had to join in the general guffaw.

Poor Jack Clarke! His exodus from the

university to enter a cavalry regiment, and die in the Crimea, was comical.

Peacefully smoking his pipe one May evening in Trumpington Street, but without academical costume, as required by university rules, he was addressed by a Proctor with his attendant bull-dogs :

'Member of the university, sir?'

'What's that to you?'

'Name and college, sir, please,' preparatory to Jack being had up and fined for being without cap and gown.

'You go to—Bath,' said Jack, and forthwith the two bull-dogs—men chosen for wind and always in training—moved forward. To borrow the line from Burnand's magnificent parody of 'Horatius':

> 'Jack made no answer, no not he,
> But he floored the bull-dog neatly
> As a man could wish to see,'

and then made for my rooms in Queen's, where the trail could easily be lost. He had knocked over the long-legged man, and the other had a bad start from falling over him, so Jack led the way down Silver Street, bull-dog after him, just in time to see him turn into Queen's Lane : two sharp turns, and he was safe. But just then, Peill, Bursar of Queen's, a heavy, dull man, was pacing forth to his evening service at St. Botolph's. Jack was six feet two, the Don short and podgy, and the crash was awful. When Clarke had pulled himself together, he found himself hit in the wind ; so, rather than surrender, he squattered through the muddy mill-pond. The bull-dog, as he said, 'warn't no duck,' and the course adopted was to send round to all the college gates the description of a tall, fair-haired man in muddy clothes. The clothes, however, were dried, and put in order at Grantchester. The next thing was how to get back into college without being spotted. If his bed was not slept in, the bedmaker would report it. It seems incredible that such a piece of Jack Sheppardism could be done ; but Clarke waited at the back of the colleges till midnight, scaled Trinity Royal Gate, got thence into the Master's garden, till stopped by a cunning *chevaux-de-frise*, which separated Trinity and John's, two neighbours who hated each other as cordially as similar bodies similarly situated invariably do—I am not alluding, of course, to the Middle and Inner Temples.

Nothing for it, then, but to plunge into the unsavoury Cam, and land on Johnian ground. Another gate had to be scaled to get into the third court, and all to no purpose, for the wet clothes told their own fatal story. Why had he not thrown them into the river? was the wonder. The bed-maker's report was made, and it was not only an offence against the college, but the university—contempt of Proctors, the damaging a bull-dog, was a crime not to be passed over, especially in a Johnian who had refused to 'cap' that very Vice-Chancellor. The summons came to appear before 'Billy Whistle.' Jack smoked two pipes, and returned expelled, sorry to leave us and the old place, as all Johnians are.

John's is the 'Prime Ministers' College,' and has produced five of them, from Queen Bess's Burleigh to Lord Palmerston; and when that worldly-wise man (can anyone believe it is only a quarter of a century since he was laid to rest in Westminster Abbey? and what would he say if he were to come back again, as to Mr. Gladstone, for instance?) opened the new Johnian Chapel, he could find no more appropriate subject than to tell his audience that he, like them, was a 'hog,' had worn 'pigskin,' and sported 'cracklin' (these all cant college names, the last as to the gown and its chevrons). Nay, more, he could tell them that within its walls he had first learned that all-powerful factor in the Science of Life, ' the art of putting things,' and advise them also to study it, as an element of the success which had been obtained by a man who, in all the histories of our land, stands first and foremost as a thoroughly English statesman.

But my time at John's was to end. Kindly Dons who knew me—Hymers, Dr. Griffin, and my private coach—had reckoned up my chances as no better than sixth Wrangler, so there would be no fellowship for me—an all-important matter. I must follow the example of another Johnian, and migrate to Queens', where it was thought I should carry off everything.

Queens', I may say, by no means approved of these interlopings ; and when I applied for admission there, Peill, the Bursar, not as yet damaged by the momentum of Jack Clarke, grimly asked for my 'bene discessit ; could I get it ?' This was the certificate of good character, but I did not know what it was, having kept out of all scrapes, and being, indeed, a reading-man. A savage sneer had to be carried back to those who had sent me; but my Johnian Dons quickly showed the angry Queens' man that there was no obstacle on that ground, and I migrated forthwith. My rooms were in the Fellows' building, approached from the cloisters by a winding stair near the wooden bridge, built without a nail in it, over the Cam. This seclusion led to Clarke's endeavour to reach it, for the only other resident in the cloisters was the President of the College, King, whose neat nursemaids and pretty children brightened the dull place as they passed through to the Wilderness, a charming pleasaunce across the river. King, a man of splendid talents and high degree, had been very wild in his salad days, and had not forgotten it. Thus, when a man was had up for breaking back into college over a glass-topped wall, sustaining severe injuries, the President rusticated him with the grim remark, 'And, moreover, sir, you must be an absolute downright fool into the bargain! When I used to get over that wall, I always had a saddle put away close by.'

My sitting-room looked across the Cam into

the Wilderness; the window seats were roomy, and much fancied by a Charterhouse man, who had been educated in slang by friendly exchanges with Smithfield drovers in the days of the old market. His delight was to chaff the bargees on a fine evening as they punted their coal-barges up stream beneath him. Of course, both their hands were occupied with the poles; to let go even for a moment would lose ground, or, rather, water; and comments about puppy pie and female relatives could not be physically replied to, so that strong men have lifted up their voices and cursed, and wept, too, at the punishment they could not retaliate; otherwise my windows would have taken in as much coal as that villa garden at Willesden Junction, which ran down to the siding where the coal-trains shunted; and whose owner kept a Barbary ape in a tub on a pole. That man would sometimes gather half a ton a day, while the B.A. was never hit once.

One incident in my Queens' life was a trip to Shelford in a dog-cart, which carried four men, two guns, some bottles, and two fox-terriers. Of course, the bottles were left behind on the return journey—twelve miles in the hour—their place being supplied by the vicarage cat, which, weakly answering to the call of ' Puss,' was caught up and set to fight with the terriers. Her end was the Master's garden at Christ's, where she had the company of many similarly captured tabbies.

April 10, 1848, was an anxious day at Cambridge. Reports at one time ran that the Chartists had forced the bridges, and that stern repression was being resorted to.

There was great rejoicing over the triumph of law and order, and the late Colonel Sibthorpe took advantage of it to remark to the late Fergus O'Connor :

' So you daren't do anything, after all !'

' My dear sir, we did not propose anything beyond a peaceful moral demonstration.'

' Just as well you didn't, or we'd have given you the d—dest hiding you ever had in your life.'

The solitary Chartist then in the House was a mild-mannered man in his way, and it was a pity when his sluggish liver led to the bonneting his next neighbour while the House was sitting, and his own remission to an asylum. Oddly enough, some years back there was another hon. member who periodically retired to a similar place for treatment when he perceived his fits of mental aberration were about to come on, and much anxiety was felt when, on a vital division, he had to be fetched out for a vote which was to decide the fate of a Ministry. However, the vote was recorded without a scene, though it was hardly part of the wisdom of the nation.

Colonel Sibthorpe was a very peculiar man, almost as much so as the late Sir William Stirling Maxwell, of Keir, who married Mrs. Norton, the novelist and poetess, when she had been bed-ridden for years. Of him, indeed, it was written :

> 'Stirling of Keir
> Is uncommonly queer ;
> Were he to be queerer,
> He'd be Stirling of Keirer.'

The Colonel had a quiet way of joking, and once told the House during a debate upon professional interests, and the way those concerned upheld them, an amusing story. Dining at the Thatched House (then a tavern, before the club was formed) he heard a tremendous row in the room overhead, as though Bedlam had broken loose. Summoning the waiter, he used some of those strong expressions which were used to that class at that period. It was then not thought conceivable that all the servants of a great Pall Mall Club—*not* the Reform, I beg to say, where I am writing this—could ever combine to sign a round-robin against one particular member for such a cause.   The waiter went, and in due course returned.

' Please, sir, it's the College of Physicianses, sir, and they're a-drinking toasts, sir ; that there last one as they made the big stamping about was " A low fever, with three times three !" '

Men spoke out plainly in the House in those days, though Lord Palmerston was once pulled up for speaking of a deputation from Bloomsbury which had waited on him on sanitary matters as ' local tinkers,' a phrase promptly corrected, as having been in reality ' local thinkers,' and misreported.

In those days all men at Oxford resided in college ; while at Cambridge, even then, many lived in private lodgings duly licensed, so that such an occurrence was impossible at Cambridge as that told me by a member of Exeter, Oxford, as having occurred there between thirty and forty years ago.

Exeter was at that time a decidedly fast college, and the son of a then well-known Bishop, who is now very much at the other swing of the pendulum, played some extraordinary pranks there. Hell Quad (named after the Empress Helena, be it understood) was the scene of curious incidents in the small hours after supper-parties. But one man was of exceptionally quiet habits, and when he sought the Rector to ask a favour, which he started by saying he knew could not be granted, he was heard with patience.

'The fact is, sir, my sister wants to see Oxford at its best, in Commemoration Week; there are but two of us, and this is my only chance of showing it her. None of the very few families I know here can take her in, being full of their own friends. Now, sir, all the men are down, and Tomlinson said she might have the next rooms to mine, and I could put her there if you would allow it. I've made it all straight with the servants.'

'IM-possible, my dear sir!'

'Of course, sir. I knew it must be so, though the poor girl will cry her heart out over it.'

Returned to his lodge, the Rector disburdened himself of the pain he had been obliged to give, and this woke up that awful real head of the college—his wife. 'Not come! why shouldn't she come? All the men are down, she can't hurt them! It will do the dingy old place good to see a nice girl about it. Tell him she is to come.'

The brother was apprised, and in due time the lady appeared, not in the least like her tall and swarthy brother, but petite, blonde, blue-eyed, having golden hair with a ripple in it. Such a vision had never before burst on Exeter—beautifully dressed, gloved, and booted, too, with the most charming innocence of being stared at, save when introduced to her brother's friends (practically at that moment the whole University, from the learned blacksmith Gaisford, Dean of Christ Church, downwards). Then a sunny smile and an absolutely intoxicating little laugh preceded the sweet low voice which came from the rosebud lips. All the Dons went simply daft. Exeter quads were mobbed on the chance of seeing her, and at last the Rectoress declared in strident tones: 'I must call on that girl.' The grim dragon went, saw, and was conquered by the girlish grace and gentle gratitude for the kindness shown to a motherless orphan, 'which could only have come from her,' and went in her enthusiasm the never-intended length of an invitation to dinner. This shook the college to its foundations. Feeds were as rarely given in that household as in the Paris Embassy in Lord Lyons' time. They were not used to such things in Exeter Lodge, and hence, in fact, came the catastrophe. The brother didn't like it; this excitement was turning the poor girl's brain, and he would take his sister away. But the Mistress had spoken, though herself frightened at the dimensions the dinner must assume, as well as at the fierce jealousies between those who must come, and those who wanted to come, but whom the room wouldn't hold. Of course her waiting staff had to be supplemented, and all the regular waiters being engaged in advance for Commemoration Week, a raw greenhorn was taken on to help. Let us hurry on to the end, not dwelling on the crowd of dull silent scholars who in the drawing-room surrounded the cynosure of all eyes—the only organ they had in use then. She had outdone herself, and the plum-coloured satin dress, with a row of pearls as white as the neck

·on which they lay, would have fetched St. Anthony himself, or his Irish equivalent, dear to Tommy Moore. At dinner she was placed next the Senior Proctor, and the innocent little *moue* thrown up in his face at the Latin grace all but made that functionary pop the question before the whole assembly there and then. Soup was served, the greenhorn was behind the lady, he tripped, and tipped the mock-turtle over the fair vision's shoulders, and down the plum-coloured dress, when the rosebuds opened and there issued from them : ' Bless your visual organs to Hades, you beggar ! what the sanguinary blazes did you do that for ?'

*   *   *   *   *

Nor among our Cambridge heads were there any like that spare little man, afterwards a Bishop, whose own grasping ways, his wife's corpulence, and his daughter's desire for attention, got for the trio the epithet, ' The World, the Flesh, and the Devil.'

My long vacation was spent at Douglas, Isle of Man, where Castle Mona was resorted to by many good Irish families with daughters possessed of true Hibernian beauty and wit—outwardly innocent as lambs, but deep as Masters in Chancery where matrimony was concerned. Although anything but a catch, they had basketed me, and likewise a wealthy young ironmaster, who was quite the reverse. We had accepted an invitation to accompany the party to their Irish home, and our baggage was to go with them to Kingstown. I have a kindly memory of the landlord, long since dead. He came to us, asked us if we knew what we were doing, told us that the same thing had happened with the same party the two previous years ; but that on arrival the marriages had collapsed, as the gentlemen's prospects were unsatisfactory. He offered to have our baggage separated, and shipped on board the steamer for Whitehaven, which sailed at the same hour as the Kingstown boat. This was neatly managed, and a pleasant run through the lake country was substituted for the Irish visit.

Among the visitors in the island was an amiable, silent, subdued, white-haired man—Keble, of the 'Christian Year'—a contrast in every way to the stout, loud, imperious wife, who bullied him and everybody else near her.

The whist-table was presided over by one

Colonel Higgins, K.H., whom I had the misfortune to dreadfully upset on two occasions. The first was a simple manœuvre by which the cards can be made to deal out in perfect suits. With the help of a friend I effected this, and the Colonel's fury nearly brought on a fit of apoplexy. How it would have been had he got all the trumps, I cannot say ; but of course one of the conspirators had dealt. The other was a well-known anecdote of his late Majesty, William IV. Beset in the courtyard of St. James's by an old crony of his wild days, the King at last managed to satisfy his importunity, and the applicant went away happy. His secretary had seen it all from the window, and congratulated the King. 'Ah! but you'll never guess how I managed it. What do you think I did, Taylor? Why, I K.H.'d him!

Among other residents was the late Mr. Charles King O'Hara, of Collooney, county Sligo, the head of that ancient family whose ancestor is said to have held Noah in such contempt that he wouldn't ship in the same boat with the dirty blaygard, but built an ark of his own. He had joined the Highlanders directly after Waterloo, and had set the watch in the Place de la Concorde on the first evening after the English had marched into Paris. On so young a soldier a great impression was made by the hostile attitude of the mob, and the savage fury which surged round the doubled sentries, none of whom, however, came in for anything worse than threats.

I am tempted to bring in here a later reminiscence or two of a subsequent occupation of Paris by the Germans, told me by a young Mayence wine-merchant, whom I met in London after 1870, and who threw open his coat to show me his miniature iron cross, one of four given to his regiment, a part of the two brigades which, spread over three-quarters of a mile, had held Ducrot at bay when, in the dark of a December morning, he had dashed across the loop of the Marne to join hands with the army of the Loire.

I duly saluted this trophy of valour as one does our own Victoria Cross, and he then told me that the original was safe at home with his branch of laurel plucked in the Tuileries Gardens when he had bivouacked there after the surrender. He described the entry into the Champs Élysées, the delay until the great gates of the Arc de l'Étoile were opened, the little undersized Uhlan officer who led the way beneath it, and the row of French troops three deep who kept back the howling mob; finally the night when, outside a similar living fence on the other side of the railings which divide the gardens from the Rue St. Honoré, the curses, cries and groans were incessant, and every minute they expected the call to arms to defend themselves.

Yet another story of a different kind of a lonely château some miles from Laon. The master and all able-bodied men were with the army—women and children almost its sole occupants. Just at midnight, without any summons, the door was blown in; a troop of Uhlans entered, and a scene of the wildest confusion ensued. When the officer called for more light, the furniture of all save the dining-room was bundled out and set on fire. When the rooms downstairs were thus gutted the officer called for the table to be spread and food brought; when this was being done in direst fear, he threw a water-bottle at the principal mirror, smashing it, and, seating himself, called for the 'Hausfrau.'

'Madame has retired for the night.'

'Tell her to get up and wait on me, or I'll have her fetched.'

The poor lady came. Meantime the cellar was opened, and she had to fill the officers' glasses; they did not, however, drink much wine, but took good care all in the cellar was smashed up. The upper rooms were scrupulously spared; and at break of day the visitors fell in. Then the unhappy lady was once more summoned, and had to be almost carried by her own servants. To her surprise the officer saluted her, and spoke in French gently:

'Madame, we have made wild work here, but nothing to what your husband's grandfather did at my grandfather's house after Jena. Everything was written down in this book' (showing one to which he had repeatedly referred). 'Every son, as soon as he could understand, was told of the outrage and the spoiler's name, and solemnly sworn to repay it in kind when the chance came. When it did come I went to General Blumenthal, and he permitted me my retaliations, confined to property only, sparing persons, though we were not spared. But you need fear no further molestation; our revenge is satisfied.'

Query—What does the young owner think about it, and has he made up a little bill of his own dilapidations for use if circumstances permit?

Another story, but the last in this digression. When Orleans was captured on October 11, 1870, a war contribution of £60,000 was imposed. The Mayor, proprietor of the chief hotel, declared that he had nothing like the quantity of wine which he was called upon to produce. On this, an Uhlan officer came up, smiling:

' Ah, bourgeois, you have double that quantity in your magazine—Rue so and so!'

' How on earth do you know that?'

' Bourgeois, have you forgotten Frantz, your head-waiter for two years?'

The Mayor gave in at once.

CHAPTER III.

Departure for Cambridge—The P. and O. Captain—The Purser
Brown—The Burning of the *Kent* Indiaman—The Middy and
the Captain : ' Pass you down, Sir ?'—The Doctor and his £200
Fee at Malta—The Life-Guardsman and the Cockroaches—
The Female Missionary at Deck-washing Time—The Missing
Gold Mohur—Danger in such Cases : The Engineer and the
Bathing-machine—The *Shannon* and *Chesapeake*—The Singalese
Millionaire and H.R.H.—The Devil Dance—The Missionary
and his Excommunicated Flock—The Buddhist Priests and
their C.M.S. Convert—Haeckel, the Jena Naturalist : his
Description of Ceylon ; his eating everything, including Snake
and Monkey—Snake Stories : my own Fright—The Rattler and
the Pony Express Man—Bear Story : a Near Squeak—An
Easter Holiday in the Cinnamon Garden—The Red - haired
Scotchman, his Olive-coloured Wife, and their Parti-coloured
Offspring—The Negombo Miracle-Play of the Passion—Colour
coming off the Angel's Cheeks—Embarkation for England—
The Ship strikes on the Bar—Instantaneous Cure of Sea-sick-
ness—Distress Signal : no Boat can come off—The Sailors'
Song at the Pumps—The Leap for Life and Escape to Land—
The Ship comes Ashore : no Hope of Rescue—A Fisherman
carries a Line—The Captain fights through the Surf to Land—
The other Six are drowned in our Sight.

A BREAKDOWN in health caused my withdrawal
from the University ; the time lost in recuperating
could not be regained, and I was sent to Ceylon,

where my father had property needing to be looked after.

Accordingly, I embarked in the P. and O. steamer from Southampton. The captain, an old stager with somewhat rough ways, was a master of his craft. It was said of him that, once when hove to in a fog in the Channel, he took soundings, looked at the bottom brought up by the lead, smelt it, tasted it, and then gave the correct course. Except in one instance, to be noted later on, he was perfectly proof against female fascinations. When, for instance, a lady asked him in her sweetest voice, 'Captain, what time does the sun set here in the Mediterranean?' he replied :

'When it sets, marm, I say, when it sets.'

Brown, the purser, had been a midshipman in the *Kent* Indiaman, burnt in the Bay of Biscay. He told us how the steward had dropped a light in the spirit-room ; how the fire spread while the gale raged, and the ship had to be kept before the wind to delay the flames coming aft ; how, for long, no sail appeared, and, when one did come, there was delay in getting her boats astern ; how his own post was to sit on the stern gallery, and lower the ladies into the boat below; how, at length, the men were allowed to follow, and all, save some poor creatures too terrified to move, though told that the magazine might explode at any moment, were safely passed down. Then there were but two left, and the middy saluted the captain:

'Pass you down, sir?'

'You plucky little beggar! if you hadn't done ten men's work, I'd chuck you into her. Over with you, sir!'

And then the gallant gentleman lowered himself down, the 558th life preserved by his courage and coolness. The ship blew up four hours after, and two hours after that an irrepressible baby, (always turning up when least expected), was born on the rescuing craft.

We had an odd adventure at Malta. The doctor, who naturally takes the lead among the passengers, was approached by two Maltese gentlemen, and went ashore with them. We missed his company, but he told us next day he had been better employed. For he had been blindfolded as soon as he entered a carriage, and taken to a large palace some way off; had performed a tedious but important operation on a young lady, been re-blindfolded, and returned to the stairs with his fee, £200, in gold. Of course, he was offered every opportunity of increasing his pile at cards, or by a little bet or two; but the medico was wary.

There was at that time no railway in Egypt. Track-boats drew us up the Mahmudieh canal to Atfeh, thence steamers took us on to Boulak, while omnibuses conveyed us across the desert from Cairo to Suez. The night in the boats was a trial, and we were roused from an uneasy sleep on benches and tables by the shrieks of a yellow-maned life-guardsman, whose perfumed hair had got filled with cockroaches.

The Red Sea, of a deep sapphire blue when we first saw it, was terribly hot in June. Ice was used up, and dysentery broke out, of which one of the passengers subsequently died. The thermometer was 102° in the shade, and, of course, the early morning, when the decks were being washed, was the most enjoyable part of the day—ladies, perforce, had to stay below till eight o'clock. One morning, however, before this time, the captain was commanding the ship in a flannel waistcoat and pair of pyjamas; many passengers in the same, or nothing whatever, were having the hose turned on them, when there entered to us, from below, a female missionary, ignorant of the eight o'clock law. The stampede was immediate; the captain bolted behind his own cabin, the door of which opened forwards, the rest of us got what shelter we could find; and an old General lifted up his voice, and cursed things in general, personal and impersonal, in a flow of language which was my first introduction to the Indian scientific vocabulary of execration. This lasted fully five minutes, during which the old gunner never once repeated himself, till a quartermaster got something on of some kind, and hustled the poor lady down the companion.

Our ship, the *Hindostan*, carried about to her dying day a memory of a grounding in the Red Sea, which she ungratefully accomplished, although her then commander, Moresby, had originally surveyed that disagreeable channel. She got to all appearance fast and fixed on a coral reef, and the captain, fairly losing his head, summoned all hands to prayers—a very proper thing, no doubt, but not inconsistent at the same time with human attempts to get her off.   The chief engineer, Peacock, who told me the story, applied to the captain for orders, but could get nothing out of him except :

'The ship is lost!   I give her up!'

'Beg pardon, sir.   Did you say you gave up command of the ship?'

'Oh yes.   We're all lost!'

'May I take charge, sir?'

'Anybody may.   She's lost!'

The big man (he was six feet diameter round the waist, and I once saw him get into a hot cylinder, and come out reduced in girth by a foot) went to the engine-hatch and called out at his loudest :

'Back her astarn!'

And with a lot of grinding and a twist which sagged her amidships for ever, the big steamer came off.   Peacock walked back to the captain, saluted, and quietly said :

'Ship's afloat, sir. Will you take the command?'

A very interesting volume might be written summarizing, so far as is known, the extent to which the fate of the world has turned upon

trifles. The subject is of almost Tupperian trite-
ness—nevertheless, its interest is absorbing. Had
not James II. been seized with violent bleeding
from the nose at Salisbury, and lost three precious
days, the afterwards Great Duke of Marlborough
might not have turned traitor, and thus ensured
the success of the Deliverer. Had not the first
Napoleon's stomach been upset by gorging on
stewed eels at dinner the previous evening, the
second day's fight at Leipsic might have gone
actually for him, as it all but did at one time.
Had Louis XVI. been able to resist the temptation of eating pied-de-porc à la St. Menéhould,
otherwise pig's trotters, when he was within some
half a dozen miles of safety and friendly troops,
the postmaster at Varennes would not have had
his suspicions roused by the well-known gluttony,
so as to arrest him ; and the French Revolution,
not over yet by a very long way, might have
taken at least a much milder form.

A similar chance saved our troops a great deal of
trouble at Tel-el-Kebir. It was mentioned to me
by Sir Charles Cookson, now Consul at Cairo,
when recuperating in England in November,
1882, and it may be worth relating here, as I have

never seen it noticed in any accounts of the battle. In the course of the night-march the two columns lost touch, and it was some time before the naval officer, in charge of the one on the right, piloting by the stars, found out his mistake. The men at once brought up their right shoulders, and regained the left column. In the loop thus left between them there lay an outpost of Arabi's men, pushed forward to that spot after sundown for picket purposes.

Arabi and his men, knowing this precaution had been taken, slept on both ears, as the French say ; but had the right column blundered upon this outpost in the dark the firing would have speedily aroused the main body, Tel - el - Kebir would not have been the hollow affair it really was, Sir Drury Lowe, with troopers almost too weary to sit their horses, would not have occupied Cairo that night, nor would the sandhill ramparts have been carried with the little bloodshed that happily occurred.

Strange things occur on these steamers. One day at dinner a passenger exhibited one of the diamond-shaped gold mohurs, called, I think,

Rampores, of great antiquity and beauty. It passed from hand to hand, but ultimately was not to be found. Be it remembered that this occurred after dinner, and that wine was then included in the fare. Forthwith every man volunteered to be searched, the captain leading the way, till at last one cool passenger declined the ordeal. The excitement culminated : he was the thief, he was to be knocked down and forcibly searched, after which the captain proposed to put him in irons, evoking at this point a word of caution from its object. What would have come of it all cannot be predicted, when there was a faint shriek, and the cause of all the rumpus dropped out of some frilling on a lady's wrist.

There was a sudden change, and everybody looked mighty foolish, until one passenger, who had done his best to moderate matters, said to the accused :

'I suppose the fact is, you've got another of them ?'

'Just so,' was the reply.

Prudence where money is lying about is very necessary, and a friend of mine, a civil engineer of eminence, is an instance of this. He was at the seaside, and wished for a bath before his train left.   On reaching the beach the last machine was putting off, and my friend dropped a mono-syllable heard by the inmate.

'If you don't mind sharing with me I'll have it put back for you.'

My friend got in, had his dip, and was nearly dressed again when the prior occupant returned, and on reaching shore he thanked him, and was going to the station, when there came a hail from the machine.

'I say, where's my purse with £8 in it?'

Rather a stunning question, but the listener, who had engineered a railway so curved that the guard can light his pipe at the engine fire as it passes him, from La Guayra to Caraccas, was not the man to be resourceless.

'If what you say be true, all I hold dear in life is in peril.   I wanted much to go to town, but now you and I don't part till we get to the station, and one of us stops there.'

By this time the accuser was on shore, and said:

'Well, if my purse was not in my pocket I must have left it in the hotel lobby in my overcoat.'

And there, sure enough, open to any thief,

the purse was found in the overcoat. And the man really wanted to apologize!

During a year's stay in Colombo I met some curious people, among them the captain of a Yankee ice - ship, for it was in ships that necessary of life got there in 1851. He was a grizzled man. and slow of speech, and it took some time to tell the following :

'It's nigh forty yeer agone, but I shall nivver forget that there arternoon, when I and a lot more as had come round from Salem went up to Boston Heads, and looked down into the roads where the big frigate was a-lying all in a bustle. They were running the guns out and in to make themselves spry with them, and there seemed no end of the men as was shipping aboard of her. She was a-flying our stars and stripes everywheer, and somewheer about noon she dropped down with the tide between the heads, and fired a gun and made for wheer that snake o' yourn was hev to. She was fit tew, and got your tyrannical old bunten a-flying all over her. We watched 'em go out to sea. and tack backards and forrards to get the weather, and about five o'clock our ship fired the fust gun, but she didn't seem cleverly handled like, and your varmint luffed up and raked her fore and aft, and then they closed, or your Britisher fell aboord of her. There was a great smoak, and when it cleared, darn me if it warn't your bunten as was a top, and not ourn. It didn't seem like ten minutes. We stopped there till we seed our noble frigate make sail for the norard a company o' yourn. It war hard. We boys sat down and cried, and Boston folk were mad like, 'cause they had got a dinner ready for 'em when they kim back, and a place for your Britisher capen at the top of it.'

The old man had seen the fight between the *Shannon* and the *Chesapcake*.

I resided in Colombo with a merchant who occupied a large house on the Galle Road, not far from the great banyan-tree, and backing on to an expanse of yellow sand called the Cinnamon Gardens. Few other trees would grow there, and it was practically a wilderness.

The house was afterwards occupied by a local millionaire, lately deceased, named De Souza, who sumptuously entertained the Duke of Edinburgh on his visit.

In 1851 Colombo was scourged with smallpox and cholera. As in face of these visitations natives in very panic return to their old gods, a devil dance was arranged. These celebrations, however, were prohibited in the town by reason of the objectionable form of Phallic worship with which they wound up ; but they were not interfered with when held a long way off, so one night at dinner a deputation came and asked to be allowed to hold the performance. My host was a man of liberal ideas, and on the understanding that the fun was not to come near the house, consent was given, and an invitation to be present was accepted by the men of the party. Accordingly, after dinner, duly escorted by torches— which every native carries at night for fear of treading on a snake in the path—we reached a spacious booth decorated with the huge heart-shaped banana bloom, the magnificent peacock flower, and the *Gloriosa superba* intermixed with the gold mohur, the sweet boodhoo-flower, and others which form the graceful offerings laid upon the tables which in the temples stand in front of the triune Buddha—past, present, and to come. Buddhism by the Treaty of Kandy is an established

Church, and a guard of soldiers protects the sacred tooth and its silver gilt coverings in the Kandy temple built for its custody.

Some relics were exposed for admiration, and the hierophant, with bells at his elbows and knees, danced solemnly in front of them, offering incense. Our chairs and tables were placed in a kind of chancel from which we could look at the long rows of silent, kneeling, white-clad worshippers, not in the least shocked by our cheroots and the modest brandy-and-soda which accompanied them. Suddenly there sneaked up behind us a man I knew, the sexton of the Church Missionary's church at Galkisse, close by. This was too much—a Church official attending a function where one at least of the commandments was as conspicuously shunted as in what is called the 'Wicked Bible' of 1632, which omits the negative from the seventh in the decalogue!

'Why, Pieris, you here! of all men, and of all places!'

'Sar, Mastar Thurston him send.'

'Rubbish ; don't tell me that, or I'll tell him.'

'Yes, sar ; Mastar Thurston him tell him

people they devil dance not go, or he scommunicate 'em. Sar, he scommunicate five that morning.'

(Now, this gentleman was an active man for a
missionary, and made a fair show in his reports.)

'Then you mean to say he has sent you here
to see how many are here ?'

'Yes, sar ; him send, sar. They ALL here,
sar.'

So that Canon Isaac Taylor's sarcastic reckon-
ing up of missionary results was true forty years
ago.

I saw something of the Buddhist priests at
Cotta, and never did I argue with such skilled
logicians. Since then a simple Berkshire curate,
sent out by the C.M.S., essayed the perilous task
of arguing with them. He was captured by the
enemy, and even entered their ranks. The Rev.
Mr. Leadbeater, till his recent return to England,
was a Buddhist priest in Colombo ; and I have
heard another has since followed his example.
One would like to know if the M.B. waistcoat and
straight collar has been exchanged for the shaven
head, yellow robe, fan, and sandals of his new
'doxy.

My friend Mr. Rhys Davids, one of the chiefs in learning among European Buddho-philes, has solved the doubt. The Rev. (?) Convert wears Unanse (a Buddhist priest) dress in Colombo, but when he called on my friend in Brick Court, was habited as an English gentleman. Did he call also at 14, Salisbury Square, E.C., on the C.M.S., while in the neighbourhood?

Colombo was a dullish place then, the break-water had not been made, the steamer port was Galle, seventy miles off, communication with which was by a line of coaches through a continuous cocoanut grove; on one side the sparkle of the sea, on the other hill-streams, full of apparent logs of timber, really alligators, and not without vistas of surprising beauty. Only one of its many visitors has ever done justice to the surpassing loveliness of Ceylon landscapes. The naturalist Haeckel of Jena, in his book, even its English version, gives some idea of their beauty. It is right to say that Darwin's favourite pupil went thoroughly in for the whole thing, and ate all put before him. Out of the many local dishes, iguana, shark, monkey, etc., he seems to give the preference to snake, in its cobra de capello form;

he rather dwells upon it, indeed, as superior to eels. In Lincolnshire they make pies of snakes, calling them bush eels—so Yorkshiremen say, at least.

As the fortifications and moat of Colombo were not then removed, the wonder was how the snakes got into the town. Yet a venomous 'carawilla,' eight inches long, was killed behind my chair in the hotel; and a friend, going one morning to open his iron safe, found a four-foot cobra coiled up thereon. Outside, of course, they abounded, and an American returned one day from the Cinnamon Gardens—which extend for miles —saying that he had, for some odd reason, run down a terrible stench to find that a twenty-foot python had been choked in trying to swallow a hog-deer.

My own fright at Bagatelle came just after getting into bed and dropping the curtain, when there came from inside the swirling, unmistakable hiss. To jump out, take one's lamp, and rout out from the veranda a sleeping servant was natural. The quest was conducted at safe distance with a pole. When sheet and blanket were removed there appeared a large yellow mantis, or 'praying insect'—so called from its throwing up its forelegs like a Mussulman at prayer. The creature was as frightened as I was, and rubbed its wing-cases together with quite a cobra-like hiss.

I may bring in here another snake story, but this time of America, and in the days of the pony express across the continent. My informant, a man of old Devonshire family, and reversioner of the next estate to my own, was brought down so low as to serve in the Confederate ranks during the war, and afterwards to become one of the express riders. He came to one of the forts where they changed, and on the curb of the well was lying one of the biggest rattlers he had ever seen. He fired at it, it fell into the well some twenty feet deep, with two feet of water in it; and Mr. Neyle, without a thought, climbed down the rough masonry to retrieve the monster. But he had soon something else to think of. His blood curdled, for out of nearly every joint in the wall protruded a snake's head, with the rattle in full go behind it. Again, without a thought, he dashed up again, and arrived safe, but only to faint dead, when escaped from such a death-trap without a hurt.

A Batticaloa cocoanut-planter, the late Mr. Palliser, told me a capital bear story. The Ceylon or sloth bear is an undersized individual, with a great propensity for carrion, so that a scratch from his long claws is more or less poisonous. Moreover, he never waits to be attacked, but charges home to hug his adversary, using the back claws to scoop out the intestines, so that if he has to be grappled with, it is best to keep his hind-quarters as far off as possible. Palliser had gone out with a double-barrelled gun, and another heavier one carried by his attendant. Reaching a ' pattena,' or open space in the jungle, he saw a bear descending a tree in the usual fashion, stern first. He stood his ground, but rather repented it when he saw the tail ends of two others also coming down. Matters looked serious, but he shot number one stone dead, and broke the hind-leg of number two. There remained number three, who came up fresh as paint and growling savagely. Looking for the other gun, he found the native had bolted with it. To run was useless, so Palliser drew his hunting-knife, and tried to prevent, as well the hug with the fore paws as the scoop-out with the back ones.

The only thing was to let daylight as often and as deep as possible into Bruin's own internals. He at last got grappled, but pluck and science had done so much mischief that when he came to his senses he found himself lying on the top of the dead bear, with number two dragging herself up to take part in the scrimmage. He showed us some of the fearful scars inside his thigh, from which he was long in recovering.

I have a pleasant memory of an Easter holiday on a cinnamon estate near Negombo. Our host was a born naturalist, and had the gift of taming animals ; thus a very large squirrel, the size of a house rabbit, and with a very red nose, would jump on his shoulders, then run up a cocoanut-tree sixty feet high in search of the small game in the top of it, descend, and jump on his shoulders as before. The top of a cocoanut-tree is a sure find for the largest centipedes, millipedes, scorpions, etc., probably attracted by the oily exudation. It is in bud, flower, and fruit at the same time, and all the year round, save when in 'toddy,' *i.c.*, when the sap is being drawn off for distillation for arrack.

Tame deer came to the table and begged for

bread, the only creatures not tamed being seemingly the thievish and evil-smelling monkeys, who, as we were not in India, had to be shot —not a nice process when the creature is only wounded, and dips its hand in its blood, and gibbers at its slayer. It is, of course, an old jungle joke that planters eat them, and· how one superintendent, rebuking his head servant for providing for dinner nothing but monkey soup, monkey eshtew, sar, monkey roast, monkey cutlet. said :

'Oh, hang all that ; I'll dine off the curry.'

'Yes, sar ; monkey curry, sar ?'

I may add that I obtained one of these squirrels. which are venerated by the natives as having once been men, to take home to the Zoo ; but in my shipwreck, possibly from fright, it emitted so horrible a stench that it had to be thrown overboard.

A German naturalist from a neighbouring estate was one of our party, but if the cobra he trod on when coming over to us had been pinned by the tail in place of the head, we should probably have missed his society.

Among our local friends was a very red Scotchman, employed as a road officer, who had married the really charming, lady-like daughter of the local chief, or Modliar, rich in land, sapphires, and amethysts the size of a cheese-plate. The pair were very happy together, but their joint production combined the mother's soft olive hue and the father's red hair and freckles.

The Negombo folk were strong Roman Catholics, and had an annual Passion play—the Crucifixion. It was performed most reverently. The tears and wailing at the close of The Awful Tragedy were affecting ; but to act the part effectually they had whitened the faces of the angels, and the colour coming off by perspiration had a ludicrous effect where it showed the black skin underneath.

Dysentery, the Ceylon scourge, again compelled my leaving the island, and on May 1, 1851, I embarked for England in the ship *Colombo*, viâ the Cape.

The south-west monsoon was just breaking, and it was ushered in by a terrible cyclone. The ship dragged her anchors, and struck the bar. I was sitting on the stern port when this happened, and the kick-up into the air which I experienced completely cured the sea-sickness which was prostrating me (this for the benefit of that part of the medical profession which goes down to the sea in ships). Then ensued a long misery; our distress flag was useless, for the lighthouse flew a signal that nothing could come off from the shore; the hammering of the ship's stern against the bar; the crash of the keel as it went to pieces; the seas which pooped us, so that we were waist-deep in the cabin; the water-casks which burst from their cleets, and waltzed about the deck till they went overboard where bulwarks had once been, will never fade from my memory. Meantime, the pumps were in full work to keep down the fast-rising water, and the sailors' song went on cheerily in the midst of the horror :

> ' And now, my boys, we're homeward bound,
>   We're homeward bound, hurrah !
> We're homeward bound, and that's the sound,
>   With a foll-thol de-riddle-lol lol-lol-láh.'

The captain, who had been wrecked in Simon's Bay, where the worst seas are supposed to run, told us he had never known anything like our weather. He called the four passengers round him—all men, thank goodness! He would not sink at his anchors, but cut his cable, and beach his ship, trying to cant her so that the masts would fall shorewards, and we might then drop off them on to land.

The orders were given, and men set to cut the cable with cold chisels, when a boat came out of the inner harbour manned by twenty men, induced by the enormous price of a sovereign per head.

She came alongside, held from being staved in by boat-hooks; the captain, cool as ever, called it a worse risk than sticking by the ship; but we passengers took the awful leap, and got safely in, more or less battered. Then we made for land. Mountainous green seas, twenty feet high, chased us, as if they would not be baulked of their prey, but we escaped. Then Captain Eyre cut his cable, and the *Colombo* went ashore at Mutwal Point. At daybreak of next day we who had been saved were on the spot. Not twenty yards from us, lying on her side, but with the masts canted seawards, and not landwards, was our ship. Some of her crew had been saved by a boat, but already two had been drowned in trying to swim through the boiling gap of surf, in which were borne timbers from the break-up, one blow from which was fatal. Lashed to the bowsprit were the captain and six others, and the problem was how to save them. The fishermen there are the hardiest of their kind, but not one would accept £20 to take off a fishing-line, and make it fast to the wreckage astern. The Royal Artillery had brought down a small mortar, to send off a rope to the ship, but the rope broke as soon as the shot left the gun. Everybody was looking on helplessly while the ship was settling deeper in the sand, and the men getting nearer the water. I got desperate, and went up to the Government agent (for he and all Colombo were there). I told him the fishermen would not go off for me, but if *he* offered the reward they would do so, and I held him responsible for my shipmates' lives. On this he yielded. At once three men entered the surf, with a line but a little finger thick; only one succeeded in reaching the ship, but he made his line fast, and then we saw the captain unlash himself, creep aft, secure the line, and lead it forward to the bowsprit,. and again secure it. None of the men would go, so he dropped himself into the surf, held on to the line, ducking when timber came near him, and at last touched ground, only just not quite exhausted. We all rushed into the surf, and carried him in ; but for the crowd of us, some must have been sucked under. Then came the end ; the six survivors untied themselves, dropped one by one over the side ; a few heads appeared amidst waves, spray, and timber, and next morning we stood bare-headed in front of eight coffins, wherein, in the attitude of fighting it out to the last, lay as many fine fellows as ever broke biscuit.

CHAPTER IV.

INDIA.

Sir Hugh Wheeler, of Cawnpore—'The Missy Baba,' the only Surviving Lady—His being ridden over at Sobraon—His Swearing-match with Sir Harry Smith before Aliwal—How a Dispute as to Priority of Seats in Church among the Ladies at Ascension was settled by Seniority—Dr. Brydone, Survivor of the Khyber Pass, at Lucknow—Death of Colonel Sibbald at Bareilly—A French Court-martial before the Enemy—Brigadier Neill : how to prevent a Train starting—Lucknow—Tiger Stories—The Merchant and the French Empress's Jewels—The Bengal Pilot Service—Bishop Wilson, of Calcutta—The Kiss of Peace : the Horse-dealing Archdeacon—Hindoo Women and their Fascinations—Captain John Theaker and the Burning of the *Earl of Eldon*.

My memories of India chiefly circle round the great agony of the Mutiny.

I knew Sir Hugh Wheeler, whose name must ever be identified with the Cawnpore tragedy, very well, and remember his telling me that, for once, justice had been done to the Company's own officers ; and that one of that body, in his own person, would command the Cawnpore division, in place of a Queen's officer sent out from England.

The alteration was the more significant because he had never quitted his regiment nor held a staff appointment.

Though, oddly enough, he bore the name of Massy, he was insignificant in size, weak in character, domineering in manner, and his chief topics of conversation were his dogs, and his 'Babas,' as he termed the Sepoys of his regiment. He had married a country-born lady; his children had never been sent to England, and showed the usual result of being brought up among natives, the only one of them at all noticeable being the youngest daughter, the 'Missy Baba,' doomed within a year to be carried off by a trooper from among the ladies when they were removed from the boats, after the massacre of the men, to a fate worse than death. She thus escaped both that and the subsequent butchery; but when eventually tracked out elected to accept her lot and a small pension, very properly conferred upon her, rather than again seek the society of Europeans.

One of Sir Hugh's favourite stories was about Sobraon, where his regiment in square was broken and ridden over by Sikh cavalry. One sowar reined up to spear the old Colonel, and bore point down upon him; but the lance hit on a tobacco-box, which he carried in his waistcoat-pocket, and always produced, that the deep dent might be seen which had saved its owner's life.

Another of his stories over which he chuckled even more was of Aliwal, or, rather, the evening before the fight. It must be premised that these were the old swearing days; no one then imagined a time would come when an officer, soundly cursed at a review by a very high official indeed, would decline to meet the inspecting General at the subsequent dinner, and be held justified in so doing. Hence, it was not thought much of when Sir Harry Smith rode up to the Brigadier as soon as he had brought his troops into line in capital condition, but a day late, and thus addressed him *coram* everybody:

' Brigadier Wheeler, I am a hot-tempered man, and sometimes say things I am sorry for afterwards; but, now, what the —— ——' (count two minutes of continuous execration) 'do you mean by coming up a day late, and risking the destruction of the whole force—yes, sir, by —— the destruction of the whole army—by ——?'

The little man drew himself up to his full height of five feet three, and saluted calmly :

'Sir Harry Smith, I am a hot-tempered man, and sometimes say things I'm sorry for afterwards ; but what the ——— ———' (time and matter as before) 'do you mean by blackguarding me—yes, sir, blackguarding *me*, by ——— before my own Babas ?   Do you know that some ———' (say one minute of adjectives to match the General's substantives) 'fool of a stuck-up idiot of a commanding officer had sent no boats for us to cross the river, and it would have served him' (more adjectives) 'well right if the enemy had destroyed him, and been a ———' (as before) 'good thing for the country into the bargain.'

Peace be with Wheeler!   The then inflexible rule of seniority had put a man into a position he was not fit for at Cawnpore.   It sometimes, however, works well, as when the ladies at Ascension squabbled about priority of seats in church there, and the Navy Captain in command of that island tender, as it is entered in the Admiralty books, wished to allot them by the rule of age, with the result that back seats had the run made upon them.

Anent the swearing, report has it that my old friend Field-Marshal Pollock and his colleague Nott had several drawn games of a similar kind.

I once met Dr. Brydone, the sole survivor of the Cabul expedition, fated to have as near a squeak for life in the Lucknow siege. He was a singularly quiet man, and kept up the spirits of the garrison by his abounding faith that he had not got off in Afghanistan to be killed in Oudh. Indeed, where wounds were plentiful, he was not once hit.

My old friend, Colonel Sibbald, C.B., commanding at Bareilly, believed in his men to the last. When finally undeceived, he would only put his horse to a walk, so fell an easy victim, and was shot through the chest. Colonel Troup, however, who among the long roll of heroes of that time claims a foremost place, dismounted, and stayed by the dying man until life had passed away, and the dead body could not feel the indignities he and those with him were powerless to avert from it, when they rode for their own lives, and saved them. Not, however, that injuries apparently fatal always prove so. I remember a story told me by Captain Willis of the assault of the Redan.

He himself was brought down by a shot in the knee, and on reaching his tent found the man who shared it lying there also. The ball had entered the abdomen and come out through the back. He was, of course, taken as doomed, and the surgeons betook themselves to cases where there was at least some hope. But the man called for his pipe, and abused his servant for delay. 'You beggars think I'm done for, but I'm not. Nor was he ; in an incredibly short space of time he was back at duty. The ball had gone round, in place of through, him. The same Captain Willis also described to me a French field court-martial. He was in their lines when a battalion marched off to the trenches. A shot was heard, a sergeant fell dead, shot in the back. There was a halt, and the murderer, quickly discovered by a white handkerchief applied to the muzzle of each firelock, put under guard. Then the company officer made a note in his pocket-book, which the Chef-de-Bataillon signed. A passing staff officer was sent off for the General of Division, who came at once, and also signed his name, leaving directly afterwards. Then the company officer went through the ranks and flicked eleven men at random with his glove. They fell out, laid down their arms, and turned their backs while one ball was being drawn and the muskets mixed up. They then faced about, and took up their muskets. A hole had been dug by the pioneers, the murderer, blindfolded, was placed in front of it, and the men fired, the sergeant giving the *coup-de-grâce*. The body was put in, the victim upon it ; the grave filled up, and the battalion was again in march. The whole affair took but seventeen minutes, of which a large part was taken up in the musket formalities. In our service the same result would have been attained after a month, with three men taken off duty to guard the prisoner.

One of the greatest heroes in that dreadful agony was Brigadier Neill. He had volunteered for the Crimea, and on return took command of the 1st Madras European Fusiliers. Moved up to Calcutta at the dread crisis when even the Governor-General's body-guard had been deprived of their arms, and mounted guard with ramrods, and when Allahabad was in imminent peril, the leading files reached the Howrah terminus just as a train was starting, and a pert stationmaster refused to delay it for a moment. Neill's grim rejoinder was to tell off three sergeants, one to him, another to the driver, and a third to the guard, with orders to keep a revolver at their respective ears, and fire if the stationmaster gave the signal to start. So the chief official passed a very unpleasant time, with the non-com.'s hand on his collar and the barrel at his ear, till the passengers had gladly vacated the carriages and the soldiers filled them. Thus was Allahabad saved in the nick of time, and the first real check given to disaffection.

The way in which Neill quieted the country was simple and practical. Anyone possessed of broken telegraph-wire was held to have been aiding the insurgents, anyone possessed of the new copper pice stored up in the Government treasuries, but not as yet issued to the public, and therefore looted, was forthwith hanged—unless, of course, they could clear themselves by evidence ; and the compelling the butchers of the ladies and children to lick up some of their clotted blood, four inches deep, under the lash of the Provost Marshal, before they were hanged, had also a deterrent effect, as destroying both life and caste.

He fell at Lucknow, a born soldier, if ever there was one, meeting a painless soldier's death in the midst of the earthquake shout of victory.

My anecdotes of the siege of Lucknow are mainly derived from my friend, the late Mr. Bickers, of the Uncovenanted Service. There was a eunuch of the King of Oudh's who had established himself in an upper room opposite the residency, from which he daily thinned the ranks of the garrison, and in an endeavour to pot him Mr. Bickers received a return service which passed through both cheeks, breaking the jaws. When the sally was made, it was found that the eunuch's pitch was unreachable by any direct bullet, while on the other hand he covered the marksman with impunity; but at last he was reached by the bayonet.

There were strange episodes in that desperate struggle! While this kind of thing was going on, Lady Inglis records the blessed peace which came upon her after the garrison were repulsed at Chinhut, when with two new-made widows, whose husbands' bodies were left on that fatal field, they read together the English Litany.

No Indian record without a tiger story. Colonel Wright assured me that when carried into the jungle by a tigress who had laid hold of his thigh, he felt no pain nor fear—in fact, was much more afraid that the rescuer who had followed them into the jungle would hit him instead of hitting the tigress.   The late Mr. Brooke Cunliffe, of the Madras Civil Service, had a similar experience, but his deliverer shot the tiger with one barrel, the other knocking out an eye-tooth, which was hollowed out to form a vinaigrette.

Most of the stories of pluck and endurance in India are either naval, military, or sporting ; but sometimes in peaceful commerce the same qualities shine out bright and clear.   An old friend of some thirty years' standing was returning home for his periodical change, when there met him at Bombay a telegram from one of the great European financial kings, briefly informing him that the Empress Eugénie was selling her jewels in hope of doing something to save the dynasty.   A market for such costly things in such quantity was not to be found in Europe, leaving out of account publicity, which was not desirable in view of a demur to be expected for many reasons from the republic just born in the agonies of Sedan.   But the native princes of India were always buyers of such jewels as these, the spoil of an Empire ; the difficulty was to find a man of sufficient influence to approach them, with at the same time stamina, mental and physical, enough to carry some hundreds of thousands of pounds' worth over road, rail, and river into territories where the Queen's writ runneth not, nor is the tramp of the constable heard in the land. In addition, the man must himself be trustworthy.

Every preparation had been made for safety and secrecy ; the jewels had been taken to pieces, 'jointed,' so as to fold flat, and could be carried in a leather belt worn round the body. My friend had the required qualifications, and accepted the task. Protected simply by a revolver, and with one trusty servant to accompany him, he assumed the belt, wore it on him night and day, waking and sleeping, and in the course of three months succeeded in disposing of its contents, though his health suffered somewhat from the terrible anxiety and strain ; for it is hard to say whether the dangers he ran were greater in or out of British territory, by day or by night.

One or two older stories are too good to omit. The marine keys of Calcutta are entrusted to a small body of men, about a hundred in number, known as the Bengal Pilot Service, now practically filled up from the Worcester and Conway Training Colleges for merchant navy officers. The river Hooghly, some seventy miles long, owing to the mass of alluvial soil brought down by the Ganges, is always changing its shoals, which are very dangerous. In fact, one of them, where a 'thwart' river comes in at right angles, the so-called 'James and Mary's' (*jal mari*, the meeting of the waters), is much dreaded, because if a ship hangs for five minutes on it she is lost; in an hour her deck is below water, and within twenty-four more her masts have disappeared. Such a river can only be navigated by day, and the service (almost all the members of which are in the Royal Naval Reserve) is peculiarly organized, having its own colony (popularly Chummery) at Garden Reach, and even its own special judge. The officers are now reported to wear white gloves when on duty, but in the old days there were rough diamonds among them. Of one of them, Bayson, some good stories were told. Thus, when cast away on Saugor Island, the sole survivor, he reflected that he had nothing to eat himself, but that the rest of the population, tigers to wit, were perfectly ready to eat *him*. He thought, therefore, that a prayer might do no harm under the circumstances; but the only one he could recall to mind was ' A Prayer for the High Court of Parliament, to be said daily during their Session.'

On another occasion having Lady William Bentinck, the wife of the then Governor-General, in charge, the sadly-bored lady asked the old man, whose sayings greatly delighted her :

' Mr. Bayson, can't you do something to amuse me ?'

' Would your ladyship like to learn " Bumble Puppy " ?'

When a Bishop is eccentric, all the world enjoys the fun ; so that the now almost forgotten Bishop Wilson, of Calcutta, was highly appreciated. He had as housekeeper a venerable lady, who remembered the duel between Sir Philip Francis and Warren Hastings, on August 17, 1780. On entering the cathedral on a Sunday morning, fully robed, lawn sleeves and all, and passing the pew where the old lady sat, he would pause, and give her the ' kiss of peace ' before all the congregation, and this although he had met her at breakfast. His

sermons, too, were racy, preaching against dis-
honesty, especially in horse-flesh, as one of the
great English failings in India.   He went on:
'Nor are we, servants of the altar, free from yield-
ing to this temptation.'   Pointing to the occupant
of the reading-desk below him—'There is my
dear and venerable brother the Archdeacon sitting
down there; he is an instance of it.   He once sold
me a horse, it was unsound; "I was a stranger,
and he took me in."'

On another point, the fascinations of Hindoo
women, he was equally pungent.   'Ah, my
brethren, I well know what they are; I have
been sorely tried and tempted by them, but by
Divine help I was enabled to escape.'

And in a visitation at Bombay, following on
the track of Heber when he wrote one of the
most musical gems in the language—

> 'Thy towers, they say, gleam fair, Bombay,
>   Across the dark blue sea'

—he singled out one little man for especial notice.
'Come to the front, Binnie; you are the best
little man of the whole lot.   They draw all the
pay, and you do the work.'

It is time now to pass 'to my twenty years' active life as a merchant in London ; but before doing so I will relate one of those quiet deeds of pluck and heroism which, in old days, met with no reward, and get but little even now.

My friend, Captain John Theaker, commanded the ship *Earl of Eldon*, homeward bound with cotton from Bombay, some sixty years since. He had a large number of passengers, and three days after sailing he had reason to think the cotton was smouldering. As it was impossible to put back in the teeth of the north-east monsoon, he quietly prepared for the inevitable, suggesting to the passengers, bored for some amusement, to play at having a fire on board ; he got out the boats, put in provisions and water, masts, sails, compasses, and told off the passengers, who, each for the fun of the thing, packed up a few requisites, to their respective seats, even making the men row with the oars for the full carrying out of the joke. They were all pretty nimble, and just getting tired of it all, when he told them the ship was really on fire, that the fire was working aft towards the magazine (Indiamen carried powder then), and that all must really embark at once.

In an hour this was done, and the stout skipper himself in one hour more had to leave what was literally the 'burning deck.' Just sixty minutes after that the four frail boats, which had lain by to await the explosion, made sail before the wind. No land nearer than the Seychelles, over a thousand miles off, but fair wind, and probably fair weather. So it proved ; the one thunderstorm filled up their water-casks, and after fourteen days land was sighted ; but it took two more to find an inlet through the reefs. This was at last effected, and when, after landing, and due thanks given for such a deliverance, the ship's company broke up, the captain, missing all his male passengers, found them up to their necks in a mountain stream. He had landed one more than he had taken on board his ship, the usual irrepressible baby having been born *en voyage*.

CHAPTER V.

MERCHANT LIFE IN LONDON.

Panics, 1825—Robbery and Escape of Stevenson from Clevedon—
Indignation of Lubbock's Cashier—Panic of 1857 : Rescue of
Money on Deposit at Overends'—Closing the Doors in 1866—
Scene in Lombard Street after Black Friday—Putting up the
Shutters at the Agra and Mastermans' Bank—Curious Robbery
from Mastermans' in 1844—The Closing of the Old Oriental
Bank—Riot in Colombo in consequence—The Man who held
Consols bought at 46—My Gun-cotton Shipment : how it
turned Two Natives into White Men—Houghton, the Plate-
layer : how he missed making his Fortune—How a Devon
Friend did much the same thing—Houghton defending the
House at Arrah in the Mutiny—How his Employer got 14,000
Acres of Land for cutting down a Jungle—The ' Old England '
Cotton Corner—Wolff, the Corn-cutter—Stratford-on-Avon—
Wales—An Archæological Meeting at Hereford—The Fungus
Dinner : ' Waiter, a Glass of Brandy !'—Opposition ousting the
Government—My New Devon Home—The Man who never
told a Lie, and was too Old to learn—The Story of John
Crossing—Heads I win, Tails you lose—The Solicitor and the
Fourpenny-pieces.

ONE cannot write of mercantile life without thinking of panics, those tremendous financial storms
which in those days sometimes destroyed in a week
the accumulated savings of years.   They are replaced for the moment by a kind of low fever with

short intervals, which may any day sharpen up, become uncontrollable, and, attacking all the Bourses at once, leave even ghastlier wreckage than 1825, when 770 banks stopped payment, and the Bank of England was reduced to gain time by paying its £1 notes in sixpences. Not that these same £1 notes were useless ; on the contrary, the accidental discovery of a large parcel of them in a box, and their immediate issue (for there was no Bank Charter restriction then), rendered great service. For the Bank lent them to any banker (all private firms, be it remembered, at that time) who could show really solid securities, unmarketable for the moment. One Stevenson, banker in St. Mildred's Court, adroitly availed himself of this to effect a most audacious fraud, escaping afterwards with impunity. When the Bank authorities visited him, he showed them a box apparently filled with Exchequer bills, then unsaleable. The top layer was certainly composed of such, and they did not think of looking any deeper, but took the key and issued Stevenson bank-notes in exchange for the waste-paper which formed the rest of the contents. With this advance Stevenson disappeared. He lay low at a little inn at

Clevedon, hearing the ' sea break, break, break at the foot of its crags,' until a Bristol ship outward bound for anywhere should pass down with the tide. In the utter collapse of trade and credit this was a long time coming, and he had therefore to keep a sharp look-out for newspapers containing his description, and the heavy reward for the person answering thereto.

Only one newspaper, and that a *Bell's Life*, ever came to Clevedon in those days. One Tuesday it arrived as usual. Stevenson borrowed it directly it came, and strolled down to the beach. A ship was coming down ; he was put on board, and got off to America, where he so employed his ill-gotten wealth as to die rich, and even respected, under an assumed name. Even had he kept his own, there was no Extradition Treaty, and Mr. Weller senior expressed the then popular belief that the 'Merrikins would never give anyone up if he had any money. A little later on and we find Sydney Smith uttering a wish to capture a Pennsylvanian, apportion his raiment, and give his coat to the widow, his waistcoat to the fatherless, and his breeches to the poor and them that had none to help them. For the witty canon was a Pennsylvanian bondholder, and the State had repudiated.

Another good story of 1825 told how a customer of Lubbock's drew out all his money, called for his tin box, locked it all up therein, and handed it back for safe custody, only to have it thrown back at his head by the cashier, who had spent his whole life in the house.

In the panic of 1857 I myself had a severe fright. I kept all my reserve in deposit at Overend and Gurney's, bargaining for repayment at call, and by an uncrossed cheque. When I applied for the amount, a sum very much more than I could afford to lose, there were all kinds of difficulties. At last I got pressing and plain-spoken, so they gave me a crossed cheque, whereon the senior partner, Mr. David Barclay Chapman, lately deceased, left the office. There was thus no partner in the place to mark it 'cash' and initial it. I got desperate. It came to my mind that the gentleman had formed one of the firm of 'Frys and Chapman,' which had failed in 1825, with ruinous loss to their customers, so I set off to hunt him up all over the house. He dodged me from room to room, and I ran him to ground in the attic, where, after using plain, even strong language, he did what I demanded. Then to Barclays' to get the bank-notes. Smilingly told to wait, when, after much whispering, and many references to the parlour, my half-hour's agony was ended by the £1,000 notes being passed over the counter. When the revulsion of feeling had subsided, I took them down to the Stock Exchange, and exchanged them for Exchequer bills at 97.

No more deposits of mine went to Overends' after that, but I saw their doors closed in 1866. The excitement was terrible as the messenger came out, put up the shutters at the entrance door, and locked it as he went in. The click was heard in the awful silence. Then ran up from Stock-Exchange way, bareheaded, a gray-haired man, who shook the handle, and burst into passionate sobs and cries. Others mounted the iron bars in some way or other, and looked in at the clerks. The one thought on every mind was that no second-class paper was negotiable now, and that even for first-class bills the rate would be ruinous.

'Black Friday,' the next day, was even more

awful.   Birchin Lane and Lombard Street, from Glyn's to Barclays', were filled with a crowd, silent, listless, but staring at the banks, as if they expected them to fall bodily down ; while inside there was not a soul, save cashiers at their posts, with open drawers piled up with gold, and boxes filled with bank-notes behind them.   When I entered to get my pass-book, one of the beleaguered citadels over which my hereditary old friend, the late Mr. Henry Sykes Thornton, held sway, a curious scene had just come off.   In these old-fashioned banks gentlemen entered as boys, and remained in the 'house' all their lives, so that it is conceivable how Mr. Rawlinson the senior cashier should become uncontrollable, go out to the front door, and address the crowd in very unparliamentary language, winding up with : 'If you've got any cheques on us, and you don't look much like it, come in, take your money, and be d——d to you.'

Later on I saw the shutters go up at the Agra and Mastermans' Banks.   There was, by the way, a mystery of many years connected with Messrs. Masterman.   About the year 1844 over £100,000 in large notes was missed one Monday morning ;

how it went was never revealed. The firm offered a very large reward, and of course, on giving guarantee, received fresh notes from the Bank of England. Only one of them was ever presented for payment, and that came twelve years later from the gaming tables at Homburg, but the guileless-looking Hebrew Teuton who got change for that thousand-pounder could not be traced.

The fall of the Agra and Mastermans' Banks was distinctly traceable to one persistent 'bear' on the Stock Exchange, and an Act of Parliament was passed to prevent his example being followed, which was of about as much use as such remedies usually are ; for an Argentine bank lately fell by the same tactics, though not one man's work only.

Many years after I joined a small crowd gathered outside the closed door of the once great Oriental Bank Corporation, many of whose managers in former years had accumulated vast fortunes. The smash, however, was not taken so quietly in Colombo, where the bank-notes were legal Government tender. There the natives were only prevented from storming the building by the arrival of troops.

I once met a man who actually then held Consols purchased by his father at 46, when the Mutiny at the Nore was in full blast. The lowest price ever touched was, however, $44\frac{7}{8}$.

I never did much on the Stock Exchange, and when I did operate, worked on the lines of the old punter at Spa. Though attending every day, he went on the theory that the bank must always win in the long-run, but that modest profits might be made in and out. He risked a moderate stake occasionally; if he won twice running, no more for that day; while if he lost twice or thrice he withdrew, his star was not in the ascendant that day. He was said to make a living out of it.

I was, however, an original subscriber to the Confederate Cotton Loan, getting out at three premium. This was my passport to the friendship of Mr. Benjamin, Q.C., of whom I shall speak hereafter.

Perhaps my most curious experience was in the Egyptian Tribute Loan of 1871; I bought at 60, saw it down to 15, and sold at 80.

In my shipping transactions I had one very curious squeak, of which I was quite ignorant till the danger had passed.

On behalf of friends who were contractors on the East Indian Railway, I had to select and send out their working staff. One of them, a would-be sub-contractor, actually shipped as packing with his baggage a quantity of the gun-cotton of those days, given to exploding without any extraneous help. Of course, if it had taken this course, I, as the shipper, should have been liable for the loss both of ship and cargo. Luckily, however, it remained quiet, and when its nature was discovered on arrival in Calcutta, it was promptly unloaded, and piled up in the Customs Square to dry. A friend of mine had business there, and from an upstair window saw the great white heap, and two natives making for it to smoke their everlasting hubble-bubbles. They sat down, put their pipes in order, and struck the match. Before the first whiff was visible a cloud of smoke hid them from view, and on its clearing away there were two *white* men rolling in agonies; the black cuticle had been burned off them.

One man, a leading plate-layer on the Blackwall line, whom I sent out, had missed the fortune then occasionally open to men of his class. I had long wanted to secure him, but he only accepted my offer when he had seen his mate cut to pieces by an engine on the sadly-cramped Blackwall line. Then he was ready for 'Indy.' He had worked with Brassey and others as 'mate,' and, following in their steps, took a sub-contract on the Great Western at the east end of the Box Tunnel, where a long, deep cutting approaches it. He stood to make thousands, as the earth would burn into brick to line the tunnel close at hand; but directly on commencing he found a shell of rock only some two feet thick, which came up from below, and rose as he went on. The trial borings had missed it, as they had the quicksand in Kilsby Tunnel, or the soft pappy centre of the St. Gothard, both of which killed their con-tractors. It was the 'roach' of the bath-stone which had drawn out all the silica of that soft and beautiful oolite, and it utterly broke him. Passengers who care to look for this unsuspected interloper can still trace it rising on each side of the cutting. In Houghton's own words—'I moight ha' been as big a man as Tom Brassey, who worn't no more than I war, if it hadn't ha' been for that theer roach, which wur as hard as nails.'

Nor is he the only man by any means who has had Fortune in his grip and let her go. A Devon neighbour of mine tells a similar story. He was in the Hudson's Bay service, crossing Lake Superior, and the canoes hauled up on a group of small islands for the night.

The Indian boatmen spoke of vast wealth lying there, guarded by a *manitou*, of whom they stood in awe.

The place had an orey look—so much so that the surveyor in the party offered to survey it for $100, which, with a further outlay of $50 for registration, would have vested it all in him. But time was pressing, and my friend did not take up his fortune. It is now one of the most profitable silver-mines in the world.

Houghton went out to India, and formed one of the garrison of Boyle's house at Arrah, where among the other expedients to dislodge them were killing the horses, so that the stench might poison the defenders, and burning chillies in large quantities for the same purpose. The latter he described to me as the worse of the two. But in each case a change of wind diverted the effluvium. Is it not written in my friend

Colonel Malleson's stirring story of the Indian Mutiny?

But the Colonel does not record the great slice of luck which happened to Houghton's employer, the contractor Burrows. It was found so difficult to dislodge the rebel Koër Singh from the jungle that Government decided to cut it down, and made it over as a free gift to the contractor on condition of his doing it. The usucapion in this instance meant 14,000 acres of fertile freehold.

Of smart operations, I only remember one, though they are always in work more or less. By the then rules of the cotton market, the contract had to specify ship, quantity, and marks of packages as well as price. An operator casually noted in the manifest that on a ship (let us call her the *Old England*) there were but 200 bales ' Northern and Western ' cotton, so he bought all the cotton of that quality by that ship that speculators would sell him, and actually secured 14,000 bales before suspicion was aroused. Then, of course, came a fidget, but not a bale could be got to ' cover,' even the 200 being a special consignment. The ship arrived ; the buyer put the required amount at his banker's, and 'called' the cotton which did not exist. There was a terrible upset; the sellers were in a hole, and it was only a question of how little would be accepted for differences. The market figure was 7*d.*, the purchasers' 2*s.*, and eventually the matter was arranged in a payment of over £20,000. Of course, the morality of the thing was not thought of for a moment, but it is always a nice question as to which of the two parties broke the golden rule. It is somewhat as Mr. Weller fancied his brandy-and-water— 'ekal.'

An extraordinary but little-known man of that day was old Wolff, the corn-cutter of Leadenhall Street. He owned to having over 1,000 annual subscribers at three guineas each, besides chance customers and those whom he visited at their own homes. These last were among the upper crust; and on one occasion an archbishop essayed to convert the old Jew. Wolff told me, with a grim smile, how he choked the prelate off: 'If your grace *will* go on talking, I shall cut you.' His skill was wonderful; he once cut off a nail, and extracted a corn out of the quick beneath, without hurting me. I kept as still as a mouse

on the grim hint, 'If I make it bleed you'll die.'
For some thirty years he had never left his place
for a holiday, having only Sunday afternoons, as
he worked in the morning—even on Sundays.
Once, persuaded by his children, he got as far as
Boulogne, but a telegram came, 'Seven gentlemen and three ladies called.' He gave it up, and
went back to penknife and loop.

From the nature of his *clientèle*, big City men
and stock-brokers, he got any quantity of tips
and hints, which he used to great profit. One
day, however, I found him mourning over
£20,000 Perus, and I remember his deep sigh:
'The only thing one really ought to hold is
Consols, but it takes such a waggon-load of 'em
to come to anything.'

Passing his days in a dingy back room lighted
only from a well-shaft whose sides were never
whitewashed, I never remember a smile on the
old man's saturnine features save when he was
receiving subscriptions — his 'corn-rent' as he
termed it—one occasion excepted. It was in the
autumn of 1870, and, as I entered his room, he
asked :

'See that man going downstairs ?'

' Yes ; I know him a little.'

' Then you know he's one of the Rothschilds ; he's just been telling me the Prussians have laid hold of all their carriage horses at Frankfort— eleven of 'em. But they paid for 'em, though —*six pound ten apiece.*'

The greatest trouble he owned to was that none of his sons would follow his craft, so when he died, as he lived, in harness, an old man of eighty-four, strangers stepped into that dingy room (now no more) in which its whilom occupant had piled up his six figures.

Of my annual holidays I have little to record, but one experience which must have occurred to many others at Stratford may come in here. I am one of those silver medallist book-worms who own a First Folio Shakespeare, and one of the still fewer out of that small body who *can't* believe but that the real author was the illustrious Bacon. Hence, going over the house at Stratford-on-Avon, I hinted some of my heresies to a most precise elderly spinster, who was then guardian of it. At that time the critical acumen of Sir William Grove had not pointed out the lines in

'Troilus and Cressida,' act iv., scene 2, where Cressida says :

> 'But the strong base and building of my love
>   Is as the very centre of the earth,
>   Drawing all things to it,'

which that most estimable of men, whether as student, philosopher, lawyer, or judge, writes me is a fairly accurate definition of 'gravitation, as the earth's attraction is from the centre,' and this, too, two generations before the apple fell on to Newton's nose. The germ of the matter had, of course, been published by Dr. Gilbert in his celebrated book 'De Magnete,' in 1600 ; but a Latin book like that would not form one of those read by a man busily engaged as actor and manager, and who wrote his name so badly that no two signatures are alike. It is even stated that many of these show the pencilling of the scrivener's clerk, as for an illiterate man. Hence my question to the lady : 'Can the scholar, practical conveyancer, statesman, linguist, who had read an Italian novel up to this time never translated into English, lover of flowers, and philosopher, whose problems in "Hamlet" are as difficult as those in the second part of "Faust," etc., be one and the same with the lad brought up at an ordinary school ; as idle, and given to mischief, and even deer-stealing, as such boys are ?' and so, forth. The answer came quickly. It must have been given to many others, for Hepworth Dixon's book was in circulation at that time :

'Ah ! I see you think Lord Bacon wrote the plays. We hear much of that, especially from a Miss Bacon who thinks she is some relation of his. *And most people think she is out of her mind.'*

The shot was so well directed that I was obliged to have a good laugh, which angered the lady even more than my heresies.

It by no means follows that Mr. Donnelly's theories are adopted if I point out that in many books of the sixteenth and seventeenth centuries an anagram is employed to ear-mark the author of the book in which it occurs. Bacon, a scholar whose research was so great, his memory so pregnant, and unconscious cerebration so perfect, that in the course of an afternoon's ill-at-ease he could dictate some three hundred apothegms from memory, would not think it derogatory to avail himself of such an anagram. It is somewhat curious that the long word of twenty-seven letters, ' Honorificabilitudinitatibus ' (' Love's Labour Lost,' Act V., sc. 1), forms the anagram ' But this I hold, Fran' ! ! ! ! ! Bacon.

Of course there may be nothing in all this, and the testimony of Ben Jonson as to Shakespeare's own brilliancy—

> ' Oh, could you but have seen his wit !
> *   *   *   *   *
> But since you cannot, reader, look
> Not on his picture, but his book '—

must always score against the Baconian theory.

I have long fancied that in Wilton House, where lived the ' two noble brethren ' to whom the First Folio is dedicated, some scraps may still exist which will throw light on the great paradox, especially as I myself have cleared up two historic doubts almost as old : the date of ' Pilgrim's Progress,' and the position in which Charles I. died. This last by bringing to light a pamphlet open to all in the British Museum and Bodleian, but which no one previously had noticed, the inborn tendency to 'd——n pamphlets' being apparently as strong as ever.

Going up the Dee Valley in Wales, the coach took up a vivacious passenger. I thought at first he was a Yorkshireman, for his accent was so broad as to recall Lord Clare's remark to a broad-speaking Irish barrister after a wedding :

'Sure, now, will I throw an old shoe after the bride?'

'Oh dear no! your *brogue* will be quite enough.'

But the man replied :

'Noa, Oi'm not soa badd as all that; I'm Lanky' (Lancashire), 'but honest. Oi'm coom dahn heer to open a pooblic, and Aw shall call it t' Fisherman's Arms. A hoongry belly and a wet seat to your breeches, ye knaw !'

An archæological meeting at Hereford gave a week's great fun. The then Bishop was Hampden —Anthony Trollope's Bishop Proudie—a shy, unkindly man universally disliked, who had one of the termagant wives such people often get hold of, probably because the man is so shy that the lady has to propose to him. My associate was a Mr. Cheese, brother of that very young gentleman on whom, when marrying his daughter, Bishop Montague Villiers had bestowed the very best living in his gift, thus, as *Punch* said at the time, accumulating 'dams on Cheese.'

Now, Mrs. Proudie—I mean Hampden—was herself great at lecturing curates, and on going over the palace my friend significantly touched a door-handle, as being the apartment where the wiggings came off. Prominent among the clique which runs such things was a Mr. Barnwell, a fussy, irritable man, whose tongue was to let him in as defendant in the great series of libel actions 'Chamberlayne *v.* Barnwell,' in which the whole county of Wilts took a pecuniary interest on one side or the other, and where the third verdict, finally for the plaintiff, proved what a mountain of mischief a molehill of malignity can make. Mr. Barnwell's son was Mr. Chamberlayne's curate. A second manager was a Professor of Botany, who will go down to posterity with the proud record of having introduced the American Weed into English rivers and canals, with the result of choking up a good many of them.

It is known as Babington's Curse. He planted a piece in a ditch near Jesus College, Cambridge, and within two years it had run like wild-fire along the canals to Napton, where the clergyman at that time was Mr. Villiers Stuart, of Dromana, who has the unique distinction of having been successively a peer, a parson fourteen years, and finally a member of the House of Commons, to be probably hereafter best remembered as an Egyptologist of nearly the first rank.

There was even more than the ordinary amount of friction at that meeting—in fact, the friction survived the meeting, and even spoiled the annual fungus dinner of the Woolhope Club.

These esculents are first collected by experts in a pleasant outing in Herefordshire woods and parks, and are sat upon afterwards by a special sub-committee, and then pass the cook at the Green Dragon, who has been heard to say : ' It's just as well I *should* look at 'em to see none of 'em goes and poisons their selves.'   But a visitor to the Archæo-logical had stayed on in the place, and was a guest.   His mental fibre had got depraved, and after tasting the vegetable beefsteak (he had previously seen it, and a frightful thing it is to look at—a kind of toad's belly colour) he. feebly whispered : 'Waiter, a glass of brandy.'

The association split into two factions, who carried on the war merrily, both at morning excursions and evening meetings.   One point

of difference nearly led to demonstrations of force
—the question as to whether an old chair in the
cathedral was oak or chestnut.   The same con-
tention occasionally surges up about the roof of
Westminster Hall, the fact being that the two
woods, when old, are undistinguishable.

An excursion to an old country house brought
matters to a crisis.   It was the seat of a Crusad-
ing family, now extinct, where the mesalliance of
an only daughter with a footman had made the
owner   more   'dour'   than   ever.   His retirement from society made it easy to strike out a
plan whereby the opposition should arrive first,
and receive the honours intended for the administration.   There   were   three   stage   coaches :
Number one, Government ; number two, Neutral ;
number three, Opposition.   At a halt in the
road the driver of number three was laid a five-
shilling bet that he was not first at the Colonel's ;
number two, that he was not middle ; and number
one, that he was not last.   The start was made in
proper order, but when a narrow road turned off,
number one pursued the even tenor of his way for
a mile and a half, and then got wrong.   Number
two took the proper road, but got bothered at a

guide-post, and went astray also, so that number three drove up by itself, was duly welcomed (for the owner did not know a soul connected with it) and put in the place of honour where the hot dishes and champagne were. In due course number two came in, and made no difficulties. But just as lunch was concluding, and one of us eloquently proposing the health of our host, in came number one people, who could not interrupt the speaker, but sat down to cold meat, sour cider, and thin perry at the bottom of the table. Their remonstrances to the butler were vain, he would not disturb his master, ' he du swear so if you put him out ;' and when the furious committee did get to him, not only was all the lunch over, but he evidently had strong doubts as to their not being impostors. The joke was so admirably worked out that the supplanted ones thought it best to let it drop.

Other visits were very pleasant, especially one to Squire Hereford, of Sufton, who showed us the charter by which he held his estate in petty serjeanty, presenting a pair of gold spurs to the King whenever he should cross Mordiford Bridge.

My city life was soon to end; the gradual fall

of the rupee exchange alarmed me, and I resolved to extricate myself from further loss—a process which took some time and cost some thousands. Meantime the sudden death of one much loved and mourned had put me in possession of a small estate in Devon, on the watershed between Teign and Dart, which Anthony Trollope calls the prettiest part of England, within full view of Dartmoor. A charming country, swept by moorland or sea breezes, according to the wind, and, oddly enough, saved from much damp and rain by the divergent action of the hills, which draw off the clouds to right and left, so that a couple of thunderstorms may be at work on each side, while the sun shines clear on the old village midway. Not that the country is flat ; it consists of low, steep hills, with deep intervening combes, so there is no need, when enjoying the landscapes, fresh at every turn of the road, to adopt the position recommended by Mr. Denton (once of the *Saturday Review*, and currently reported to have been weaned on pickles) as making a pleasant variation in a familiar view : ' Put your head between your legs, and look at it that way.'

Not only is the neighbourhood lovely, but traces

remain of nearly all the races who have ruled over the pleasant land : round barrows, some of them bearing Semitic names, early British camps, Roman entrenchments, memorials of the French monks who held it till Henry V. abolished the alien priories—all are there. Close by, and, thank goodness! *not restored*, is the old fortified house known as Compton Castle, the family home of the discoverer of Newfoundland, Sir Humphry Gilbert, who was to sink beneath Atlantic waves with the touching words that Longfellow has rhymed so well :

> ' " Do not fear.   Heaven is as near,"
> He said, " by water as by land." '

And with him lived his half-brother, a bright boy, afterwards to be known as Sir Walter Raleigh, whose life one follows with pity and admiration until, everything worn out but his dauntless spirit, the old man calmly ascended the scaffold (erected where now stands Marochetti's Cœur de Lion), a sacrifice to the inveterate malignity of Gondomar by the first of the Stuart dynasty, whose own son was to meet the same fate a hundred yards off.

Truly St. Margaret's. Westminster, is one of the holy places of Anglo-Saxondom.   There rest the ashes of two great leaders, who, bursting into seas till then silent, gave it two new worlds to conquer, promptly occupied, resolutely held. Caxton, the founder of the English press, which disseminated English literature all over the world, has a meet companion in the grave in Raleigh, who colonized Virginia, and established the imperial race in its great possession over the sea.

*　　*　　*　　*　　*

Yes—

> 'Every prospect pleases,
> And . . . .'

—the drawback is the people.

I am engaged in developing the evidence which goes to prove that they are the survival of a colony of Phœnician, that is, Carthaginian, stock. The name of Baal occurs in the names of contiguous closes over one hundred times. The Ballhatchet family held the tenement of Baalford, under Baal Tor, from father to son, for time out of mind, recalling the Purkises of Lyndhurst, who drew the Red King's body to its grave in Winchester Cathedral, and who only died out in 1851; the Wapshots of Chertsey, similar land-holders, from the days of King Canute, and others. Baal and Ashtoreth go together ; and in this village Ballhatchet (Baal-achad : Baal is first) lives opposite to Easterbrook (Ishtarb'ruch : Blessed of Astarte).

The Ballhatchets held their little plot of land by seisin, not even by that simple form of conveyance. five hundred years old, and in full force now—

> ' I, John of Gaunt,
> By this deed do graunt
> Unto John Burgoyne
> And the heir of his loin,
> Both Sutton and Potton,
> Until the world's rotten.'

One of the late Conveyancing Acts did indeed provide a statutory form of land transfer as simple as this, but it did not suit that terribly powerful body, the English solicitors, to adopt it, and things go on much as they did before.

The village has one other Semitic inheritance —' Punic faith,' much aggravated by broken men coming to reside there with their wives (not unfrequently other people's), and the evil spread to weights and measures. A ton, to buy, was twelve hundredweight ; a pound of butter twelve ounces ; nine pints could be squeezed into a one-gallon jar ; while paid accounts were demanded over again, on the chance that the receipt had been mislaid. No bargain was worth anything except in writing, and as for veracity, no prize could be offered at the athletic sports for the 'lying' race, as the whole population was qualified for it, saving only one brilliant exception, a man of some sixty years old, who personally assured me that he had never told a lie in his life, and was too old now to begin to learn! The whole place was distinctly demoralized, and my friend, the present Vicar, who some four years ago manfully tackled it, has told me that, when he accidentally omitted repeating the eighth commandment, he comforted himself by reflecting that it was useless as a moral lesson, and merely a needless irritant.

Our village has only produced one man of capacity—the late Jack Matthews, who, being allowed, for experiment's sake, to call for as much cider as he pleased, got through twenty quarts on one Saturday afternoon.

And its name occurs but once in the State Papers, and that in Commonwealth times. One Crossing was a clothier, and so rich as to send to his agent in London woollens to the amount of £200 (as good as £1,500 now). It was sought, and successfully, too, to arrest these goods in the agent's hands by reason of the owner's delinquencies, as what follows will show :

Crossing had bribed the captain of a merchant ship, loaded in London for Genoa, to put into Dartmouth, then held for the King; there the merchants' cargo was sold for £1,000 (£7,500), the captain taking £100, and the clothier £900, after which Crossing fitted up the ship to cruise for the King; many vessels were captured, really by piracy, but at last Crossing was driven to sell the ship herself for £1,000, divided exactly as before, and the victims' redress granted by the Council of State did not help them much when they got it. This Crossing family died out at a neighbouring village, where there exists another odd proof of the 'slack-twistedness' which seems to run with the land. A Vicar who died in 1662 utilized the old altar-slab, with its five crosses or 'wounds,' as a flat tombstone for his grave in the chancel.

They are a curious people. During some thirty years I have never seen a man run, save once to stop another making off with his cider-keg. Of time they have no idea, except as a vehicle for wages. A good telescope brought to bear on a workman in the fields will show marvellous little exertion on his part. The story about a train on the Ashburton railway halting at Staverton while the guard picked some watercresses for his tea has probably some foundation ; it is paralleled by another train on the Somerset and Dorset pulling up to allow the driver and stoker to settle their differences in a wider ring than the foot-plate, a jury of the passengers being requested to see fair play in an adjoining field.

'Homer sometimes nods,' according to Horace, and a legend of the South-Eastern Railway may be a revelation in its way to the astute genius who presides over its fortunes.

A train which started from Tunbridge pretty much to time, as they work it down there, stopped, however, erelong for an unconscionable while. The guard got out, and was much heckled—so much so that, when moving on again, he vouchsafed to inform them :

'Cow on the line.'

But after a time came another hang-up, and the guard, after the interval due to his dignity, revealed the reason why, repeating :

' Cow on the line.'

' Why, you're always having cows on the line.'

' Certainly not,' said the official indignantly; ' it's the same cow, only we've caught her up again.'

Superstition exists not in our village ; we have not a ghost. Wit, as such, is unknown, save topical taunts—' I feel like the Totnes man, not inclined to do any work ;' but there is a practical kind of humour; such as when a neighbouring Rector was sinking a well, and offered the men five shillings when they should show him water in it. Next morning there were several bucketsful, and the men got their money ; the water, however, soon evaporated, as they threw no more down. His successor tells some good stories ; one, of his experience as a curate in the Black Country, where he used to visit and read to the good-looking wife of a Bilston puddler. The chapter under exposition was Daniel and the fiery furnace. The puddler interviewed the instructor, and forbade any further visits—was, in fact, unreasonably violent.

' I allus knaw'd tha war a liar, but naw tha comes and reads to moy woife about heating t' furnace seven times hotter nor it war afore. Tha coom to moy furnace, and try to heat that seven times hotter if tha can ; if tha comes again to moy woife, I'll poonch thy head !'

Such are the perils of missionaries !

One is glad to think that within the last four years a change for the better has passed over our village.   A new Vicar, a high-bred young Scotch-man, has effected much good, though it is a case of a thoroughbred harnessed to a coal-waggon ; a better class of gentry are returning to the place, and it is to be hoped the rising generation will avail themselves of a better example than that set to their parents—it could hardly have been worse.

Joking in Devonshire is usually practical.   A recently deceased solicitor at our market town had a weakness for tossing for champagne at the hotel bar.   He invariably produced a sixpence to toss with, which he handed to the other man, invariably calling 'heads' and winning, inasmuch as the coin, which he once showed me, bore on one side the heads of William and Mary, and that of the Deliverer alone on the other.   It got remarked, of course, and monotonous, but led to a rough-and-tumble between the man of law and one of the bibulous ones of our village, in which both parties exchanged damages. The legal gent had a large collection of fourpenny-pieces, and when no longer coined, he would bring up the subject of their scarcity in the hotel smoking-room. Bets as to whether two hundred of them were producible in the town within a given time would follow, and the lawyer would turn up exhausted, just as the clock was striking, with the required amount quite unexpectedly made up. After some three or four *séances*, however, the landlord suggested their discontinuance, for from £20 to £50 had changed hands about it.

In bounce, as distinguished from mouthing, the people are deficient. There is one story of it from Chagford, where is a long, hilly lane so narrow that two carts cannot pass each other, and one has to back till a gate is reached and a field can be turned into. A heavily-laden cart, with a long man as driver, was going down the hill, when there met it a light load and a short driver. The long man pointed out the rule of the road—to wit, that the man coming up hill should back, as the one going down could not. The short man significantly replied :

'If you don't go back, I'll serve you as I did the man the other day.'

On this the long man crumpled, and backed his heavy load all the way up the hill, not unnaturally asking, as the short man passed him :

'What might you ha' done to that there man the other day ?'

'Well, you see, he wouldn't go back, so I had to.'

My final change in life arose from the fact of this curious people coming to me for advice in law ; I gave it them, and it was wrong, so I was upbraided by one client.

'If so be as you tells us what the law is, it seems to us as how you ought to have knowed it yourself first.'

The hit was just ; I could only say, 'If ever I do advise you, or anyone else, again, they shan't say that to me,' so I entered myself forthwith for the Inn of Court, which is my last subject after a few details of social life have been given.

CHAPTER VI.

FOR many years of my life I was too busy to join
either clubs or societies. The day over in the
summer-time, Cremorne was a pleasant change;
and I remember the great Derby-night row there,
which, indeed, I innocently started.

I had been to the race, and dined with two
friends—one of them Frank Blomfield, a son of
the Bishop of London, who told me that the
then current story about the paternal nursery
was correct. The Bishop, left a widower with
a family, had married a widow lady similarly

situated, and a joint household was carried on, while a joint family appeared in due time. The Bishopess once invaded the episcopal study :

'My dear, your children are fighting my children, and making our children cry.'

Adjourning to Cremorne, I met a big hussar doctor, whom I knew, and, walking round, came behind a person whose hair was hanging down behind so exactly like bell-pulls that I was tempted to use them as such, and give a good pull ; the person turned round, and though I walked unconsciously away, gave me a kick, which I felt for some time. Meantime the Bishop's son was accosted by the woman's companion, who got knocked down for his pains. Things went on ; there was a free fight, the bar was stormed, and a day after my hussar doctor turned up badly damaged, with divers marks of a signet-ring on his face, which he declared had come from a big man he had seen with me. I then told him that it was the sign-manual of the son of the Bishop of the diocese. Poor Frank! A shipwreck in California closed a somewhat rackety existence. Church dignitaries' sons are not always saints, and Frank Buckland was another instance. When on his fishery inspections he travelled third class in very common clothes, and carried his short black cutty-pipe in the band of his somewhat dirty felt hat. Hence, when the High Sheriff's carriage was waiting to fetch the fishery inspector from the station to a county meeting at Hereford, the footman refused to take such a person up ; and though cheerfully told, 'You beggar, tell 'em I'll walk up, and they must wait!' resolutely guarded the platform-door against the supposed tramp when he got that far, until someone came out to see what the row was about.

Fuimus Troes; the days are gone by when at daybreak residents at the Hummums and Tavistock Hotels would wind up by organizing market-women's races round the market, with boys in the baskets as handicap weights. And the driving a hansom down the Central Avenue can no longer be arranged at Evans', then close by. Waterfordism died hard.

My first society was the Royal Geographical, to which I was introduced by Sir Bartle Frere, whose shocking bad hat was always the same. It was, however, a chimney-pot, not of peculiar shape like Lord Tennyson's, or dear old Sir

Richard Owen's, or the bashed-in pot-hat which Mr. Quaritch puts on when he is going to pay more than £1,000 for a book. There is one capital story of Sir Bartle being in Zanzibar with his son ; he was hungry, and went into a hut for food. There was nothing eatable there, but in a corner was a chatty full of little black balls. These Sir Bartle insisted on having, though the owner was reluctant. The meal was eaten, and it came out that the owner had been a great warrior in former times, and had cut off and preserved as trophies the ears of the slain, which ears had now been curried and consumed by her Majesty's representative.

His experience resembled Lord Elgin's at a state dinner in China. Liking very much a dish he had tasted, and which he took to be duck, the envoy forgot St. Paul's warning against asking questions in such matters, and said to the servant behind him :

' Quack-quack ?'

The man bowed low as he replied :

' Bow-wow !'

Another acquaintance was Dr. Rae, the solver of the fate of the Franklin Expedition.

At a recent soirée, he was exhibiting a real Esquimaux lamp of his own, fed with blubber, against Dr. Nansen's neat little alcohol stove, which had warmed and fed that 'hardy Norseman' when crossing Greenland. The doctor still held fast to his being best.

In 1872 I joined the Savile Club, then in Savile Row, and an exceedingly social little place, social without being Bohemian, far more comfortable than now, when it has removed to Lord Rosebery's old home in Piccadilly — a house never built for a club. It is still, however, 'The Prigs.'

In the old days before it received this title, many curious stories used to go the round of billiard and smoking-room. One of Dr. George Harley's was of an execution by the sword in Baden, just before they ceased—the culprit bound in an armchair, the executioner behind, the level sweep of the sword, as clean as Tarquin the Elder cut off the poppies, the spirt of the blood three feet high. I have a print of the process in Luiken's 'Theatre of Martyrs' (Antwerp, 1578). Another of the Franco-German War, was told by a guest, an Englishman naturalized in France, who had served in a mitrailleuse battery at Gravelotte, and had evidently been taken prisoner. The question under discussion was: 'What is courage?' and this gentleman gave us his own experience. He premised that his gun carried 1,800 yards, and could not fire again until the enemy was 400 yards nearer. The first shot cut a clean gap, one man getting forty-five balls from his gun, and ten from the next. The second cut an equally clear gap, but by this time the German shells and needle-gun were in play. The ground was muddy, and they stood upright in place of lying down till the shell burst. In the midst of all this his captain said: 'Would you like to walk behind that tree?—there is plenty of time.' He actually did, but found the fire so fierce that the shelter was useless. His captain then said: 'No good, eh? My captain at Solferino did the same to me.' Then just at the last round a round shot cut his subaltern in two. In place of running to help him, there was but the one idea of revenging his death, and he 'saw red' like Humboldt; to kill was the whole impulse then.

One evening a Communist dined there, who described the defence of the Place Vendôme against the Versaillais; and I remember a professor from the Hôtel Dieu relating experiments on guillotined heads, with his own firm conviction that sensibility was not even then extinguished.

In 1874 I joined the Reform, the most comfortable house in London, though not social. But few good stories attach to it. The best is, perhaps, that of Sydney Smith, who, when shown over it, remarked: 'I prefer your rooms to your company.'

Among the members was an old man, unmistakably a gentleman, though his coat was green with age. One passed him with a slight creepiness. It was the O'Gorman Mahon, who had shot his dozen men in duels, and any quantity more in promiscuous soldiering everywhere, a veritable survival out of Lever's novels.

One of the memories of the Reform is the great ballot on the question as to whether the election of members should be confined to the committee, or remain by open ballot as before. Two of the Messrs. Chamberlain had been rejected, and a good deal of feeling resulted, ending even in a libel action. The meeting was a stormy one. It was that celebrated occasion when Mr.

Bright thought fit to express his opinion that if they were 'gentlemen,' the club would give up their personal veto, a speech which militated strongly against his view in the result. I was one of the scrutineers, and unless very much mistaken, fancied that many men personally conducted to the box by the committee twisted their wrists in the direction unfavourable to the change. As the whip was strong, and over half the club voted, it was interesting to see if the head coffee-room waiter would know the names of all the voters. The hall porter also, who remembered Lord Beaconsfield as a member, was also an object of interest for the same reason. He has since retired, possessed, it is said, of £10,000, the result of tips in money, and tips in advice judiciously employed. In the result the hall porter answered the test, but the head waiter had to ask one name. As the particular member lived in the south of Ireland, and had not entered the house for a quarter of a century, the waiter did, however, very well.

The Jubilee Ball, however, was the greatest event during my seventeen years' membership. Although the crowd was as thick as on a fine illumination night in Savile Row or the night of the Peace fireworks after the Crimean War, yet one has some pleasant memories of how the Prince was fairly beset, and on asking a gentleman to take his elbow out of my ribs, it proved to be the Speaker.

My acquaintance with Peers has been very limited, but I heard some good stories about the hermit Duke of Portland, who had turned the public roads round Welbeck into gas-lighted tunnels, so that no one should see him. When he came up to town it was in a closed carriage, and on one occasion the servants, ordered away that they might not see him get in, halted on the road for a drink, discussing their master freely, in entire ignorance that he was listening to them. Suddenly a squeaky voice broke in on them :

' You lazy scoundrels, if you don't go on I'll dismiss you !'

One day there came to Welbeck a shabby individual, who went up to the front door, and opened it, saying to the astonished attendant :

' It's all right.'

He went up the stairs into the Duke's room without knocking, and said to its inmate :

' I have to serve your grace with a subpœna in the case of So-and-so. This is the original, and £1 1s. conduct money.'

He got clear off the premises, and was quickly followed by the head servants, who had forfeited their places and been dismissed for letting him run the blockade. At the trial, however, the Duke attended, a wizened, not-over-well-dressed man, and gave evidence. On one occasion in the last year of his life he summoned to him his successor. On arriving at Worksop, the guest found no carriage sent to meet him, and went back by next train—materially mending, it is said, his own prospects by his independence.

The late Marquis of Westminster, who figures on the walls of the Reform Club as a Knight of the Garter, had queer economies. On one occasion he went to Grosvenor House, and informed the butler he had brought his lunch with him—producing a penny saveloy. It was duly served up on silver plates; he ate half, and directed the remainder to be kept till he came again.

He was equally parsimonious with envelopes, readdressing those he himself had received to his own correspondents. There is a story also of his calling upon a local clergyman and handing him a small packet which he would 'find useful.' The Vicar was puzzled : was it for the schools ? or church restoration ? or the new reredos ? or the poor ? It was too light, however, for money, unless a cheque or banknotes. At last he opened it ; it contained all his own visiting-cards, left at Motcomb with great frequency for a long period.

The Marquis liked, however, to have value for his money, and the storm which broke out when he found that his servants, who had received second-class fare, were travelling third, was for long a good story in the neighbourhood of Motcomb. He turned them all bodily out, and made them change both class and tickets. He was not a bad landlord when anyone could get at him, and when a posse of Wiltshire tenants once waited on him in a body, he not only granted their requests, but asked them to lunch, which was just over. Fresh plates, etc., were soon arranged, and the leading man sat down at the head of the table, and said : ' Now, then, I'm going to drink the Marquis's health in his own wine.' He soon put it down, with a wry face : it was toast-and-water.

I knew the late Mr. Aston, for many years

accountant to the Ecclesiastical Commissioners. He assured me that he was the only Christian left in that office, constant contact with bishops having undermined the faith of all the rest, and sorely tried his own. If all his experiences were like that he had with Lord Auckland—who, when he called on him at Wells to ask payment for sundry luxuries at the Palace, paid for out of the fund, roundly abused him, and told him to 'get out of the house!'—this might well be. Mr. Aston, a barrister, and master of a great City company, had to open the front door for his own exit, but left it to somebody else to shut.

A friend of mine, passing up St. James's Street some two years ago, saw an unexpected sight. He met a gentleman coming down that thoroughfare, and at once made way, uncovering as he did so. The salute could not be returned in the usual way, for the person saluted had both hands occupied, so a genial smile, nod, and laugh took its place. The whole thing was so surprising that my friend could not believe his eyes, so he turned and followed the gentleman, who passed under the Palace clock-tower, giving the same return to the sentries as they presented arms, indulging both simultaneously in two of the broadest grins of which Tommy Atkins is capable. Other sentries performed the same manœuvres, facial and manual, and when the shadowed one went into the Duke of Edinburgh's house, no doubt remained that the Prince of Wales had been observed carrying a parcel, and a good-sized one too.

It is a not uncommon practice to concern one's mind with the present condition of relatives who have passed before us into Silence ; and an eminent M.P., who runs a society journal, appears to have found it profitable. The senator in question had an uncle in the House of Lords, and an acquaintance of his got it into his head that the relationship between peer and commoner was that of father and son. Calling on the M.P. at the House, he remarked :

' I've just been listening to a speech of your father's in the House of Lords.'

' Well, now, *that's* satisfactory ; the poor old gentleman died some years since, and we've never been able to make out what had become of him.'

CHAPTER VII.

SOCIAL REMINISCENCES.

Failures *ab initio*—The Duke's Son among the Convicts—The Bridegroom does for himself—'They've got the Cab by the Hour'—Dr. Pusey's Sacrifices—'Wusser than a Canon'—My Son's Maiden Speech in the House of Commons—The Old Lady in the Wig—'Who's that Preaching?'—Disraeli pats him on the Head—'You're a young 'un to come in here, anyhow'—'Thee'st a loiar, 'cos I bay'—A Great Wreck of a Great Man—Orthodoxy and Heterodoxy—Brunel and his Half-sovereign Investment—His Hour's Ride to Bath—Mr. Horatio Love and his H's—'Like to see the Man who took you in'—The other McNab—The Cherry and the Stone—''Tis I, sir, rolling rapidly'—Unsuccessful Fraud—The Scenter—Gratitude due to a Burglar—The Peat-charcoal Patentee.

IT is extraordinary how some men contrive to handicap themselves at the very beginning of their career, and to do it irretrievably too, so that no place of repentance lies open to them. Two amusing instances occur to me in quite different spheres of life. Up to the time when the Australian Colonies settled the Convict question by refusing to receive any more convicts, annual debates on the question took place in Parliament, and one of the Duke of Richmond's sons, Lord Alexander Gordon Lennox, went out to study the subject on the spot. On his return, as a new member, he received the customary favourable hearing on his maiden speech. ' Sir, having had considerable experience in a penal settlement——' He got no further ; the peals of laughter silenced him at once, and for ever. There have been few who could say, like Disraeli, 'The time will come when you *shall* hear me,' and I remember no other who has ever done it. The second is a recent episode in the life of a simple country clergyman. He was marrying a couple, or rather preparing to do so, and a pleasant-faced, neatly-dressed damsel was the most prominent figure. The Rector could not make her out, and asked the bridegroom :

' Is that the bride ?'

' Noa, zur, she bain't ; I wish she wor.'

Little contretemps often occur in these domestic offices, as when a zealous young curate substituted for the usual exhortation which ends with ' amaze-ment ' a still longer homily of his own. The parties fidgeted, and at last the clerk interposed :

' Pray cut it short, sir, they've got the cab by the hour !'

A good story is told of another ecclesiastic in the early days of the Oxford movement. He was travelling in a railway carriage when a lady, with whom he was in conversation, lamented the turn things were taking in Ritualism.

'There's that dreadful Dr. Pusey, he sacrifices a lamb every Friday.'

'Really, madam, you must be mistaken.'

'Oh dear no, I am not! I have it on the best authority that he sacrifices a lamb every Friday.'

'I really do think you must be mistaken, for I am Dr. Pusey, and I really do not know how I should begin to set about it.'

'From the sublime to the ridiculous is but a step,' and a compliment turned topsy-turvy is the reverse of flattering. A clergyman in a cathedral city found himself too unwell to do duty, and sent off in all directions for a substitute. None, however, could be found, and at the last extremity the Close was applied to, and one of the Canons at once complied and performed the service. The old clerk's gratitude was effusive:

'How kind it is, sir, of a great man like you to come and help us down here. We've tried everywhere for a wusser, and could not get him.'

He meant, of course, a man less dignified in rank, not higher in moral character.

On a certain occasion I was within measurable distance of that very serious matter, contempt of the House of Commons. I had been down with my boys to the Docks to see a poor neighbour's son for whom I had got a berth on board ship, and on the way back the eldest, a lad of seven, asked what that big building was. I was then showing him the place where Raleigh had mounted the block with almost as much cheerfulness as Sir Thomas More had done before him ; and the pedestal of Cœur-de-Lion's statue, which occupies its place, telling him the story of that monarch's clemency in sparing the life of the archer who shot him.

' So the poor fellow got off, papa ?'

' No, my boy ; after the King died his people flayed poor Bertrand de Gourdon alive.'

Leaving the Marochetti statue, we went into the Central Hall, and a member came up to me :

' Is that your boy ? Would he like to go into the House ? I'll take him in ;' and before I could interpose the boy was led in through the members' door.

I followed as far as I could, distinctly fore-
boding that the Clock Tower would be the end of
it all.   However, back came Roger Eykyn with
his usual genial smile :

'The boy's all right ; come in yourself.'

I found him in the seats under the gallery,
where a rail only separates them from the House
itself.   The boy was getting a little scared, but
brightened up when I came in, and forthwith, to
my horror, began to talk in a loud whisper :

'Papa, who's the old lady in the wig ?'

'Hush ! Lyla' (his name).

A speaker with white hair and very short sight
was in possession of the House.

'Papa, who's that blind man ?'

'Mr. Robert Lowe, my boy.'

By this time some members whom I knew had
come up expecting some more fun, and they got it.
Mr. Macfie, formerly M.P. for Leith, was moving
a resolution for greater accuracy in Australian
statistics : 'When I conseeder, sir, the magnitude
o' the interests which unite the mither country
with its great dependency, and the valie o' the
information which a better seestem o' stateestical
details wad pat in oor hans——'

' Papa, who's that preaching ?'

The shout of laughter which followed, and the cry of ' Order, order !' from the Chair, warned me I had better withdraw my little man at once ; but, as I was doing so, our introducer told me :

' I don't think the boy noticed it ; but, as I was bringing him in, Disraeli met us and patted him on the head, saying, " Well, you're a young 'un to come in here, anyhow !" '

The boy, now a man, is exceedingly proud of that pat on the head.

Bystanders do not as a fact always meet advances in the way expected from them, as once happened to a blue-stocking lady—Lady Emmeline Stuart Wortley—when on a visit to Gorhambury. Riding along the road, the gate was opened for her by a small yokel, on whom the lady bestowed a trifle, adding, with her sweetest smile :

' I'm sure you're not a Hertfordshire boy, because you are so polite.'

' Thee'rt a loiar, 'cause I bay.'

I was once a passenger by Great Western from Paddington to Taplow ; the train was full, and I had almost to force my way, so much did the occupants ask me to go elsewhere, into a carriage which contained but three inmates, the principal one being a man of fine features, and originally strikingly handsome, but, from the effects of excess plainly enough written on them, become a total wreck. The eye of the elder man was one of command, wonderfully like that of a Navy captain, that of the subordinate equally powerful in a dissimilar way. When we entered the carriage, for I had a friend with me going down to boat at Skindle's, the elder man told us quietly :

' I can't prevent your getting in, but you'll be sorry for it.'

Before we started, a gentleman came to the carriage, looked in and exchanged a meaning nod with the other, who had used to me what at first looked like a threat, but which turned out unpleasantly different. Quickly as the passer-by had looked in, he had been noticed by the patient, who tried to lift a palsied hand, and stammered out :

' Ah, Mitchell, that you !   I'm not very well.'

' So I'm sorry to see, Sir Edwin.'

' I'm going down with our friend the doctor

here to stay at his little place by the river. Good-bye !'

The interlocutor hastened away, the train started, and we *were* sorry for having got in.

Before leaving the train I, by mere chance, looked on the once noble features, and asked :

' Who is he ?'

' Didn't you hear what Mitchell said—that was Mitchell, of Bond Street—it's Landseer !'

It takes a great building to make a great wreck, but both were here, and the Landseer pictures invariably now call up, when I see them, the face of the gifted artist as I saw it for the last time.

*   *   *   *   *

How the human face divine can change under the influence of passions was also made evident to me by another occurrence of quite a different nature. I once knew a Hampshire village where resided a heavy dragoon who, giving way to an inclination for social suicide, had married an Irish actress from off a provincial stage. Wonderfully handsome the lady was, and of conduct as blameless as Miss Costigan herself, but quite uneducated, and with an Irish brogue and Irish temper. Of course, no lady in the regiment would associate with her, and the 'heavy' had to leave the service. Some attempts were made to educate the wife, but to little purpose ; so they vegetated on, the husband going to races, hunting, and playing billiards, the wife going with him to concerts, theatres, and public balls, at which last, however, ladies can contrive to scratch pretty keenly in a quiet and even silent way.

At last the Colonel took to being much from home, chiefly riding over to a garrison town where there was a very handsome shop-girl —*petite*, golden-haired, low-voiced, sweet smiling, and all the rest of it. Then he must run over to California to look at a property which he thought of buying. So the wife accompanied him to Liverpool, and saw him off. She was the last to leave and go on board the tender, so did not notice a golden-haired little woman standing by. But that golden-haired person was the little milliner, for whom the 'heavy' had provided passage and outfit, and with whom he went off as cheerfully as did his neatly humbugged wife in her self-congratulations that she had seen him off safely, and there was no 'hussy' to be feared. And in this placid self-assurance the lawful wife, let us call her Orthodoxy, remained for two years, when the news came that the Colonel had returned, and was living in Jersey, though corresponding with his family and home through the somewhat round-about postal channel of Pinos Altos, Cal., U.S.A.

The Irish blood was up, and the lady started for Weymouth. Arrived on board, by that curious list towards mischief which occasionally seems to get a clear run away with the ball, there met her on board the boat an old gentleman, very courteous to the queenlike beauty, whose every motion was untaught grace. Was she going to Jersey to seek her husband? Was he living there? In Montpelier Road (let us say), and number 67? Why, he himself lived in Montpelier Road, and the very next door; he must know him. Popkins —Colonel Popkins (no military gentleman of the name of Hopkins is to consider himself indicated hereby, as both name and arm of the service are unreal)—of course he knew him! They took their morning walk and smoked their evening pipes together—were like brothers, in fact!

'But, my dear lady, did you say Colonel Popkins was your *husband?*'

' Of course he is, and I should like to see any other woman who dared to call him so. Is there one ? Tell me !'

Here the old man tried to shamble away, but was held by a strong hand. Escaping, he was followed to his cabin and everywhere else, with the demand for full particulars. Now, details have a strange attraction, and I have only known one man (never a woman) resolutely set his face against hearing them, and that was Sir James Hannen in the Divorce Court.

However, the lady got her particulars, and stepped on shore, finding her way up to a pleasant road where well-to-do-people lived. They are early birds in the Channel Islands, not like Theodore Hook, who used to say he shouldn't know eight o'clock in the morning if he was to see it.

So the house was reached. A nurse with a baby came to answer the door, but retreated to make way for a golden-haired little woman in a fascinating morning wrapper. The door opened.

' Does Colonel Popkins live here ?'

' Oh yes ; my husband has just gone out for his morning walk.'

' No, you hussy, he hasn't. *I'm* his wife.'

It must be remembered that Orthodoxy had never seen Heterodoxy to her knowledge. And with that the grand Irish woman literally went for the little South Coast beauty. The savage was literally uppermost. Blows, tearing out of hair, scratches, and flowing of blood, kept step with the litany of curses that Irish volubility poured out without intermission, when, just as the neighbours were being attracted, and the unhappy old man who had let the cat out of the bag was timidly peering round the corner, there turned in at the gate, fresh, cool, and smiling from taking his dog for a morning run, the joint protector of the two combatants. To prevent murder the Colonel pulled the woman who lawfully owned him off, and turned her out of doors to cool, while the weaker vessel was being removed to a place of safety, and put together again ; but meantime the injured one had found a pile of road metal handy, and brought him to her side once more by smashing the windows. A truce was, of course, quickly arranged. The lady wanted neither scandal nor arrest; the Colonel neither more scandal, which he said had already been enough to drive him away from the place, nor damage to pay for.   So money-terms for a separation were agreed on ; but a year or two after, the Colonel could not pay for either ' Doxy,' both his appendages having to come on their own friends for themselves and their children, and now they are once more where they started from, only half-a-dozen miles apart.

I had a little acquaintance with the younger Brunel, and could not help noticing the sad and pained look which he carried about with him after the peculiar accident which for a very long time not only incapacitated him for work, but gave him daily and continued pain.   Playing with his children, and ' palming ' a half-sovereign, it slipped down his throat, and lodged in the trachea, whence all efforts to dislodge it proved futile.   At last, after everything else had been tried, gravitation was resorted to, and the patient swung pendulum-wise, with his face downwards and mouth open, for months.   Patience was again almost exhausted, when one day the harassed victim gave himself a wrench for very weariness' sake, when it fell out. Chink ! he was delivered.   He had the coin mounted as a pin, and wore it till he died.   '

There was a story of his going from Paddington to Bath in an hour. It was an engine and tender only, the last carrying a heavy weight of iron to prevent its hinging over and doubling up in case of anything going wrong. The line was set clear, and away she went—up the Moulsford banks, down the Box Tunnel, with the fearful curve beyond it, not then made safer by heightening the outer rail. The experiment was carried out successfully, but Brunel never expressed a wish to try it again, and both driver and stoker declared that if he did he wouldn't have either of them with him on the footplate.

My acquaintance with George Stephenson was confined to his coming to a house where I stayed as a boy, when Midland stock was at 37, and Manchester, Sheffield, and Lincolnshire about half that figure, with no buyers for either. I myself have held Great Northern at below 50.

I remember some of the Eastern Counties Railway meetings in the old stormy days, where it was my wont to take the part of dissatisfied shareholder. The chairman had but one answer to all complaints—a more or less decent form of 'the lie direct.'   By the merest chance I found out the way to practically disarm the enemy by putting him in a furious passion in the simplest way, which is, I think, useful to know whenever one has to deal with similar vulgar, blatant bullies. Mr. Chairman, a born Londoner, left out his *h's*, and did not like being reminded thereof, so it was only necessary to allude several times running to the 'Alesworth and 'Addiscoe, to fetch him finely —not that he did not return the fire otherways. Almost the only 'silencing' I have ever thoroughly succeeded in was with one of the great missionary societies, which, at that time, when any of their own acceptances was overheld, directed their bankers to refuse payment, and refer the holder to them.   I was protesting against such a stupid way of giving needless trouble, when a sancti-monious clerk smugly said :

'We have made this rule because a man once took us in.'

'Have you got his photograph ?'

'No ; why do you ask ?'

'Because I should like to see the man who could take *you* in.'

During the pause which followed the 'palpable

hit' of this shot, I had time to get off the premises. Perhaps, after all, he would have taken it
quietly, like the Scotchman in Canada who called
on Sir Allen McNab, the universally admitted
head of that clan, and left his card with the words,
'The McNab.' The challenged chieftain in due
time returned the call with his own card altered to
'The other McNab.' A good specimen of the
'reproof valiant' is told of an Eton boy called
Cherry. Some thirty years ago, that young
gentleman, learning 'humanities,' as the Scotch
phrase is, used to think it a capital way of passing
Sunday afternoons to pebble the bargees hand-
somely from the tow-path. But one afternoon
Cherry, who was a dead shot at this kind of fun,
was himself met when floating down-stream by
three bargees, who hailed him with a few *cursory*
remarks, and then opened fire with brickbats,
bottles, and anything else that was handy. Cherry,
however, was prudent, and carried in his pocket
three carefully selected pebbles ; the first cut a
bargee's eye open, the second took out a few of
another's teeth, and the third put the remaining
bargee to flight. The retort may sometimes be
given in retreat, as when Theodore Hook, very

much 'on,' indeed, knocked in a very random manner at the door of the room where Campbell the poet was sitting.

'Wha's that drunken beast?'

Hook was already tumbling downstairs, but the joke would not be denied:

''Tis I, (*Iser*) sir, rolling rapidly.'

As in the case of Bishop Wilberforce, and all other diarists, one would like to get at the good stories which careful editors have kept back from vulgar ears.   They get to light sometime or other; old Pepys' are to be published in an un-Bowdlerised form, and the same thing must sometime or other be done with Mr. Greville's.

When by any chance a fraud does not succeed, the merriment is usually great.   The Bank of England's way of cancelling a bank-note is to tear off the signature.   In the old days before the private banks admitted the joint-stock banks into the Clearing House, a Bank of England clerk was collecting money at the counter of one of these latter institutions, entering the note-numbers in his book and tearing off the signatures.   Just as he had done this, another person at the counter tipped an inkstand over in his direction.   It was summer weather, the clerk's pantaloons a light fancy gray. He at once skipped away, and when he came back his pile of notes was gone. But in place of being struck with consternation, he burst out laughing, in which he was joined by the gentleman behind the counter. The notes stolen were absolutely worthless.

I know a man who owes a deep debt of gratitude to a burglar. My friend was executor and general factotum to a worthy old lady who had been his nurse. Among other property she held some foreign bonds, which, as the safest place she could find, she deposited in a trunk among old dresses. She went away, leaving her house unguarded. The burglar came, broke the box carefully open, tumbled out all its contents, and paused only at a brown-paper parcel at the bottom. Foolish Mr. Sikes! Had his legal experience been acquired in front of the dock in place of behind it, he would have known that it is advisable to read every word of a document, and hence to open every parcel in a box. For in that brown-paper receptacle, tied up with a piece of tape somewhat soiled by wear, there was nearly £1,000 in bearer securities, transferable from hand to hand.

The old lady was so thoroughly scared at the risk she had run that she presented my friend with the bonds *nunc pro tunc*, as they say in the Chancery Division ; in other words, gave him the money there and then instead of at her death, up to which time he respected and esteemed her, and after which he venerated her memory, feeling a certain amount of gratitude to the burglar as well.

When the direction of railway works in England was transferred from the rough underground coal-viewers, with whom it first started, to a professional class, and when 'kid-glove' articled pupils came on the scene, there was naturally a little friction with the navvies, and they had odd ways of showing it. For instance, a highly-perfumed young gentleman gave them great offence, and as he passed a gang at work, the first man he passed would make a great sweep with his arm, and religiously hold his nose ; the second would follow suit, till at last some twenty or more would be standing at ease, all holding their noses. This did not suit the contractor, and the 'scenter' had to be sent somewhere else.

Previous to this, however, it had been arranged that, at the point where the gang were getting out mud, a plank should 'tip,' and the unfortunate dandy got nearly smothered in consequence.

I once met a patentee of peat-charcoal, who planned working his wicked will on Dartmoor as he had on Yorkshire and Lancashire moorland. He had, indeed, tried it in the far North, but got dismally swamped, though favoured by the two great ruling powers, the laird and the Churches. His Grace of Sutherland not only took him up, but even 'tuned the pulpits' in his favour. It was a happy moment for it, a kind of blessed though unnatural peace in the Churches. For a wonder in Scotch theology all the denominations were at that moment in harmony, having combined against a ranter who had been thinning the congregations of all three—Establishment, Free, and U.P. alike. The man was incorrigible, even by 'wut,' and had survived a scrummage with the toughest 'meenister in the haill toun,' this wise :

The doctor had met the Philistine face to face on a bridge, and expostulated with him on his contempt of all authority in matters of religion, and when answered promptly, ' I canna help but speak what's in me, meenister. The Lord has opened my mouth, ye ken,' had rejoined, ' I ken weel, Jamie, that the Lord once did open the mouth of an ass, but I can't find it written that He ever exercised His power in that direction a second time.'

But the peat processes did not take ; the natives only said, ' Fat's it for ?' and ' Fat's ta guid ?' It was ill work teaching an old dog new tricks, and the Lord of Dunrobin lost his money.

CHAPTER VIII.

TOWN AND COUNTRY REMINISCENCES.

Always Buy before you Sell—Ancient Lights as Troublesome as Ancient Livers—The Ordeal by Whisky—When is a Welsh Doctor drunk?—'It's only the Cockles'—The Red Jesuit—Why did not the Austrians shoot Napoleon III. when they had the Chance?—From Palace to Scullery, a Come - down—Why Garibaldi suddenly left England—Bishop Wilberforce, the Two Men in him—Sunday Afternoon at Luton: Two Thousand Women with never a Man among them—How a Shower of Rain made Harmony—The Duchess must not kiss the Duke—Bees, Toads, Tomtits—The Blind Man and the Stock Exchangers—Did Sadleir, M.P., really poison himself?—The Bank Manager never away for a Day—'Wāāk ōōp, Scōtt'—A Little Mistake in a Bank-book—'Stop her'—'Overboard'—Ironies in Death—The King, the Merchant—More Inversions—The Religious Trustee—Paris in 1851—'On tire sur Cinq Personnes'—How to abuse a Solicitor to your Heart's Content on the Cheap! and get Hush Money on the same terms.

MY own experiences of corners in trade was a very small one. There was no Saturday half-holiday then. Offices were open till post hour, and banks till four o'clock, so that an indigo-broker found me in on that day.

' I want you to buy 200 chests of Kurpah. I

must sell it to-day, and some people have kept me humbugging till now, and want me to give an answer on Monday. Will you buy it? Price 1s. 9d. ; deposit this day fortnight ; three months prompt, and I'll guarantee you shan't lose.'

'Yes ; I'll take it.   Send me the contract.'

Before I left the contract was brought, and I locked it up in the safe.   On Monday the broker looked in.

'Got that contract all right?   If you repent it I can get another man to take it.'

Next day : 'There is some mistake about that Kurpah   Would you mind cancelling the contract for, say, 2d. profit?'

Following day, 'I can get you 3d.' brought the answer:

'Bother you and your Kurpahs!   Come again two months hence.'

Eventually the daily nuisance got so great that I insisted on knowing what it all meant, and the reply was astounding.

'Well, before I came to you I was in treaty with Wolff and Lambe' (the names are fictitious). 'It turns out they had sold this parcel to their people in Germany, but would not buy from me unless I took 1s. 8d.   I told them I must sell, and that I knew a man who was sure to be in, and I must sell if he would buy.   Now, they've got to get this parcel of yours somehow.'

'Oh, then, they've been trying to screw you down, and I think I remember they got in my own light some time ago.   So, now tell me what ought this stuff to be a year hence?'

'Last year it was 2s. 9d.   This is a big crop; two big crops never come together; it ought to be worth 2s. 9d. next year.'

'Very good, then I'll keep it till next year, or your people may have it at that price now, less interest at five per cent. for their money.'

There was wailing in Jewry; but I got my cheque for the shilling a pound difference on the Saturday, and a very good week's work it was, for there were a good many pounds avoir-dupois.

Much money can be made by a seller with plenty of elbow-room from a buyer who must purchase—is, in fact, cornered; thus, in a quiet way, 'ancient lights,' in the present rebuilding of London now in progress, have yielded a good deal to their fortunate possessors, who have only to threaten an injunction to get all they ask from the building party, to whom delay is almost ruin.   I had myself to do with a company which had this claim set up with regard to a little window, three feet by two, never used for light, but blocked up with cigar-boxes.   The freehold was in the Bank of Ball's Pond, Limited, and to get the window closed cost my company £5,000 one way or other.   The ragged gaps in the rear, which thin to a shell Temple Avenue houses where they back on to the Inner Temple, prove that ancient lights can be as troublesome as ancient livers.

Big drinking in the bygone days was a fine art, regularly trained for, and I once met a man who had been champion for the defeated side in the great standing contest of Dundee *v.* Glasgow, with the invariable result of the eastern city's twenty-four tumblers of toddy beating the Glaskie bodies' twenty-two.   I remember, indeed, a tournament of the kind in 1847 at Dunoon on the Clyde, where both champions died, the one on the field, or rather carpet ; the winner after a week's illness.   The ordeal was conducted pleasantly enough.   It began after a one o'clock dinner, and ended with one of those substantial

suppers of which we read in ' Pickwick.' In
fact, but for the presence of umpires of the
opposite party to 'tally' the tumblers, no re-
straint was visible. One shudders at the feat;
yet it is being daily repeated in our midst. A
distiller's traveller once told me that if he did not
drink with every landlord he called upon, his
goods would not be bought, and that he had that
very day emptied forty-eight liqueur-glasses of
various spirituous compounds—about his usual
quantity. Inquiry brought out that he drank only
water on Sundays, and that his predecessor had
died after three years. But my informant had no
fear for himself—it was just business!

Soakers of a similar type abounded many years
ago in Wales; but they drank beer, or *crw*,
beginning about ten a.m.; one glass would follow
another till the end came, and another kind of
end too, Llanfyllin (pronounce it, please, Thlan-
vuthlin), for instance, being noted for young
widows. All ranks who could afford it were
alike—parsons and doctors too—in fact, these
last were not believed to have their inspiration or
awen unless they were tight.

I was talking to a lady who lived at Barmouth.

' I saw your cousin, Dr. Williams, last night.'
(The man has been dead thirty years.) ·

' Yes.   Was he well ?'

' Oh yes—very lively indeed.'

' Ah, I see, you think he was drunk.   Tell me, now, was he fighting ?'

' No.'

' Could he speak ?'

' Yes.'   ·

' Could he stand ?'

' Yes.'

' Then ' (scornfully) 'he was not drunk.   We like him like that.   He once had to operate on my sister, after a period of some hours had elapsed, and promised to return at a fixed time.   No Doctor Will. came.   So I sent off our man with the carriage, and told him to stop at every public-house on the road to Dolgelly.   He found Doctor Will. half-way, and brought him along.   When he reached our door he had to be led in, stammering out, " It is only the cockles, Miss Gwen."   But as soon as he touched the handrail he sobered himself at once, went up, and performed the operation with a firm hand.   Bless you ! we like him when he's like that.'

Executions were not in my line, though on one occasion, when in Ceylon, I went to the place where five men were to be strangled next morning, and stood on the drop with the beam above me. My nearest experience was from the lips of an Under-Sheriff, known as 'White Choker Wilson,' whom I met returning from the despatch at Newgate of the five pirates who had captured the *Flowery Land*, and destroyed all evidence against themselves on the theory that dead men tell no tales. There had been fear of the five little fellows uniting once more when brought out, and storming the gaol. So precautions were taken, but the creaking of the beam when it took the little fellows' weight had completely overpowered my big Scotch friend, and he who had borne unflinchingly a personal address from the then Master of the Rolls, in which that functionary repeatedly expressed his regret that he could not remove that solicitor's name off the document of which he was official custodian, was absolutely and completely unstrung. The pinioning apparatus is, of course, a nasty-looking thing, and when, after a week's service on the Old Bailey grand jury, some of us used our privilege of inspecting the prison, and nearly succeeded in buckling the straps round the burly form of the unsuspecting foreman, that functionary was perhaps justified in resisting. Some of us were handcuffed for the fun of the thing, which soon passed off, and the whole party were locked up in the Black Hole, and while there mercilessly chaffed by the chief warder, whose own joke consisted in inability to find the key to let us out.

* * * * *

In the year 1868 I became acquainted with an extraordinary man, who did not conceal that at one time, if not actually so then, he had been a Red Jesuit. He was externally an Italian Hercules, the exact likeness of that splendid figure whom Raffaelle has placed in the foreground of the ‘ Dispute of the Sacrament,’ and of which the painter’s original sketch has been discovered by my friend Mr. Louis Fagan, and is now to be seen in the British Museum Print Room. Externally very poor and almost sordid in appearance, he was acting as curate in an ultra-Ritualist church from which repeated ’vertings have occurred, among them a nephew of the Archbishop of Canterbury, formerly also curate there.

My Italian friend liked a good dinner and a bottle of Asti after it, and as he was one of the finest amateur billiard players I have ever known, I got to know a good deal of him over the green cloth towards the small hours. His story pieced together like this, and in the few instances where I could confirm it was corroborated; in fact, the existence of a big Anglo-Italian in the thirty-six-hour forced march after Magenta came out clear on inquiry from men who were in it.

In the year 1831, the revolutions in France and Belgium had provoked an outbreak in Italy. It was speedily suppressed by the Austrian troops, who shot a good many of the leaders, among them, at Forli, Prince Louis Bonaparte, the only one of his two nominal sons whom the father, Louis Bonaparte, once King of Holland, ever acknowledged. Had the White-coats shot the other brother as well, the face of the world would have been changed; thousands of lives already sacrificed would have been spared, and the catastrophe of Sedan would not have created the Franco-German rancour which may any day bring about a bigger butcher's bill. However, Queen Hortense had powerful friends, and the Austrians let

the future Napoleon III. escape from Bologna ;
but among those they did shoot was Prince
Colonna, the reigning head of that great house.
He had married an English wife, from whom a
son was born ; the destitute mother with her child
got back to England and there married the
chaplain at St. Helena, whose name was Helps ;
the child took his name, and became known as
William Stephen Helps, in place of Giulio Stefano
Colonna.

When the boy was nearing manhood the party
returned to England, and the son made for his
native land, where there were plenty on the
estates who knew him and even helped him with
money. The estates had been transferred from
the revolutionist head to the next brother, on
whom devolved the title and duties of Senator of
Rome, who, when the Pope says High Mass in
St. Peter's, stands in front of the whole congregation. There can be no doubt that at this part of
his life the disinherited one entered the Society of
Jesus, and seems to have been employed by
them, on the strength of his father's name, to
enrol himself at the same time in the ranks of the
Carbonari. It will be remembered that Orsini

justified his attempt to assassinate Napoleon III. on the ground of his having violated the Carbonaro oath taken by him when he threw in his lot with the victim of Forli.   .

He thus became one of those spies in the enemy's camp, whom the Jesuit policy has from all time maintained; and while reporting everything to headquarters in Rome, was a Carbonaro commissioner with Garibaldi in 1859.. He formed part of the column which, after the victory of Magenta, by a forced march of thirty-six hours, got in the rear of the Austrian right wing, harassed them, and gave them no rest till they had fallen back behind the Mincio.

Colonna's position in the Jesuit Society must have been an important one. I will give one instance of it, premising that 'he' means Beckx, the General; 'house,' the Jesuit College at Rome; and 'it,' the Society. 'I went to the house one day and saw him, and while I was talking they brought in the name of a big swell at Vienna Court, confessor there, and up to everything among the great folks. When he came in he did the usual thing, crossed his arms on his breast, knelt down and made the Cross three times with his tongue on the floor. "Rise, my brother!" brought him on his legs again ; and then "he" said, "My brother, our poor house requires periodical cleansing ; let it be your duty to perform it ;" so the big man took pail, soap, and scrubbing-brush, and was a couple of days washing all the stairs down—nice dirty job it was! And when he went into Refectory, he had to make the Cross in the dirt again, and lie down full length while they all stepped over him. I suppose his bones wouldn't stand that work long, so one day when I was with him "he" sent for the Vienna man and set him to clean up all the pots and pans, and act as cook's scullion in the kitchen. That went on for a week, when "he" sent for the man again when I was by, and told him, "My brother, we have now made experience of your obedience and humility," and then told him he was to go out as adminis-trator (that was not the word used, however) of the whole of South India.'

But this mysterious man even claimed that Garibaldi's very sudden departure from England was brought about by him. He told me one evening about mid April in that year :

'I have not been to see him yet, though I have

written to him ; *they* don't like his being here, and
have told me I must go and tell him so.   Nobody
knows who I am, and so I can go to Stafford
House without a fuss.'

A day or two afterwards came the news that
Garibaldi had actually gone without notice of any
kind.   The shabby curate came in the same evening, and lighted a big cigar.

'Well, you see he had to go, and he's gone.'

'Did you see him, then ?'

'Yes ; he made a bit of a difficulty at first, but
very soon saw there was nothing else for it.'

If this were true, *they* could only mean the
secret societies.

About this time I made the acquaintance of
Bishop Wilberforce, of whose marvellous powers
none of the published reports speak highly enough.
No more accomplished man of the world ever
existed, and it is doubtful, perhaps, whether his
father's impecuniosity did not develop his own
money - making abilities, and his father's long-
winded preachments bring out his sacerdotalism.
How completely the two men in him—the outside and the inside—differed, is plain from his
diary, as to which the story goes that his son was

reproached for having published so much that was contrary to the popular idea of his father. The answer is said to have been :

'If you talk about that, you should just see what I've left out.'

I have omitted all references to my London Sundays, invariably spent in some of the pleasant outskirt places, for the most part at St. Albans, which all the ages have found a pleasant little town, from the ancient British Prince Tasciovanus, who minted his gold coins there, and the Romans, whose amphitheatre is just the size of that at Pompeii, to Nicolas Breakspear,* who loved the abbey where he had entered as milk-boy and gone out as Cardinal; where still can be traced the baker's shop where Henry VI. was taken prisoner (bakers' shops are immortal by reason of the oven), and still can be seen the home and grave of Francis Bacon, the greatest practical benefactor to Humanity that ever existed. Battle-fields and camps, of all ages and all races, the tower of the Saxon king's palace, the fortified outlook, the

* Adrian IV., the only Englishman ever Pope of Rome. Died 1159. Tradition hath it he was choked by a fly.

church with its beacon turret, storied nooks such as that where Warwick the King-maker died fighting against fearful odds—all go to prove that the land was deemed well worth fighting for, and the record is daily added to.

Thus a piece of waste land, as repulsive in aspect as that great battle-field now called 'No Man's Land,' whereon was fought the second battle of St. Albans, proves to have been one vast pitfall, in which a whole company of horsemen appear to have been engulfed and rotted where they lay. All these incidents, and such as these, with the unrivalled Bass's beer and tawny port to be had at the 'Pea-hen,' come back to memory; and with them Luton, in the pre-railway days, ten miles off, where on a fine Sunday could be seen the elsewhere impossible sight of the 'Park Road.' On this highway, some two miles long, were to be seen 2,000 young women smartly dressed, and some of them beautiful, taking the air with never a man among them, their male belongings, where they had them, shrinking from being swamped in such a posse of petticoats. These were the operatives who during the week made up the straw-plait into bonnets and hats. Now John

Chinaman makes the plait, and Bedfordshire men, women, and children no longer take their walks abroad twiddling straws. The glories of the Park Road have departed. In the old days one felt there like a Devonshire servant of mine, whom, duly escorted by a London one, I ran up against at the Royal Exchange. It was his first visit, and he was just then giving his astonishment mouth.

' Bain't they never going to ha' done coming ?'

Or nearer town was Whitchurch, where was the organ on which Handel had played, and the plain wooden rail which records the name of 'William Powell, the harmonious blacksmith' and parish clerk, into whose smithy a most blessed shower of rain had driven the organist, to posterity's everlasting benefit, to pass away the time by noting down the clink of the hammers, so endowing the world with a deathless melody.

Under the church could still be seen the velvet-covered coffin of their common patron, the great Duke of Chandos, who could tell his second wife, when she kissed him (rather a queer personage, that Duchess No. 2 !): 'Madam, my first wife was a Percy, and *she* never took such a liberty,' but who is now only remembered as the owner of Canons, for whom that somewhat uncouth and coarse German organist aforesaid wrote some never-to-be-forgotten anthems, so called.

Handel remained, indeed, the same all his life as when he ordered a supper for four, and asked why it was not brought up.

'Waiting for de gompany, hein? I am de gompany.'

Farther afield, outside the Chiltern Hills, was Aylesbury, with its White Hart Inn, where, in the old mad days, Mytton, or some other like him, had his hunter brought up the great oak stair to the first-floor, and made him clear the dining-table.

Or pleasant nooks in the Chiltern Hills, such as Velvet Lawn, ankle deep in soft turf, with, close by, Chequers Court, held by descendants of the Protector Cromwell, where could be seen the portable property—watch, Bible, and sword—of that great natural-born General who never lost a battle.

Much of this country I studied in a novel way, taking the first turn either to right or left, and chancing where it would lead me. Old churches, old halls, old farms, with a climb up an outlier of the Chilterns for a more extensive view, filled up many a pleasant day's ramble. One's knapsack ensured perfect independence, and if the way were in doubt, then, and then only, would the Ordnance Map be appealed to.

I had some acquaintance, though but slight, with the late Dr. Cumming, of Crown Court.

At the time—1852—while that divine was giving the world at large but five years more of existence, he was renewing the lease of his pleasant house on Tunbridge Wells Common for fourteen, so he could have set little practical store on his own predictions.

He greatly enjoyed bee-keeping in that honey-making spot, and not unfrequently brought it into his sermons in somewhat far-fetched analogies.

It was said of one great pulpit orator who got into a sad mess, that where there was so much profession practice would naturally be the weak point ; and Dr. Tyler tells a story of his Heidel-berg Professor, who, when advocating the application to the human skin of an alkali in combination with a fatty acid in conjunction with warm water, went on to say :

'It is wonderful how rarely one carries out one's own theories, even in soap and water.'

I remember but one Stock Exchange joke apart from that practical form which seizes on that body when business is dull, and a stranger has inadvertently strayed into the sacred spot. Then is raised the cry '1400,' and the intruder, hustled, bonneted, cuffed, and converted into a walking inkstand by the quantity of that fluid poured down the nape of his neck, escapes mauled and battered from precincts where law and order are held to be of the highest value, to judge by the way prices are put down when their opposite obtains in any country possessing public debts.

Thirty years ago there carried on business on Waterloo Bridge, not then toll-free, a blind man who read the Bible in an audible voice from a volume in raised type. He was quiet, respectable, old established; taken to business in the morning and removed at night, and regularly paid the income-tax for which the neighbouring Somerset House assessed him. To this harmless practitioner, so thoroughly trained in his trade as not to swear when half-a-crown was held out to him and subsequently pocketed, entered two

Capel Court people for the purpose of deciding a small wager. Let me pause to suggest that this half-crown palming combines the advantages of detecting a fraud and a little harmless fun as well; while, if the man be really blind, he is not disappointed. It should be done in quick time, so as not to give the man time to think. The victim noticed their stopping, and went on with his recitation: 'And it came to pass, after they had pitched in Gilgal, at the going down of Beth-horon, that Saul said unto Samuel:'

'Who the sanguinary blazes has been putting sand on my book?'

*   *   *   *   *

It is gruesome work following the trail of a suicide, marking each point where the helpless and hopeless hunted one dashes from one side of his tether to the other, till the point comes when it dawns upon him that escape can no longer be thought of, and the scorpion's fate is elected rather than the disgrace to those belonging to him, which comes in when the father is a convicted felon. Nearly forty years ago I followed up the track of that mystery, John Sadleir, to his last day in the City, the last farewell—'Good-bye,

McKenzie! I'm going a long journey and shan't see you again '; the visit to Bedford Row, where the solicitor held the ropes tight; the return home; the thought that now there was no time to marry the heiress and replace everything; the call at the chemist's; the untraceable journey to Hampstead Heath to reach that hillock in the muddy marshes where, without a speck of dirt on clothes or boots, the body, with its white face turned up to the sky, was to be found on that wintry morning.

Far different from the thin saturnine Irish Lord of the Treasury was the man whose end I was next to ascertain. White-haired, stout, Scotch, and pawky in its most Glaswegian sense was the manager of one of the biggest of Scotch banks. He was the great man of the time, a leader in a place where local business qualifications are keenly discussed—witness the case of that drover who was tried before a jury of his peers at Falkirk Tryst, for selling more of the unpolled stot of Galloway and the kyloe of the Mearns, worse beasts and at better prices too, than his mates, and held justified by his plea that he 'found a fool.'

In his way the manager was a remarkable man.

He had never taken a holiday for fourteen years, knew every depositor by name when he brought his 'buik' to have the interest put in, ha'e a bit 'crack' with the manager, and be personally attended to by the head himself. Inside the counter, too, his praise was loudly sung ; he kept the deposit books himself, so as to ensure the accuracy of the minutest detail. And in the kirk, one of the three-thirds of a hair into which Caledonian polemics have split the Seamless Robe, he was paramount, so that when the bedral died the manager must see him laid to his rest.

A man of mark in his way, that bedral! Was he not the man whom Dr. Candlish had singled out for somnolency in the ninety-fifth minute and twenty-seventh head of his discourse, and, after a marked pause had failed to rouse the sleeper, then shouted out ' Wāāk ōōp, Scōtt '?

No! bank or no bank, the manager must see the last o' Sandy ; and with reverently bowed head the ruling elder of the kirk sorrowed over one of its humblest officers.

Meantime the travelling inspector had unex-pectedly turned up at the bank, had heard why the well-known presence was not there, had ex-

pressed sympathy with both man and reason
why, and was leaving the bank to come back in
the morning, when there entered a depositor who
wished to withdraw a small sum.   The book was
produced, compared with the ledger, cheque paid.
Then spoke the cashier :

'There's no matter o' hairm, Jam's, in your
telling the warld oot lood that ye've got seven
ninety-three saxteen aught in here, but ye need
not hae tauld it me, for I ken ye've no but saxty-
seven twelve nine.'

'The manager aye tuck my money, and pat it
down his sel', and the interest tae.'

'That's a' vary weel, Jam's, but the interest is
wrang, too.   Ye'll hae made a mistak.'

'Deevil a mistak, mister !'

'Weel, weel, ye'll hae to come in the morn.   *I*
canna put it richt.'

The inspector was all ears, of course ; and when
the manager, who lived over the bank, came in,
he replied—when the book was compared with
the bank ledger—'The man is just daft; the
book's no written up.'   But he went out of the
bank dressed just as he had come from the funeral
and never returned.   Some three weeks after it

was found that the depositors' books, all made up by him, were in excess of their credits with the bank by £27,000. The money had gone in personal expenditure over many years.

In mercy to the rest of those employed, bank defaulters must always be followed up, and the manager's case was exceptionally flagrant. It was, however, six weeks before he was run to earth, and it was then too late by ten minutes. He had put up at a little fourth-rate inn at Conway, lying close all day, only going out by night, and invariably leaving the common room when any strangers entered. On one occasion he had come back in the small hours thoroughly drenched, as if he had essayed drowning. The man became daily more and more broken down, till one day, while the family was at dinner, he passed into the stable, and was found hanging there by the neck when two strangers called to ask for him by his assumed name. Justice was too late ; as well perhaps that she was, for the lesson reads almost as awful as if he had actually joined the felon herd.

The face of an intending suicide is an awful thing. I shall never forget that one which I saw on a Thames steamboat. It was an elderly respectable woman of the lower classes, and the grim set expression of her features drew my attention as she clawed at her face with a long thumb-nail. It was raining, and I offered her a share of my umbrella. Snappishly refused, I feared my civility had got me into trouble, as she moved away towards the stern.

All at once came the cry, 'Stop her! Overboard!' And the poor creature went struggling with the tide till sucked under a tier of barges at Lambeth. After some inquiry I ascertained that at the inquest the reason given was 'Trouble.' But the helpless, despairing look is present to me now.

The ironies of death are almost as sardonic as those of the life which it closes. We can throw on the screen two shadows of pleasure, wealth, and ambition. When the worst of the Stuarts—that solitary one, of whom not one good word can be said—was entering his last evening of life, he whispered to his successor :

'Don't let poor Nelly starve.'

The ex-fruiteress had duped the man who sold England for the French King's gold, just like his other mistresses. My friend, Mr. Hilton Price, informs me that the King's English —— (say doxy, for decency's sake), as she styled herself, died worth many thousands of pounds, in addition to that solitary house on the south side of Pall Mall, which alone of all there does not belong to the Crown, having been diverted Nelly-way by the free-handed monarch.

Take again the money - maker, Blumberg, originally a huckster of German glass. When told that the door of the stately mausoleum at Norwood which Sir Charles Barry had built for him at a cost of £4,000 was opening for his entrance, he said to the physician :

'Doctor, I'll give you £10,000 to save my life.'
The sorrowful, pitying smile follows.
'I'll . give . . you . . . twenty . . .'

* * * * *

One curious reverse of fortune came to my notice. There are, of course, plenty such in Shoreditch lodging-houses, whither drift the broken-down gentlemen of the West-end clubs. But this was a woman—the grand-daughter and heiress of one of the West India sugar kings in the days before Emancipation.

His will contained something like 200 bequests

of this nature : 'To Bill, £10 and his freedom,'
'To Sal, £10 and her freedom,' said legatees being
his own children.   But the hon. gentleman's
heiress was a great catch, and her £50,000 fortune was equal to that of her husband.   So the
two started with £100,000 between them—a large
sum in 1831.   Before, however, the decade was out,
the money was spent, the father missing, and there
were some eight children to be fed and started
in life.   The lady herself became a housekeeper ;
the sons clerks ; some of the daughters domestic
servants or unspeakably worse ; and a somewhat
sanctimonious relative was resorted to for small
loans, which finally ceased on account of the applicant's liquory condition when appealing for
them.   The refusal roused up fury.   Old recollec-
tions were pieced together, and a sporting solicitor
brought the case into Court, when it turned out
that the pious relative was surviving trustee of a
sum of £10,000 Consols, provided by the grandfather for the contingency of poverty, which had
really occurred.   As desired, the trustee had kept
the matter very secret, likewise the half-yearly
dividends, which, together with compound interest
at five per cent., the Master of the Rolls compelled

the good man to refund. It was, however, necessary for legal purposes in those days to find the long-lost father, and he was eventually discovered as a writing-clerk in a solicitor's office in the next house to that where two of his sons filled similar positions. So small is the world!

I had a friend in Somerset House who ran over to Paris in the early winter of 1851, and took up his quarters in one of the side streets near the Madeleine. He had his wife and son with him, and on the following morning went out for breakfast. Opening the door, he came all but in contact with a bayonet, and was gruffly told :

'On ne passe pas.'

The street was full of cavalry and infantry, and the nearest officer was appealed to. He, however, could give no information ; but as an Englishman was concerned, he agreed to pass him through the troops, the passage under horses' heads for a stout man being the reverse of pleasant. However, the Boulevard was at last reached. Great was the joy when a well-known French friend and his wife were encountered ; yet the natives did not return the cordial greeting, but moved away, till the Englishman got angry.

'After all I've done for you, Langenbeck, you are treating me *emphatically* badly.'

The reply, given ten yards off, quickly altered matters :

'On tire sur cinq personnes,' and sure enough came the sound of the troops firing at the windows, and the heavy guns cannonading the houses at point blank—a massacre which cost hundreds of innocent lives. If Dr. Arnold thought he could see the finger of Providence in the Moscow Retreat, what would he have seen in the downfall of a dynasty founded on such crimes as these, in the lurid flames of Sedan and Bazeilles?

Utterly sickened at the slaughter, my friend and his people got away by the next train.

The Reform is not a very social place, but is not quite so chilly as its neighbour, the Athenæum, where members are usually very silent. Nor has it any such member as the Senior United Service possessed, who was only known to speak once, as he made his wants known in other ways. Once, however, he was given half a sovereign short in change. The man was detected, and his conviction made

known to the silent member, who then spoke for
the first and only time :

' I knew it.'

Huddleston had but one bench story, and even
this he did not repeat much in later years. It
related to

> ' A farmer of Ciceter
> Who went to consult a solicitor.'

' Zur, what would you be a-charging me for
telling what I can call a man without his having
the law of me ?'

On this, reference was made to one of the text-
books on slander, all of which (British public,
please take note) contain a vocabulary of the
epithets the law has in decided cases held to be
mere abuse when used verbally—not in writing,
however, my B. P., nor to a man in connection
with his trade.

' My fee, Mr. Smith, is 6s. 8d.'

The amount being produced, the adviser continued :

' You can call a man a rogue, a liar, a scoundrel,
villain, etc. (for some forty of them), and also a
thief, if you thereby do not intend to suggest that
he has committed larceny.'

' Then, zur, you be a röog, you be a loier, you

be a scoondrel, you be a villain, etc., and you be a d——d big thief, not meaning to saäy as you never stole nothing.'

A perfectly novel form of competition is not easy to find, but one cropped up the other day in Change Alley. Two musicians, violin and harp, both of them artists, had taken their pitch opposite a restaurant, and one lingered to hear a few bars of the fine music which was sure to be heard. The violin tuned up, the harp used its key, and a few wailing notes from the leader showed a treat was coming, when from the crowd by their side a dingy-dressed woman, with a face that told its own tale of how the fall had been brought about, commenced an Italian bravura song, with so much music in it as to show the voice's natural gifts had been carefully trained. Violin looked down, and harp said something ; but of course the singer had as much right as they had, and kept the field, while the crowd laughed vociferously, which culminated when the men abandoned the contest ; accompaniment being, as it usually is, nowhere in comparison of singer. Evidently the lady thought peace must be paid for, and wanted for herself literally ' hush-money.'

CHAPTER IX.

LITERARY TREASURES.

Hunting all Game—'Jimmy, my Lord, not Tommy'—The Great Duke of Wellington : His Moral Lesson—He would like to *bury* St. Edmunds—The Salisbury Bookseller and the Caxton MS. —'Knock me down, and walk off with Shakespeare's Autograph'—Mr. Piccadilly—The Bunyan Warrant—A Slice of Luck in a Sale—Groans of the Wounded—'You've no Business to have this : its Place is here'—Her Majesty's Gracious Condescension—Dr. John Brown and his Lucky Guess—Bunyan in America—Keble's 'Christian Year' taken up by Scotch Presbyterians—How Charles I. met his Fate—The Red Pamphlet—'Eyes and no Eyes'—New Touching Details as to the Closing Scene—Did Sir William Penn write it ?—The Queen graciously accepts the Valuable Document—'Eikon Basilike'—Photographs of the Skulls of Richard II. and his Queen—How the Clergyman got his Jaw-bone—Kings' Brains are Sweet—The Skull of Mary Queen of Scots—When shall Cromwell's Head go back to Westminster Abbey ?—'Roll up the Map of Europe'—Luther's Bible —Don't trust Grandees with Autographs—How the Windsor Chapter treated their Caxtons—Who wrote the 'Imitation of Christ'?—Milton's Poems, Wesley's Unique First Hymnbook—'The President goes to Court now'—On Forgeries generally—A Prayer-book from Whitehall Chapel, burned in 1698—Commonwealth State Papers—How the Peer came to part with them, and his Vain Regret—Secretary Thurloe—The Event which doomed Charles I.—The Warrant for the Arrest of Charles II. after Worcester : £1,000 Reward—The Proclamation of the Commonwealth—The Last of the Cromwells—'Life gets Harder' —The Portsmouth Royal Charter of Edward II.—Not so Tough all round as our Forefathers—A Pretty Picture-book.

HUNTING is a passion born in all animals, and therefore very human. There is a story about it connected with the late Earl of Mornington, who, as Tilney Long Pole Wellesley, attained distinction as a *roué* and spendthrift even in the days of Gorgeous George.   His broken-hearted wife attempted to remove her son from the contamination of such an evil example, and in the course of the Chancery proceedings which ensued, there was handed up to Lord Eldon a letter written by father to son, in which occurred the words : ' Hunt all game, from the flea in the blanket to the elephant in the forest, and play —— and Tommy.'   Such surroundings as this interested the stern old man, whose own bringings-up had been of a far different kind, and who could look back to the time when a sheep's-head, bought for 4d. in Clare Market, with its 'fine confused feeding,' had to satisfy the hunger of himself and his wife ; and he dwelt upon the last paternal instruction, but pronounced it ' Jimmy.'

' What —— and Jimmy can mean the Court cannot authoritatively settle, but it is evidently something which no proper-minded parent should set before his son as a career to be followed in life.   —— and Jimmy !   Jimmy !'

This was too much for one of the junior

counsel, on whose fine and sensitive ear the mistake grated :

'Beg your lordship's pardon : —— and Tommy, my lord, not Jimmy.'

The Chancellor referred to his notes.

'—— and Tommy it is, Mr. Shadwell, not —— and Jimmy.'

Hunting, however, does not always succeed. There is an amusing story of the great Duke of Wellington seeking an introduction to Mdlle. Mars. The great actress declined :

'He is said to have given my countrymen a moral lesson, and I gave him one in return—I told him to go home to his wife.'

In my own case book-hunting was innate, although I am no way of kin to the celebrated bookseller of Covent Garden. When very young, I had picked out the oldest book to be found in the house, and given it its precedence as *doyen d'age ;* while Snuffy Davy, in Scott's 'Antiquary,' who bought Caxton's 'Game of the Chesse' for 2d., and sold it for twenty pounds, was my boyish hero. Not that a schoolboy's pocket-money, nor the bookshops of the Brompton Road, gave much opportunity for exercise of the twist in one's mind ; that had to come later on with time, leisure, and what I suppose a late trial will add to the English language as 'oof.' One peculiarity, however, of old-book hunting is that there's always game afoot of some kind. A friend of mine was once curate in the ancient town of Bury St. Edmunds. His stipend was of the most modest ; a wife and two boys had to be provided for out of it, yet this admirable gentleman, on whom poverty sat as a crown, and who had taught himself Hittite for a school lecture, told me that nearly every week he picked up books at the stalls for a few pence which, disposed of elsewhere—doubtless in London—would realize as many shillings. Here, then, pleasure and profit were combined, carrying out that great system of COMPENSATION which is as powerful a life-factor now as in the days of the manna, when they who gathered much had nothing over, and they who gathered little had no lack. The problem has been little studied, but it will bear a great deal of study, for in the adjustment of everything by the scale of individual enjoyment rests one of the great balances of social life, without which, indeed, it could not be carried on.

To get back to book-hunting. The ignorance of men who are really experts in some part of their book-trade is almost judicial. I shall give many instances of it, but will open by a little incident which occurred in the Salisbury Close.

Bookseller's shop ; a customer enters.

' Got any black-letter ?'

' No, nothing worth speaking about. I've got a manuscript, though, if you care about that—it's very cheap.'

' Let me see it.'

It *was* a manuscript, and a very peculiar one ; but the customer rather suspected something.

' What's the price ?'

Fifteen shillings, eventually lowered to 12s. 6d.

The purchaser took the first train back to town, and the next morning went to the one place where information is always freely and frankly given, and where no time is thought wasted that can assist a student—the British Museum. He knew a little of Mr. Bullen, and saw that gentleman opening it :

' A manuscript—the " Recuyll of Troye " it is called.'

' My *dear* sir ! didn't you *know*, by the feel of

it, that this was a Caxton, printed with Colard Mansion's type ?'

It was shown in the Caxton Exhibition, and was remarkable for its beauty and condition even there ; and its value was nearer £500 than the 12s. 6d. so judiciously laid out in its purchase.

The story got about, and the unhappy book-seller, a man of sterling worth and attainments in his trade, but who had missed the great chance of his life, was thereafter continually pestered for manuscripts, until he would rush away in agony. There is a whisper, however, for which I am not to be understood to vouch, that a funny kind of retribution fell upon the man who had won the prize, in this form : that, not recognising he had exhausted his slice of luck at one shy, he went about buying rubbish in a silent, secret way, in the hope of a second innings ; and that the outlay thereby incurred took a good deal of gilt off the Caxton gingerbread when his library came to the end of all things literary—the hammer.

I was one day with Mr. Bullen comparing my Luther's Autograph Bible with that in the Museum collection, when he took up a small folio and said :

' Now, then, all you've got to do is to knock me down, and walk off with this.'

The volume bore one of the autographs of Shakespeare, on which some little doubt, however, exists ; and I was obliged to point out to my friend, who had suggested so startling an end to our confab, that, supposing everything else, and that I *could* knock him down, the book was marked all over with the Museum stamp, and that I could no more sell it than the stolen Duchess of Devonshire picture of Agnew's could find a market.   I had, however, one parting shot :

' I have, Mr. Bullen, some books that bear your mark already, notably an Erasmus Testament with Cranmer's autograph in it.'

The chief looked rather glum ; it was one of the duplicates sold out of the Museum many years before, and they had made a little mistake over it.   They don't sell duplicates now.

Not, however, that experts are above trying to get things cheap.   Not many years ago a very successful ' knock out ' came off at a London book auction.   There was a First Folio Shakespeare put up, and the ring got it for £25 ; at the subsequent resale £400 was the figure reached, and cheap at that; so the four parties to the deal cleared over £90 apiece.

The Americans have a proverb: ' It's the longest pole that fetches the persimmon ' (which means a plum), and the cleverest man with the longest purse comes to the front in the book-trade as everywhere else. London has an excellent specimen—let us call him Mr. Piccadilly—whose talents first blossomed in a little shop at the bottom of St. Martin's Lane, but have since raised him to an eminence which few of his craft have ever attained to. Guy, of the Hospital which now bears his name, enriched himself, not so much by his trade, as by cashing sailors' advance notes. Our present subject has a keenness almost amounting to an instinct, and has been known to detect a *princeps* of Izaak Walton's ' Angler ' in a lot of cookery books, and to secure the lot at the price usually given for books suited for the twopenny box. When he goes down to battle in a very old felt hat bashed in at the side, it is known the veteran means business, and that £2,000 won't stop him. In fact, he has given the largest price ever given for a book for business purposes, *i.e.*

to sell again, for the £13,000 odd given by the Duke of Roxburgh for the Valdarfer ' Boccaccio ' was simply a contest between two rich men, like the late Lord Dudley's purchase of three Dresden china chimney ornaments a foot high for £11,000; and both the articles have since passed the hammer at very large reductions from these figures. However, Mr. Piccadilly gave £4,950 some years ago for a Mentz Psalter, and one regrets to infer from its continued appearance in his latest catalogues that he has it still. Naturally there are but few people who can afford to lose interest to the tune of half a sovereign a day for looking at the back of a book, though the nation loses some £7 a day in like fashion for the sight of the Marlborough Raffaelle in the National Gallery.

To return to Mr. Piccadilly, a perfect master of the difficult art of buying, and rarely failing to depreciate at the first start the lot he means to have at any price, it is hardly conceivable that he should ever be off his guard, and let anything of any kind worth having go past him; but in one instance he did so to my own great personal advantage, and as the document in question settled a historical doubt, fought over almost as keenly as what Lord Beaconsfield called those never-to-be-settled controversies, Mary Queen of Scots and the death of her unhappy grandson, Charles I., namely, the date of ' The Pilgrim's Progress,' the story may be worth telling.

Some 220 years ago there practised at Bristol a physician called Ichabod Chauncy, the son of a very eminent Cambridge Professor, whom the relentless malice of Laud had reduced to beggary, and who had received his own pathetic name as having been born in that agony of privation and poverty. The father eventually got over to America, where his name is recorded as the Second President of Harvard. The son, originally an army chaplain under the Protector, in which capacity he had shared in Oliver's capture of Dunkirk, which was to be sold back to the French King in the second year of the Restoration for a million sterling, availed himself of his medical degree as has been said. He was the great stronghold of the persecuted folk in the West, attended the prisoners in the crowded gaol, fought hard for better air and better food for those imprisoned for conscience' sake, and thus saved many lives.   But he did even more than this: he advised them in their legal difficulties, as to whether and when an appeal would lie.   It must be borne in mind that the severity of the Draconic laws then in force was mitigated by the power of legal quibbles.   Chauncy had in this way procured the release of 'Saint's Rest' Baxter from the kind-hearted Lord Hale, who had quashed the warrant under which he had been arrested.   And so famous was he in this way, that the local grand jury presented Ichabod for prosecution as the 'Dissenters' Attorney-General.'   The distinction was a perilous one, and on his second conviction, in 1684, he was exiled, with forfeit of land and goods, returning, however, after the tyranny had overpast in 1688, to resume his practice in Bristol, till his death in 1691.   Now, in 1670 a case had occurred which brought Chauncy as a legal adviser prominently to the front.   It was long known as the Bushell Case.   When Quakers' meeting-houses were closed by the New Conventicles Acts in that year, the City disciples of George Fox resorted to a peaceful but most irritating rejoinder.   On each and every Sunday they repaired to their shut-up place of worship in Gracechurch

Street, and remained there in silent meditation during the period usually occupied by their service. Arresting them did no kind of good, for as soon as a Quaker was let out of gaol, the next Sunday saw him back again as provokingly as before. So the Lord Mayor thought fit to call this dumb protest 'a tumultuous assembly,' and for this offence William Penn and another were duly indicted at the Old Bailey, and the trial showed what everybody knows, that very good people can be very irritating ; in fact, the founder of Pennsylvania gave back almost as many nasty speeches (in truly Christian phraseology however) as the Recorder sent at him. Bushell was the foreman of the jury, which refused to convict, so the Recorder in question locked them up for thirty-six hours, without fire, light, food, and drink, or indeed anything. This had no effect, so the Court fined them forty marks apiece, with imprisonment till the fine was paid. This last straw settled it. Bushell was a spirited man, and he took counsel with his friends and Chauncy, by whose advice he brought his conviction, by writ of Habeas Corpus, before the full Court of Common Pleas, with the result that it was quashed as contrary to the principles of Magna Charta. People in those days were thankful for small mercies, and Bushell was quoted as a second Hampden, so that when the old tyranny broke out again, in 1675, his case would be fresh in all men's minds, especially at Bedford, where Quakers abounded, and where a case of great oppression had just been carried out, notable even among the many of which the records of that time are full. Bunyan, after twelve years' imprisonment, had been set free in 1672, and licensed as a preacher; he had used his freedom with his wonted energy, and during the three years in which his churches had rest had largely multiplied their number in the half-dozen counties round, so that when the Danby Ministry had passed a new Act against Nonconformists, he was singled out as the first victim.

A warrant for his arrest, prepared by Cobb, the Clerk of the Peace—an enemy who had brought about his first imprisonment — was laid before thirteen justices, and by them signed and sealed. The form of this instrument of torture—but for which 'Pilgrim's Progress' would never have been written—may be worth introducing to a generation which for conscience' sake puts up tamely with Salvation Army bands, and allows the traffic of London streets to be disorganized for half a day by one of its funeral processions a couple of miles long.

' To the Constables of Bedford and to every of them

Whereas informaçon and complaint is made unto us that (notwithstanding the Kings Maj^ties late Act of most gracious gen'all and free pardon to all his Sub-jects for past misdemeano^rs that by his said clemencie and indulgent grace and favo^r they might bee mooved and in-duced for the time to come more care-fully to observe his Highenes laws and Statutes and to continue in theire loyall and due obedience to his Maj^tie) yett one John Bunnyon of yor said Towne Tynker hath divers times within one Month last past in contempt of his Maj^ties good Lawes preached or teached at a Conventicle meeteing or assembly under colo^r or ꝑtence of exercise of Religion in other manner than accord-ing to the Liturgie or practise of the Church of England. These are there-fore in his Maj^ties name to comand you forthwith to apprehend and bring the Body of the said John Bunnion bee fore

J Napier

W Beecher

G Blundell

Hum: Monoux

Will ffranklin

us or any of us or other his Maj[ties]
Justice of peace within the said County
to answer the premisses and further to
doe and receave as to Lawe and Justice
John Ventris shall appertaine and hereof you are not
to faile Given under our handes and
seales this ffowerth day of March in the
seaven and twentieth yeare of the Raigne
of our most gracious Soveraigne Lord
King Charles the Second A°qʒ D[ni] juxta
&c. 1674.

Will Spencer
Will Gery St Jo: Chernocke W[m] Daniel
T Browne W: ffoster
Gaius Squier'

The document itself is very good evidence. It is in beautifully clean condition, with but one small tear, is neither rubbed nor soiled, so could never have been in the hard horny palm of a constable. Bunyan very probably went and surrendered himself on this his last imprisonment as he had done at his first. But the key once turned, his friends obtained this warrant from Cobb, and despatched it to Chauncy in the hope that some flaw might be found, in which case Habeas Corpus would lie. He was, indeed, at that very moment following up a similar trail. His own minister at Bristol, Mr. Hardcastle, with two

others, Thompson and Weekes, had been lodged
in Bristol Gaol on February 10, whence three
weeks' foul quarters had released Mr. Thompson
by death, all Ichabod's requests for removal to
purer air having been disregarded. The Habeas
Corpus brought up on behalf of the survivors was
heard on May 15, but the mittimus had been
carefully drawn, and all the Court could do was
to direct the Sheriff to place them in a healthier
prison.

How Bunyan was released by a motion to the
Lord Keeper under the Act of 35 Elizabeth
need not be told here, but the warrant itself,
rendered useless thereby, went back into Dr.
Chauncy's pigeon-holes, where it slumbered until
brought some few years ago to the hammer by
his family, who had an abiding faith that among
their collection of MSS. was a treasure worth
£1,000 : and they were right in their faith, though
quite wrong in its object. For the seven MSS.
of Pope, ' Essay on Man,' ' Dunciad,' etc., which
Dr. Chauncy had obtained 'from the poet's friend,
the novelist Richardson, were not the treasure in
question, though they realized some hundreds of
pounds, but a simple half-sheet of foolscap paper,

which it was fated should escape the notice of the keenest experts, both trade and amateur, till after the hammer had fallen. It was catalogued thus : ' Bunyan.—Letter to the Constables of Bedford relative to the imprisonment of John Bunyan for preaching. Autograph signatures and seals, March 4, 1674 '; and was on view, as usual, for two days previous to the sale.

It attracted no notice from the many who for pleasure or profit look in at Wellington Street almost daily during the sale season, but the entry caught my eye, and on examining it two things were clear. First, that it was a criminal warrant, but with an inexplicable waste of judicial power, as though their worships had thought strength lay in numbers. Second, that it might be worth looking up Bunyan's life to see what it all meant. A stroll down to the library of the Reform, and a reference to two or three biographies, especially Dr. Brown's exhaustive Life, but two years old, in which Bunyan's successor had insisted that there was a third imprisonment specially of the ' Progress,' made it pretty clear that one was on the brink of a discovery which would settle the date of the book itself. But beyond this came a little

uneasy reflection. ' Plenty of others must have
seen this and looked it up, the thing is so plain ;
and it is, moreover, not a common sale. The
Pope MSS. will bring down all the great guns,
and the British Museum as well ; while, as for
Mr. Piccadilly, he'll never overlook it. One can
only hope to see it sold ; to bid is useless ; the
thought of having it for one's very own is vain.'
A second visit the next day showed no diminu-
tion of the apathy. It had not been put apart
in a special place, like rare things are. I had a
twinge, however, when a really good antiquary
with a nose on his face took it up ; but he, too,
laid it down with a puzzled look. Still, all this
was quite consistent with a rapid rise in biddings
once they were opened.

At last the sale-day arrived. The scene of
action was the old top-lighted upper room where
for more than a century buyers have fought out
their contests, · and where the largest sum ever
given for a book—£4,950—has been given out at
the fall of the hammer. Round a hollow square
of tables, within which walks the shewer, sit the
giants of the old book trade, men whose names
and catalogues are known from China to Peru ;

so many Americans of the higher culture com-
memorating their visit to Europe by placing on
the shelves of the libraries of their local town—
but lately a cluster of wooden huts by a water
privilege in Michigan—a book published in the
day-dawn of printing. Mr. Piccadilly wears the
bashed-in felt—or fighting-hat, as it is called—
has secured the Pope MSS., and has just spread-
eagled two or three minor planets, who wanted a
cheap lot while he was not looking, when the
' Bunyan ' is put up. The great man opens the
sheet which contains the precious document, sniffs,
screws up his eyes, purses his mouth, and actually
throws it down, to be taken up by Mr. Bond
Street, who has often been an exceedingly good
second to his famous neighbour. But indifference
is catching ; he, too, lays it down. A third—let us
call him Mr. Tother'un, does the same ; the rest
don't care to look at it. The biddings are in
shillings, and take long to reach a pound. Indeed,
it is knocked down to my bid for less than two
sovereigns, but afterwards put up again. I did
not dare to press my own right, for fear of draw-
ing attention, though it began to dawn on me that
nobody knew what it was. ' I might be happy

yet.'   So with head bent over a Piranesi's ' Rome,' and measuring a pier of the Milvian Bridge, outwardly calm, and apparently unconcerned, I telegraphed behind my back to my agent, 'Go on !' The only competitor slackens, the bids get slower, and after that provoking delay with the hammer which always occurs when you want anything quickly knocked down, it falls, and the prize is won.   The next thing is to pay for it, and get possession.   Then the flush of triumph can no longer be restrained, and one can say to the courteous, silver-haired president, just descended from the rostrum :

' I suppose you know what this is ?'

' No ; what is it ?'

' It is the warrant on which Bunyan was apprehended when he wrote '' Pilgrim's Progress.'' '

'Ah ! did you know that when you bought it ?'

'Certainly.   I can read Court-hand, and know a little English history.   No person who gave it a thought could mistake this.'

' If I had known it, though, you would never have got it for the price you have.'

Chorus (in the person of a big black amateur) :

'No; and if *I* had known it you would not have got it, either.'

The first thing was to protect it by a frame, the next to approach the vendor for information as to its pedigree, courteously accorded by the family solicitor to the effect stated. It is true his first words were: 'I want my £500 for that Bunyan warrant. We knew we had a treasure worth £1,000, the price asked for the Pope MSS., but never dreamed of its being that.'

It was next submitted to the then head of the MSS. Department at the British Museum, since worthily advanced to its highest post, and his remark was:

'You have no business to have this; it ought to be here. Did you know what you were buying?'

'Certainly I did, and was even stupid enough to tell some people what there was up for sale at Sotheby's. Luckily they did not turn up there.'

'It's strange, very. Why was I not told of this? Why didn't Mr. Piccadilly tell me about it?'

'Because, sir, Mr. Piccadilly did not know it

himself; nor did anyone else in the room till I told them.'

I put a short note in the *Times* announcing the find, and it was very largely copied. One of my sons reported its repetition in the New Zealand papers, another in the principal Indian journal, the *Pioneer*. It was autotyped, and my paper, read before the Society of Antiquaries at the opening of their session, met with the approval of that body, followed subsequently by election into their number—an unexpected honour.

Subsequently the society have paid me a compliment of so high a nature that one feels almost awkward in relating it. I am engaged in an investigation of an entirely new kind, and carried out on new principles—strange as both may seem at the present time—and wished to lay the results of my work up to 1890 before the society. They declined it on the ground that they had no one capable of discussing it. Here is their letter:

'Society of Antiquaries, London,
'Burlington House, Piccadilly, W.,
'*January* 15, 1891.

'MY DEAR SIR,

'The Executive Committee, while fully recognising the zeal, care, and learning which

14

you have bestowed upon " Phœnician Vestiges in South Devon," consider it unsuitable for reading at a meeting here. The subject is quite new and very difficult, and should be treated in an independent work, so that the abstruse evidence produced may be more leisurely examined and commented on by those who are specially competent to do so. Justice could not be done to it by those who may happen to attend on one of our evening meetings. I therefore return the paper in a registered cover, with many thanks.

'Your obedient servant,

'H. S. MILMAN.

'W. G. Thorpe, F.S.A.,
'Gloucester House, Lark Hall Rise, S.W.'

I declined to accept such a compliment at the hands of my co-fellows, many of them far my superiors in attainments ; but the director persisted, adding verbally :

'We have not a man who can deal with it, but we hope to have one soon ;' and one of the Executive Committee, standing by, added :

'A man was put up who could have discussed it, but he was pilled, worse luck !'

Yet the few who saw the paper thought it very

interesting and pleasant reading, and among them was a publisher!

Oddly enough, the delay has advanced the investigation. New facts have come forward, and new analogies—among them a gold ingot mould, brought by Mr. Bent from the ruins of Zimbabwe in South Africa, which he attributes to an Arabian race. The mould, although of course much smaller, is on the same plan as that of the tin ingot dredged up in Mounts Bay, of which a cast is in the Jermyn Street Museum. The idea of the pattern of both moulds came from the same centre, and the same people, under similar conditions; and hence one more link between Cornwall and Carthage is established. .

Later on a better reproduction of the Bunyan warrant was made by Van de Weyde, of Regent Street, looking very much older than the original, and with the seals reproduced in red wax. The first impression printed off was graciously accepted by the Queen, and by her orders placed in the library at Windsor Castle, where a relation recently saw it.

Indeed, her Majesty would seem to take a special interest in Bunyan, if such an inference can be drawn from the two letters from Sir Henry Ponsonby which follow :

'Windsor Castle,
'*March* 2, 1888.

'SIR,

'I am commanded by the Queen to thank you for the reproduction of the Bunyan Warrant, 1674, which you have been kind enough to present to her Majesty, and which the Queen was glad to receive. The account of this curious paper in the proceedings of the Society of Antiquaries has not yet reached me ; but when it does, I shall have much pleasure in laying it before the Queen.

'I have the honour to be, sir,

'Your obedient servant,

'HENRY F. PONSONBY.

'W. G. Thorpe, Esq.'

'Windsor Castle,
'*May* 8, 1888.

'SIR,

'The Queen has placed the reproduction of the Bunyan Warrant in the library here, and, in thanking you for the description you have been kind enough to send her, desires me to inform you that it has been now given to Mr. Holmes, the librarian, to place by the side of the document.

> 'I have the honour to be, sir,
>
> 'Your obedient servant,
>
> 'HENRY F. PONSONBY.

'W. G. Thorpe, Esq.'

And following out the idea of 'Pilgrim's Progress,' it is earnestly to be hoped that the Queen is an exception to the rule that monarchs with large families are much worried individuals. At all events, the late Emperor William was one, being standing referee and arbiter in all the family squabbles about everything, anything, or nothing. And the old soldier felt very helpless about it; so that the victor over Austria, the unifier of Germany, the conqueror who as such had twice ridden into Paris, could but repeat a formula which never had much force at the first, and weakened the more it was used, 'Say nothing, do nothing; all will come right in the end.' Which it usually did, like Lord Palmerston's correspondence. Asked how he managed to get through so much, he answered, 'Well, some I do, and that is not much; some, others do, and that's a good deal; some does itself, and that's more than you'd fancy, and the rest doesn't get done at all.'

The second impression of the Bunyan Warrant facsimile was forwarded to my friend Dr. Brown, Bunyan's successor at Bedford, where it was placed with the other objects of the Bunyan Cult, greatly venerated by our American cousins, who visit them as a matter of duty, just as they do the Nidus of the Washingtons, or the plain Quaker's Yard, where, in a place mercifully not exactly known, otherwise they would have had them up, rest the remains of the founder of Pennsylvania. When Dr. Brown did me the honour to call and see the document which turned his clever guess into a positive fact, I was somewhat amused by the various tests with which he had provided him-self—tracings of signatures, casts of seals, and so forth. He was not aware until I told him that my friend Dr. Maunde Thompson (whose quick-ness in research is an instinct) had within five minutes traced all the seals save one to their owners, the signatories.

Of the seven or eight impressions taken, one

is in the Memorial Hall, which commemorates Bunyan's fellow sufferers for conscience' sake, and another in Harvard University library, placed by my valued friend, Dr. Justin Winsor, near to Bunyan's Bible, presented to the College (where the name of Chauncy is still known and honoured) by Mr. Charles Sumner, for Bunyan is a living power in America even more than he is in the land of his birth. The New York Missionary Society alone prints annually some 12,000 'Progresses.'

Nor has he strayed away from the affections of people whom he first charmed, like the 'Christian Year,' for instance, which Dean Howson now tells us is the great delight of Scotch Presbyterians. This is not so much to be wondered at, since Keble's biographer—the late Sir John Taylor Coleridge—has already told us that the author was not a 'Christian Year'-man any more than Jack Wilkes was a Wilkite.

But this is not the sole 'historic doubt' which I have had the good fortune to settle. A controversy which had long raged as to the position in which Charles I. met his death, with that placid courage, as Macaulay has it, which has half redeemed his fame, broke out virulently again two years ago when Mr. Croft's fine picture of the tragedy was on the line in the Royal Academy, and it was wonderful how little positive evidence was forthcoming either way. Such an authority, for instance, as Mr. Reginald Palgrave wrote to *The Times* on May 10, 1890, that 'there was no help from any contemporary account.' Yet all this time there existed a book—in the British Museum Library two copies and a facsimile, a third in the Bodleian, and a fourth in my own collection (now, by her Majesty's gracious acceptance of it from me, in her library at Windsor Castle)—which not only solved the mystery, but added many other unknown and touching facts to the doleful history. It certainly did its best to attract attention ; it was entitled ' The Bloody Court, or the Fatall Tribunall,' and was even printed in red to resemble blood. Blind, indeed, were the eyes and deaf the ears of those who turned over those much-rubbed copies and missed the point. It dates itself to a nicety as having been at press before June 18, 1649, and the new matter is from an eye-witness, evidently an officer of high rank on the Parliament side, but having

internally strong sympathies with the King.   He
tells us that he stood 'neer' the King at the trial,
and trembled with 'feer' lest the soldiers should
murder him in Westminster Hall; saw them open
the bar where they put the King, and blow
tobacco, 'which he could not endure,' in the
King's face; he could visit St. James's Palace,
where the King was lodged so that he might not
hear the sound of his scaffold being erected—a
fatal scaffold, constructed for a wrestling-show
during the marriage festivities of the Prince of
Orange and the King's daughter, which went on
in full swing during that week throughout which
Strafford waited for death, vainly imploring the
weak master for whom he had sacrificed everything to veto his bill of attainder.

The scaffold was to end his own days, the
marriage to oust his dynasty.   Our writer could
interview the housekeeper, learn how the King
bore himself up, see his sad parting with his two
children—'it would have drawn the tears out of
a rocke heart to have seen this parting'—accompany the fatal procession through the park, tell
us the number of the guard—500 in front, 500
behind, with 30 partizans on each side—enter the

Banqueting House, and there witness the King's last communion ; be present, too (all this is new matter), when, the Act against the proclamation of any successor having been passed, a sudden message came to the Monarch that the hour-glass was turned, and he had but that hour to live. A ghastly chill fell on the little company, but the King said to the Bishop :

'My lord, do not you pity me. After one hour is expired, I shall pity *you*, and all the people in my kingdom.'

Our author tells us that the King had contemplated a forcible resistance on the scaffold, but had been dissuaded from it in view of the fact that mechanical means had been prepared and stood ready to meet such a contingency. This was known from the Venetian Ambassador's letters. Our author accompanied the King on his way to the scaffold, and noticed the nerve displayed as well when he passed his open coffin, as when he saw the mechanical appliances, no longer required but still full in view. He seems to have here quitted the King and gone in company with a gentlewoman—probably the housekeeper at St. James'—inside the ring of troops which surrounded the scaffold, from which he heard the King's speech, which, however, he does not report, as shorthand clerks were there to do it on the part of the Government. As this rare book is not likely to be reprinted, the account of the catastrophe may be extracted here :

'The sun shined that morning very clear until the King came to the fatal block, and then *lay down* (the first clear statement of his position), and then a dark thick cloud covered the face of the sun, so that a gentlewoman standing by me to behold the dreadful tragedy cried out, Look, look, sir ! the sun is ashamed and hideth his face as if loathing to see this horrid murder ! Immediately upon her words the fatal blow was given.'

The pamphlet lends itself especially to interrogation as to who was its author.   He was a politician, bitterly hostile to Cromwell and Ireton ; was a strong Presbyterian, deep in their councils, and able to inform us that many of their congregations continued the whole night before the execution in prayer for the King's life.   But he had some influence with the stern Ironsides and their commander, Colonel Joyce, so that he could do seven things at least, for any one of which any but an officer of high rank in strong favour with the soldiers (all-favourable to the King as he really was) would have been locked up in the guard-room, to wit :

1. Frequent St. James's Palace during the three days of the King's detention there.

2. Witness the King's parting with his children, and even take down the words !

3. Converse with the housekeeper as to the King's conduct.

4. Join the dismal procession through the park to Whitehall. (It must be remembered that the park then was surrounded with a wall, and the Horseguards not yet built.)

5. Enter the Banqueting House with the King, watch his last communion, be present when the dread summons came, observe his demeanour, and take note of his words.

6. Walk by the King's side through the Banqueting House and note his features when he saw coffin and scaffold.

7. Though not with the King's friends upon the scaffold, be allowed to enter, with the housekeeper aforesaid, inside the ring of troops sur-

rounding the scaffold, and go away without being held responsible for the housekeeper's remark upon the ' horrid murder.'

8. Be on friendly terms with Colonel Joyce, the commander, and even commend him for his humanity to the King.

All these particulars point to one man. Sir William Penn, father of William Penn the Quaker, an Admiral of repute, second only to Blake, but whom Cromwell had committed to the Tower some nine months previously : whose Irish estate had been sequestered by Ireton, and who subsequently offered to carry the whole fleet bodily over to Charles II., had that monarch possessed either money or stores, or a harbour in which to receive it.

The fit receptacle for the last copy of this curious revelation, which had not up to that time found proper appreciation in public possession, is indicated in the enclosed letter to me :

' Windsor Castle,
' May 20, 1891.

' DEAR SIR,

 ' I need scarcely assure you that the Queen was extremely pleased with the very curious pamphlet you have so kindly sent to her Majesty, together with your description of it. And I am to thank you sincerely for this valuable present.

'Yours faithfully,

'HENRY F. PONSONBY.

'W. G. Thorpe, Esq., F.S.A.'

All the four copies are much thumbed and worn, showing the demand for it; hence it was expanded seven-fold, and reprinted at the Hague in 1651, under a different title.

I possess a fine copy of the first edition of the 'Eikon Basilike,' a book written by Gauden during the King's life, and published on February 8 following his death. It is said that had it been brought out before the catastrophe, the then ruling powers would not have gone to the last extremity. But my friend, Professor Rawson Gardiner, tells me that anything was permitted to be printed up to and long after the fatal 30th of January, and a Government which could allow such strong-speaking matter as 'Eikon Basilike' and its folding plate to pass through the press must have had confidence in its own strength.

Together with my first folio of Shakespeare I

keep a memorial of another English king as unfortunate as Charles I., but differing from him in
that he neither shed his subjects' blood nor did they
shed his—the unhappy Richard II.   Now one of
the late Dean Stanley's peculiarities was a par-
tiality for exhuming ancient corpses ; and, as this
could be indulged under cover of a general restoration of royal monuments, the Dean had a pretty
good innings.   Thus the tomb of Richard II. and
Anne of Bohemia was thoroughly explored, and
the bones re-entombed afterwards.   What was
left of them, that is ; for the King's jaw is said
to be in the possession of a clergyman in Kent,
who, when a Westminster boy, went a-fishing in
the mausoleum with a hook and a piece of string,
and pulled out that for himself.   Anyhow the skulls
were found, and with them a piece of the King's
brain, which, following the precepts of a former
Dean (Buckland), 'always taste all bones,' I
put to my tongue and found quite sweet.   (Not
that he tasted them only.)

I held in my hands the heads of both King
and Queen (the last, small and polished like ivory,
as I am told, was that of Mary Queen of Scots
when exhumed); and, thinking of their tremendous

downfall, the words put into Richard's mouth by Shakespeare—'Within the hollow crown that rounds the mortal temples of a King keeps Death his court'—seemed to have a double appropriateness. I can almost recall the feeling now, as I possess a set of three very fine photographs of the full face and each profile of these memorials of the past, of which I believe only eight were taken.

Sooner or later—better of the two if sooner, as involving no questions at present even smouldering—the doors of the great temple of Silence and Reconciliation must swing back to receive, for the last time and finally, the head of, in Macaulay's words, the greatest Prince who ever ruled in England—a soldier by intuition, for he never lost a battle, and the manœuvre by which he won Dunbar was repeated by the victors of Austerlitz and Salamanca—a statesman who in but four years could raise England from the position of a country harassed and exhausted by civil war to treat on equal terms with Louis XIV., and have all his demands submissively complied with by the very Dutchmen who, fourteen years later, were to burn Chatham Dockyard ; who was to obtain redress from the Grand Duke of Tuscany for persecuted Protestants, and to compel the Algerines to surrender their English captives by the threat of Blake's guns; who inscribed the first name, that of Jamaica, on the long roll of England's colonies ; who passed the Act establishing the first Missionary Society on the express ground that it was England's duty towards her Red Indian subjects, and who but three months before his death captured Dunkirk—a conquest of such importance that, four years later, the French King purchased it back from the third Stuart at the price of a million sterling, equivalent to about six of them now.

The indignities offered to the senseless corpse it could not feel, as Charles V. knew well when he compelled his fierce Spanish infantry to leave Luther to rest peacefully in his grave ; and the outrage was avenged by the story which gained currency at once, how the body of Charles had been removed from Windsor and placed in the Protector's grave, its occupant's remains being laid reverently to rest on Marston Moor, where his innate soldiership had brought up the cuirassiers, who turned the tide of battle and conquered its liberties for England.

The story found many to believe it, and in Mr. Inderwick's pleasant 'Side Lights on the Stuarts' there is reproduced a contemporary print of Henrietta Maria doing penance at Tyburn on the theory that the King's body lay there. But be that as it may, there is a Cromwell Road in South Kensington, a Cromwell statue at (I think) Manchester; and my friend Mr. Palgrave's 'Vindication,' ironically so-called, fell as flat as anything from his pen could fall.

The time must soon come when the Protector's head, now in pious hands at Chislehurst, shall be returned with due honour to the place where it was laid when that hush of helpless, resourceless fear fell upon the nation, such as we have heard our fathers speak of when the victory of Austerlitz killed William Pitt, and the swollen tongue could only just enunciate before its eloquence became silent for ever, 'Roll up the map of Europe.'

I am the possessor of one other volume unique in private hands—a large folio copy of the second issue of Luther's Bible, 1542, in which the Reformer has written seven holograph lines, signed ' Martinus Luther, A.D. 1542,' beginning, ' Ich bin der Weg, die Wahrheit und das Leben.'

Only some six of them are known.   They were
gifts to favoured adherents.   That at Erfurt was
destroyed by the fire which burnt out Luther's
cell there in 1872, on which occasion, in reply to
a wail in the *Pall Mall Gazette* on the irrepar-
able loss, I was able to inform the editor that
like copies existed in Windsor Castle, the Berlin
Library, the British Museum (it cost them
£367 10s.), at Munich and Stuttgardt, and lastly
in my own library.   I have since heard that the
Windsor copy, which the late Prince Consort
greatly prized, is not to be found.   If this be so,
the skilful abstractor, if he were such, would have
saddled himself with as hopeless a white elephant
as the person who has got Messrs. Agnew's
Reynolds' Duchess of Devonshire.   It may perhaps have been borrowed ; they did queer things
in libraries in the fifties.   And a friend of mine
who was then about the Court has told me that in
a Windsor canon's house he one day noticed in a
window-seat an old vellum book supporting a
recently-watered flower-pot, from which the water
was soaking on to it.   It was only a Caxton, that's
all, and worth £600 or £700 ; and when my
friend had taken it up, carefully wiped it dry, and

carried it himself to the dignitary who had borrowed it from the Chapter Library, his reception was as if he had committed an impertinence.

But the Reformer's Hebrew Bible, with notes and autograph, is in the hands of that eminent orientalist who has described the Moabite Stone.

I went to see him in the British Museum, when he showed me the Shapira forgeries—a clever attempt by the Jerusalem tradesman of that name to reproduce a MS. of the Book of Deuteronomy of the period of the Captivity. Such things, of course, exist in the shape of the Samaritan Pentateuch ; and the man would be bold who affirmed that search in Ptolemaic tombs might not yield up more of them, as well as MSS. of Homer, and papyri of Aristotle. But these of Shapira's were blown upon in Berlin first, then in Great Russell Street, and the unhappy man committed suicide subsequently. These shown to me, my friend broke out in a fresh place :

' Have you got your Luther yet ?'

' Yes ; have you yours ?'

' Yes ; but I nearly lost the autograph the other day. A very great man, a grandee, asked to see it, and I left him with it at my desk. But something said to me, " Go back, go back," and I found he had doubled down that leaf, and was going to tear it out.'

' Of course you kicked him out ?'

' No! But I told him what I thought of him, for after all, you see, there was something to be said for him.'

Here I differ from the learned doctor.

Books and coins, however, are a great temptation, and antiquaries are not always honest, as is testified by Mr. Oldbuck. In fact, on one occasion I took precautions against myself. It was at Clumber, then unoccupied by his Grace of Newcastle, the owner living in apartments in Park Place on an annuity of £2,000, doled out by his mother-in-law, who, by buying up the Duke's debts, had acquired possession of all the estate. Not a pleasant life to lead! So at the age of only forty-five the despairing man turned his face to the wall and died for very weariness of it. He had strawberry-leaves only, neither fruit nor cream with them. There had been a fire in the great house, and I visited it in company with the architect who was to rebuild it. He went off to his work—I to the library, in the next room to which the fire had stopped.   Had it gone on, the library was insured for only £9,000!   It was a charming room, only one press wired over, and that not locked, with, placed here and there, a notice signed 'Newcastle,' which directed persons taking books out of the library to leave in their place a paper bearing the taker's name.   It was a tempting invitation.   There were six 'Caxtons,' all perfect but one ; twenty 'Wynkyn de Wordes,' in condition to smack one's lips over ; an absolutely perfect First Folio 'Shakespeare,' with 'Thos. Holles, 1630,' written in it ; the 'Sonnets,' also a *princeps ;* some quarto plays, and altogether such an overwhelming mass of treasures that it struck me, 'If any of these are missing after you're gone it won't be nice.'   So I went to my friend and told him my difficulty.   He was an antiquary himself, but not a bookworm, so laughed at my dilemma, eventually, however, getting the house-keeper to come and watch me.   The poor old lady never looked once at me, but gently knitted till she nodded herself asleep.

But as to *stealing* books.   The thing is not only sometimes lawful, but even meritorious, and one man will go to heaven for it—in fact, has gone

there already. The mode in which Tischendorf
ran off with the ' Codex Sinaiticus ' in 1839 may
be described as anything you please, from theft
under trust to hocussing and felony ; but it
succeeded, and all Christendom was glad thereof.
It is the custom of the Greek monk to worship
like Jacob, standing, leaning on the top of his
staff, and he protects his feet from the cold ground
by putting under them a good thick volume from
the library. Such was the position occupied by
this priceless treasure, perhaps the oldest MS.
of all we have got to trust in, when Tischendorf
first saw it ; and he resolved to rescue it somehow, for they would not sell it. The great
German was equal to the task ; he provided himself with good store of Clicquot and Hoffmann's
cherry-brandy, which, mixed on Mr. Weller's
' ekal ' principle, form a compound called ' Prince
Regent.' He then set himself to drink the Abbot
of St. Catharine's on Mount Sinai blind-drunk,
and it took him three days to get that Churchman
under the table ; then the library key could be
got from under his petticoats, and the priceless
volume carried off, all the rest of the caloyers and
lay brethren being kept on the booze by minor

agents.   The escort kept in readiness was at once summoned, and Tischendorf himself carried the precious volume.   Onward to Suez, across the desert, when a pursuit was descried.   Someone had woke up, detected the theft, and the Bedawin, who depend on the monastery, were started in hot chase.   Indeed, it was only by two hundred yards that the Russian Consulate was gained in safety, after which ample money satisfaction was forthcoming, and the story was hushed up.

Among other books I have a pretty little 'Imitation of Christ,' black letter, Paris, 1499, in which the printer had put the author's name as Gerson, indignantly corrected with the pen, both in title and colophon, by a contemporary hand. This controversy it has been attempted to shout down, but it is one which will never be settled, both the claimants' other books being so utterly inferior to this masterpiece which took the world by storm, and has since held it, just like the 'Pilgrim's Progress,' that one would very much incline to believe it composed by neither of them.

A pretty little copy of Milton's poems, first collected edition, gives me the pleasure of reading 'L'Allegro' and 'Il Penseroso' out of what is practically the first edition, though they appear in the previous one. Partly because it was a unique copy of a hitherto unknown *princeps*, and also as being the first example of a hymnal as we now have them. I secured the solitary first edition of ' Wesley's Hymns ' known. It had previously been facsimiled by the Wesleyan Book Committee, and the Connexion will probably have to wait for my decease before they get another chance of placing it, together with Mr. Wesley's Bible, in the custody of the president for the time being. By the way, what would Mr. Wesley have said if anyone had told him that such president would very properly go to Court, and be duly presented there? Was 'prodigious' a word of Mr. Wesley's as well as Dominie Sampson's ? And when such chance as aforesaid is open to the Connexion, they may have to encounter some representatives of the fourteen or fifteen American and other Wesleyan connexions. Such, at least, was the opinion of my friend, Dr. Justin Winsor, librarian of Harvard, when he was looking at the little volume. It is in common sheep binding, weighs two ounces, and was originally for sale at sixpence, as easy to pocket as a pear-shaped pearl, and perhaps even a hotter chestnut to handle in the long run by any purloiner. It is odd that books are so impossible to forge without detection ; a facsimile stray leaf very often gets passed, but never a whole book. Yet everything else can be forged. Only the other day there were shown to the Society of Antiquaries some flint implements which failed because of their very perfection—an easy method of detection in emeralds, which they always make too good, as they do the sapphires at Colombo, manufactured out of blue finger-glass bottoms, which are any price, from rupees 100 to rupee 1 when the steamer is just leaving, to the great disgust of purchasers who have bought earlier in the day, and nearer the former figure.

Pictures, of course, are always in doubt ; and when her Majesty honoured the Society of Antiquaries by exhibiting a portrait of Mary Queen of Scots, acquired by the Prince Consort at a marvellously low price, it was hard to keep one's countenance when Mr. Calderon, R.A., demonstrated that one pigment used was not even known till 1816. There have, of course, been whole collections of forgeries, such as that of old masters bequeathed to the National Gallery by

Mr. Gower, of Marseilles, which Sir Frederick Burton had regretfully to decline, as there was not a genuine one among the lot which were 'named.'

Leaving forgeries—for are they not so various that the science of Equity has never ventured to define fraud, since, in that case, justice would have been forthwith flouted by something morally within, but legally without the line?—I would speak of a book in my library that has been much handled, and probably by about the greatest set of scoundrels ever created—the Courtiers of the Restoration. Be it remembered that at that period the taking the Sacrament three times a year was not only a mark of loyalty, but neglect of it was punishable by fine and imprisonment. Now, this volume, which is a copy of the 'Sealed Book,' or first edition of the Prayer Book of 1662, bears on it 'W. H., 1662,' and was therefore a copy in use in the chapel itself—not the Banqueting House, lately so called, which has never been consecrated, but the old Court Chapel, burnt down with the rest of the palace in 1698. What hands must have turned over these leaves! Are not the names written in the diaries of Pepys and Evelyn, both regular attendants there ? Clarendon and Ormond on the honest side, but against them Rochester, Wilmot, Clifford, Shaftesbury, Buckingham, Arlington, and the Duke of Lauderdale, famous for fitting on to Scotch Covenanters' legs the iron boot invented by the future James II., into whose reign the book lasted, as his name is substituted for his dead brother's. Of all the persons who opened this book, it is permissible to doubt whether ever one devotional thought was suggested to them by it, so utterly bad were the hands which made use of it.

I am the possessor of an almost perfect collection of Commonwealth Black-letter Proclamations and State Papers, commencing January 16, 1648-49, and ending 1658, being the official copies handed at the time to two Government functionaries, and filed by them. The first portion was collected by a person named Henry Liddell, who has written his name, with the date, April, 1652. He was of the Ravensworth family, and his collection stood on the shelves of a peer connected therewith till early in 1891, when his lordship's bookseller removed it to make way for newer books, to the owner's great disgust. For,

among the collection were three Acts passed in
January, 1648-49, which speak of the King as
living and awaiting execution. It is impossible to
read without deep interest the Act to prevent the
proclamation of any successor, until after the passing of which, at the afternoon sitting of January 30,
the King's execution was delayed. There are
several Acts passed in order to substitute the
style '*Custodes Libertatis Angliæ*,' for that of the
kingly title, even down to removing the Royal
Arms from churches, and some of them are passed
die Sabbati, which shows that Parliament on emer-
gency sat the week through. On that day, indeed,
May 19, 1649, is dated one of the gems in the
book in most pearly condition—an Act for de-
claring and constituting the people of England,
and of all the dominions and territories thereunto
belonging, to be a Commonwealth and Free State,
and that without any King or House of Lords.
There is an Act passed in view of the events
which led up to the Battle of Worcester, enjoin-
ing the departure of all Scots out of England on
pain of suffering death as traitors and enemies, with
forfeit of land and goods (How Dr. Johnson would
have rollicked over this!), which penalties further

attach to any person publishing Charles II.'s declaration from Edinburgh in August, 1650. Then comes the thanksgiving for the victory of Dunbar, from which we learn that the battle-cry was 'The Lord of Hosts.' In November, 1650, it is ordered that all law proceedings be henceforth in English, afterwards re-enacted in consequence of the steady opposition of the lawyers. Then matters sharpen up again in view of the coming battle of Worcester, and there is a proclamation in September, 1651, for the arrest of Charles II., reward, £1,000. It is wonderful how any copies of this proclamation exist. One side would post them up to perish as broadsides do, the other would pull them down as quickly as they dared; yet there are four in the British Museum, one sent in 1760. My own has been folded wet from the press, and shows the transfer.

The gap between the two series is filled up by a fine copy of ordinances by the Lord Protector, from December 16, 1653, to September 3, 1654, when the new Parliament was about to meet.

The second collection was made by Secretary Thurloe, and I am able to prove this by very curious internal evidence. Among the public

papers is a copy of a bond for good behaviour by
one Gamaliel Capel, of Rookwood Hall, near
Abbess Roothing, in Essex, it being the only
private document out of a large quantity of public
ones. The question naturally arises, how did it
come there? The natural reply is, it was put with
them because connected with public duty. And a
little investigation clears all this up. Thurloe was
the son of a Rector of Abbess Roothing, of which
Sir Gamaliel Capel, of Rookwood Hall, was the
Squire. Hall and Rectory were not sworn friends
before the Civil War, as they have ever been
since ; quite the reverse, indeed, Squire treating
Parson with disdain, of which Macaulay gives
instances. Things were even worse here in
Essex, for the Rector held with the Puritans, and
had put his son in the train of an implacable
enemy to the Church party, Oliver St. John,
that stern, hard, dark man. whose speech on the
Hampden Ship-money trial was to ring through
England, as a note in the register of Abbess
Roothing states. St. John had Thurloe for his
secretary at the Uxbridge negotiations, and the
two remained close friends. so that when St. John
was deprived of his Chief Justiceship in 1660

Thurloe was able to save his stern patron as well as be himself asked by Charles II. to continue in his own office. As the Duke of York, afterwards James II., expressed his deep regret that St. John had not been included in the fated twenty who were excluded from the general indemnity, it will be seen that Thurloe's power must have been very great. But as Secretary of State and Postmaster-General under Richard Cromwell, Thurloe had greatly fostered the Restoration. I may just note here that there was a tie between my kinsman, Francis Thorpe, and another man for the honour of being twentieth in that black list of butchery, and that on a second division the other man succeeded. Thurloe had chambers in Lincoln's Inn Gateway, still in use, where, some century ago, his private papers were found behind a papered up cavity. These chambers have heard much English history while it was being made, for from them there started in that long summer evening the two private soldiers who went through Staple Inn to the inn yard of the Old Bell in Holborn, inside much the same as it was then. The men sat down and drank while a packhorse train was being loaded for the West, till

a smart page came in and gave the driver a
packet, which he carefully sewed up in a pack
saddle. Then the men left. and returned to
Lincoln's Inn, but the horses were stopped on
the Oxford Road by troopers, and the horse bearing that saddle carried off. The packet contained
letters from Henrietta Maria to the King in reply
to his. Cromwell and the Parliament leaders
were to be fooled at any price, earldoms, pensions,
land, and so forth, until power could be regained,
and then they were to die the deaths of other
used-and-done-with tools. The men who read
this charming little programme were Cromwell
and Ireton, the two soldiers in question. After
this the King could no longer be trusted, and
Charles, by the fatal Stuart insincerity, had lost
his last chance.

Thurloe did not forget his grudge against his
old landlord's family. When the Syndercombe
and Gerard plots against the Protector's life had
thoroughly scared society, after some years of peace
under a strong Government ; when Charles II., as
the price of French aid, had, with incredible base-
ness, promised to place an English seaport per-
manently in the hands of the hereditary enemies

of England ; when the judges on circuit at Salisbury were seized, taken to the gibbet to be hanged right off in their robes, and only just rescued in time, the Government called out the militia, and locked up many of the country squires, who might be able to hamper its usefulness.

Among these was the reigning Squire of Rookwood Hall, a young man of about twenty-three, who was carefully conveyed to Yarmouth, and there confined. Release was easy from the first to those who would submit and sign a bond, binding their estates as security against plotting or being privy to it ; but either Gamaliel Capel would not apply, or his release was deferred until a bond of ultra stringency had been prepared, when, after more than six months' imprisonment, the prisoner was released on signing it, his estate having been previously decimated, or taxed to one-tenth of its then annual value—£400—to pay for the expense of the army, just as police taxes are levied now in Ireland when any outrage occurs in a given barony. The obligee of the bond, Major Haynes, sent up a copy to his superior, Thurloe, so as to be always in readiness if the offence were repeated. But Gamaliel had grown wiser by experience ;

he married and settled down, and this terrible engine of oppression, worked, in case of need, without legal process by an extent from the Exchequer, remained harmless till the Restoration took the sting out of it altogether.

Both sides used this kind of weapon. The Commonwealth Lieutenant of Derby was, after the Restoration, confined to the limits of his own little township; the petitions of himself and his neighbours had no effect, and not till the Deliverer came, in 1688, was the embargo removed.

The Thurloe collection of State Papers is more complete than that in the British Museum or in the Society of Antiquaries. It contains five specimens of the seal — *Olivarius Dei Gratia Angliæ Scotiæ et Hiberniæ Protector*—a legend which makes the coins which bear it, notably the crown piece, worth £5 or more ; and among the documents are: 'The Humble Petition and Advice of Parliament to the Protector to assume Supreme Power on 25 May, 1657, with the reiteration of it on 26 June, 1657, and the Proclamation consequent therein assuming such Power.' 'Had either of his surviving sons inherited his splendid talents as patriot, soldier, and statesman' (I am quoting

from the *Daily Telegraph* of Christmas Eve, 1891),
'a white-haired man would not have gone up to
the throne in the House of Lords in the days of
Queen Anne, and said: "It's just the same as
when I sat there."   It was Richard Cromwell.'

The Protector's lineal descendants are still
among us ; the last male of his name, Oliver, died
1821 ; the last female, Susan, 1834.

Londoners, whose coals have been doubled in
price within a week for the un-Adam-Smithian
and contra-John-Millian reasons that pithead
stocks are so unmanageably large and demand
so restricted that coal-owners have to call upon
their operatives to share their loss with them in
the shape of a reduction of wages, will be charmed
with the simple way in which the first of the
Stuarts kept prices at a reasonable and satisfactory level in the year of his accession.   Not for
him, any more than for coal-owners, merchants,
porters, or the black gang generally now, any
questions of demand or supply.   For him, as for
the young German Emperor—*voluntas regis,
summa lex :* Henry Beauclerk's foot and forearm
had fixed the standards of length ; whenever
the Emperor of China plays whist he looks at

his hand and then names the trump suit: so wherever Scotch Jamie went he fixed the tariff.

By the terms of the probably unique broadside in my possession (copied on next page) the prices of 'corne,' victuals, lodging, 'horsemeate,' or any other necessaries were to be fixed by the clerk of the market of the King's household, and hung up on the gates. Any person selling or buying at any other prices, or keeping back his goods because he liked not the figure he had to sell them for, was punishable by fine and imprisonment.

⇥ A forme of Proclamation to be proclaimed by the
Clerke of the Market, and he to fee it executed touching
prices of Victuals.

He Kings Maieftie ftraightly chargeth and com-
mandeth, That euery man doe obey and keepe all such
prices as is and shalbe prized and rated by the Clerke
of the Market of his most honourable houshold, And
the Iury before him or his Deputie by the authority of
his Office sworne and charged from time to time, And
so fixed and set vpon the gates of the Kings Highnesse Court and
other places within the Verge : And that no person or persons of
what estate or degree soeuer he bee, doe in any wise pay more for
Corne, Victuals, Horsemeate, Lodgings, or any kinde of Victuals,
then after the Rate and forme aforesaid, vpon paine of imprisonment, and further perill that shall thereof follow, The same punish-
ments to be inflicted as well vpon them and euery of them, which
doe or shall presume to pay any more, for any the things before
mentioned, As vpon them and euery of them, which shal vtter and
sell any maner of things contrary to the true meaning of this Proclamation.

And moreouer the Kings Highnesse straightly chargeth and com-
maundeth all Maiors, Iustices of Peace, Bailiffes, Constables, &
al other his faithful Officers, and euery of them, aswel within
Liberties as without (within the Verge of his Highnes Court) from
time to time, when and as often as need shal require, diligently within their authoritie, to endeuour themselues to see execution & due
reformation of the premisses, according to Iustice & prices as aforesaid.   And further it is ordered, That no person or persons, now
vsing, or which of right ought to vse to serue any City, Towne, or
other place within the Verge of his Highnesse Court, with any
kinde of Corne, Victuals, Horsemeat, Lodgings or any other necessaries, aswell vpon the Market day, as at any other time, be any
thing the more remisse or slacke in making prouision for the same,
then they or any of them heretofore haue bene, nor hide, lay aside, or
vse any colour of craft to deceiue the buyers thereof, whereby the
Kings Highnesse Traine within any Citie, Towne, or other place,
and the inhabitants of the same should not bee aswell serued, and
plenteously furnished in euery behalfe, as it was before, or of right
ought to haue bene, in defraude of this his Highnesse Ordinance,
nor take or receiue any more then according to the prices which
from time to time shall stand & be declared in maner aforesaid,
vnder his Graces Seale of the Office of the Clerke of the Market,
vpon paine of imprisonment, And further to make fine vnto the
Kings Highnesse vse, for his or their contempts therein.

God saue the King.

⇥ Imprinted at London by Robert Barker,
Printer to the Kings moft Excellent
Maieftie.   Anno 1603

To show how James's personal parsimony contrasted with his liberality as to Crown property, it may be noted that he requited the Spanish Envoy's gifts to his courtiers by some 50,000 ounces of gold and silver plate, amongst it a matchless enamelled gold cup, recently recovered for the nation at a cost of £8,000—only £130 per ounce !—by Mr. Franks, of the British Museum.

It was the custom of Mr. Dunn Gardner, a collector of half a century back, to decline to answer any inquiries as to where he got his books, or what he paid for them, on the ground that half the world would say, ' What a fool he is !' the other half, ' What a liar he is !' the real reason probably being, ' I got those things middling cheap ; if I say where it is, no more chance of any good bargains there.' It was so in my own case. I knew a shop where the man had a good nose but not much reading. It was in Vinegar Yard, and I once picked up a ' Fust and Schoeffer' there for 3*s*. 6*d*. I noticed, however, that, in the language of the venerated Master of the Temple, who, of course, must know all about it in order to preach upon it, 'life was daily getting harder,' and prices too. **One** day the mystery cleared itself up. I was in his back shop, looking over a parcel, when I heard a well-known voice outside. It was chaffering for books! A thrill shot through me. I went out to find the voice that of Don Pasquale de Gayangos, afterwards Government archivist at Simancas, but then buyer for the late Mr. Huth. So I spoke :

'It's you, is it ?—quæ regio in terris tui non plena laboris ? Now look here, Mr. Dealer ; this gentleman buys for the richest amateur there is ; he will give any price for a rare book, and he's as good as gold—-make him pay for what you sell him.'

I thought that nothing more was left for me to find out, and that my luck was exhausted by settling the date of ' Pilgrim's Progress,' and the way in which Charles I. died ; but only recently I came across a parcel of externally dirty deeds, and secured them. One of them turned out to be the original Royal Charter of Edward II. to the town of Portsmouth, dated February 12, 1313, and though the outside was black the inside was as clean as the day on which it was engrossed. By the kind permission of my friend Dr. Maunde Thompson, the principal librarian of the British

Museum, always forward where students ask assistance, I was allowed to have it flattened out and framed by Mr. Hunt, expert in the manuscript department. It has been so beautifully handled that it looks like new. By Dr. Thompson's direction, I sent a printed copy of it to the Portsmouth Corporation, and a local paper published a note on it, suggesting that it had been stolen. My own theory, however, and I have evidence in support of it, is that when Charles II. called in the Charters in 1683, rather than give them up, the owners distributed them, ' consigned them in a safe quarter,' like Mr. Pell's client in ' Pickwick.' This was certainly the case with the Charles I. Charter of 1627, which was bargained away to the Duchess of Portsmouth, Madame Karwell—'the leg of mutton which came home from France,' as the jingle ran—for a couple of loving-cups, and repurchased by the local M.P. in 1688. My Charter seems to have been offered for sale not only to Sir Frederick Madden, of the British Museum, in 1863, but to the local historian, Mr. Saunders, two years earlier. I was greatly amused by the comment of an American :

' Whenever you sell this, you'll find Amŭricans

quite willing to take it away. There's a Portsmouth in New Hampshire as well as in Old ; and there's more of 'em in Virginia and Ohio, and mighty proud of such a title-deed will be the one that gets it. Don't you forget that *our* history is *your* history up to Independence-Day.'

When at that costly fiasco the Eglinton Tournament, some fifty years since, it was found that would-be combatants could not get into plate-armour which their ancestors had slipped on like a glove, it was clear that in body at least we were stouter than our forefathers ; that we are as stout in heart is proved, so far as cold blood is concerned, by Maxse's solitary night-ride through Crimean woods and Cossack piquets to summon the allied fleets round to Balaclava ; and by Stoddart's clinging to the faith in which he was born, when a word would have released him from that absolutely dark Bokharan dungeon, where the sheep-tick was cultivated for the torture of prisoners. Not to speak of Gordon's Bayard-like putting on his uniform in which to die.

For our stoutness in hot blood we also equal them. Think of Willoughby and Forrest ex-

ploding the small arm magazine at Delhi, and
themselves with it ; of Home and Salkeld blowing in the Cashmere Gate ; and Corporal Bur-
gess, mortally wounded already, lighting the fuse
just before the shot which made the wound a
death : while among them stands the bugler,
thrice repeating, by Home's command, their regi-
mental call which summoned the gallant ' Die
Hards ' now, as at Albuera, to advance. Not
that such antique courage is our own solely.
Willoughby may have thought of that splendid
Dutchman whose sloop-of-war was left on the
mud of the Scheldt in the Belgian Independence
struggle, and who, when summoned to surrender
by Antwerpers chuckling over an easy victory,
went below and blew up himself, his ship, and a
good few bystanders. Why can't our War Office,
which has copied so much from the Continent,
adopt their system of rewards for such devotion
as this ? So long as a Dutch War Navy exists,
so long is a ship bearing his name (Bahr, or
something like that) to be always in commission.
And Napoleon carried it further, into the very
ranks. In the regiment of which the First Grena-
dier of France once formed a part, his name is

still called first on the roll, ' La Tour d'Auvergne.'
The second man answers for the hero, ' Mort au
champ de bataille.'   Were our Admiralty to name
a ship the *Broke*, can one fancy her surrendering
to an American cruiser ?   The hero himself had
told the *Shannon's* crew that it would never do to
be beaten on a first of June, when Lord Howe
had thrashed the Frenchmen so soundly.   And
the memory told, and stirred the blood ; and
history once more repeated itself.   It was once
again philosophy teaching by examples.

But in one particular, inflicting and bearing
cruelty, and enjoying after a fashion the sight of
it, our ancestors were far tougher than we are.
Public executions, till done away with, drew spec-
tators by thousands.   (Can it be that out of sight
is out of mind, whence it is that outcry has ceased
against Messieurs the Assassins paying their stake
when they lose, so that even when women turn
fiends there is no exception now for the fair sex ?)
But our forefathers carried it a little further ; if
they could not see the real thing, they would
have it served up cold in the form of copper-plate
engravings.

I have one very rare book ; there is no copy of

it in the British Museum, and Brunet seems only to record the sale of one, perhaps this of mine. It is called 'Théâtre des Martyres,' by Luiken, 1738, is in three languages—German, French, and Flemish—and contains 104 spirited engravings of pretty nearly all the forms of torture, ancient and modern, ever invented as means of bringing about a change of opinion on those mysterious theological dogmas on which man seems all the more desperately certain because the ALL WISE has left them in doubt. Why flaying alive and impalement were omitted from the catalogue of Spiritual Convincers is doubtful. Burning alive hardly supplies their place fully.

We will merely run through this table-book of a century and a half since, premising that the engravings are fully equal to the art of the period.

A description of this book is given, in order to show what pleased our ancestors (being Dutchmen) 150 years ago; but as it may not please their descendants now, it is well that all whose nerves are not over-strong should skip the residue of this chapter, for, as the Fat Boy said to Mrs. Wardle, ' I'm goin' to make your flesh creep.'

The greater part of the 103 etchings are of the Alva cruelties in the Low Countries, but sixty years past when the book was published, though the two creepiest, reserved for the last, are of earlier date.

Certain martyrs for Christianity as a whole precede those put to death for sectional disputes on matters of opinion subsequently developed.

Thus, Vitalis is being buried alive ; Cassianus, the Imola schoolmaster, being knifed to death by his own pupils (how the young rascals do enjoy the fun !) ; Dulcia is being cut to pieces, one executioner holding an amputated arm, and with his knife in his mouth straightening the other for work upon it, an assistant meantime cutting into the victim's knee. One man's fingers are being cut off by chisel and mallet ; a baker, bound to a ladder, is being thrown backwards into the flames, a woman sharing the same fate in the Alvan horrors later on.

Algerius, at Rome in 1550, is having melted lead poured on his head, preparatory to the burning-alive process. Plozier, at Antwerp in 1560, and two women, are being drowned in sacks, and the process is shown in detail. Thus, the man is being sacked ; one of the women lies on the floor trussed up ready for her plunge ; the third is being immersed in her cask, an attendant behind holding the covering which is to smother her. Eemkens, at Utrecht in 1560, is fastened to a stake, and by means of a flaming truss of straw is being 'browned,' as a cook would ' brown ' with a salamander, a monk superintending. Ursula Schulmeister, suspended by her wrists, is being flogged, after which the rack and its attendants await her before the flames mercifully come. Pinder, stretched on the ground, is having his neck sawn through. Misel is beheaded by the sweep of the sword, as was Anne Boleyn. The blood spurts up three feet high, as I have already told was seen by my friend, Dr. George Harley, who witnessed the last of such executions in Baden.

Cornelius is hung up by his left thumb, a heavy weight tied to his feet to keep him steady, while the two soldiers play at cards, and the executioner watches their game, till the time comes for the rack, standing close by. Smit hangs from a gallows by his left leg.

Then comes a more human, though by no

means more humane, picture. Marie Wems has been burnt with an iron gag in her mouth ; her son, a lad of nineteen or so, comes to the foot of the charred and smoking stake, from which the chain still hangs, to seek, among the smouldering ashes of what was once his mother, for this ghastly memorial of her sufferings. A little child looks on with its hand in its mouth unconcerned.

Anne van der Hove is being buried alive at Brussels. Everything is earth-covered, save a sweet, calm face, on which a man is about to throw a heavy shovelful that will conceal it for ever. By the side kneels a priest with biretta, holding up the crucifix !

Perhaps the most purely horrible is the death of another Herod, in the shape of Hunneric, a Vandal king in Africa, A.D. 484, though how such a persecutor has found his way into a book of Christian martyrs requires explanation. The tyrant is being devoured by worms, and loathly insects of all kinds are plenteously in evidence. A foot and hand have rotted off, and are being carried away by attendants, whose one great care is to hold their own noses.

But the most terrible of all, which ought

only to be looked at on a very hot day, is the martyrdom of the Apostle Bartholomew. The saint has been affixed head downwards on an X-shaped cross, and is being skinned by two men. They have got down as far as the armpits, when a pectoral muscle stands out, gives some trouble, and requires scraping with the knife. The performer, whose left arm is covered with flaps of skin, remarks about it to his mate, who, however, with his knife-blade between his teeth, is stripping down the epidermis while listening to some remark made by a third man close by.

The countenance of the victim is absolutely freezing with horror, contrasting with the common, matter-of-fact expression of the executioners, and the gloating look of a Jew who stands near.

The practice is said to be still extant in some parts of Persia, or the even wilder country to the east of it, though both it and impaling are no longer performed in public.

CHAPTER THE LAST.

THE MIDDLE TEMPLE, WITH ITS TABLE-TALK.

Does anything ever perish ?—Do any Traces of the Old Templars still remain in the Society which succeeded them ?—Finest Town View in London—Two Noble Leaders—Mr. Benjamin, Q.C.—Talking Nonsense to Fools—Lazarus and Dives in Pump Court—Benjamin's Ghost—The Voice from Aleppo heard in Bloomsbury—The Maximum Fee of an English Barrister—The Minimum Ditto—An Attorney-General's opinion of his Position—Sir John Holker—Chief-Baron Kelly once a Grocer in Oxford Street—As to the Salubrity of Bethnal Green Air—Lord Lyndhurst—What is a Woosbird ?—Chief-Justice Bovill—Chief-Justice Jervis—'I thought I'd said it ; not you'—Mr. Glass, Q.C.—The New Judge and the Annual Practice Book—Mr. Commissioner Charles Warren—Serjeant Ballantine—How I first knew him—'Don't point that Gun at my Head'—The Serjeant and the Preaching M.P., Q.C.—Whist at Blenheim Points for Thirty-six Hours—The Great Indian Fee —'Mind whom you take with you'—A Law Library exchanged for French Novels—Sir John Campbell and Lady Stratheden — Robert Hall's Courtship — Bar Women — The Northumberland Street Tragedy—'It was all about me'—The Serjeant's Final Collapse—'She wor a Mooggletonian'—The Last Survival of the Bad Days of the Regency, and its Morals—Judges' 'Sets' at the Bar—'Meant for my Brother Bacon'—Wit no longer extant in the Chancery Division—Sir Lancelot Shadwell and his Injunction granted on the Thames — Advertising for Two Hundred Ballet-girls — The Judge and the Deaf Juror—Lord Westbury—Plain Speaking by Father and Son—Mr. Baker Greene—'What Number, pray ?'

—His Correspondence with his Tailor—Mr. Bottomley Firth—
Ayrtonism as a Fine Art—' You're all afraid '—The Tichborne
Claimant : ' Why not ?'—How Jean Luie came up—The Lefroy
Consultation—The Late Lord Redesdale—' It was the Dog
that died '—How Justice Maule brought about the Divorce Act
—The good Lord Shaftesbury—His Successor's Suicide
in Shaftesbury Avenue—Irish Thais—The same and Lord
Brougham—The same and Jung Bahadur—What happened to
the Nepaulese Jewels—Thais married—The Lawsuit about the
Dressmaker's Bill—A Magdalen with a Vengeance—How she
read Grace at Lord Shaftesbury's Dinner-party, and what the
Host said—A Bishop's Prayers declined by an Archbishop—
A Second Charles XII.—Mr. Baron Huddleston—How he
thought Twice about tackling *Truth*—His Feeling towards
Cyclists—How he managed to do so much Harm—The Quaker
and the Black Cap—' Ten to One on the Rope '—Comical
Cross-readings in Reported Cases—' The Man in the Boat got
out and ran away '—Judges on their own Trial—' Which shall I
put in : the Half-sov. or the Sixpence ?'—The Old Servant not
a Bad Master—How the Litigants shunted the Judge—Mr.
Justice Witty—The Sanguinary Bore—How we dine in Hall
during Commons—Difference from other Inns in this respect—
How they managed Two Hundred Years ago—The Call to
Mess by blowing a Horn—The Benchers' Procession with the
Mace—The Three Mystic Knocks—The Grace—Withdrawal
of the Mace : the Sacramental Meal—Return of the Mace—
The Three Mystic Knocks again—The Return Thanks—Return
of the Benchers' Procession down the Hall—Variations on
Grand Nights—Old Ceremony when a Judge appointed during
Term-time was excluded from the Inn—Calls to the Bar—High
Jinks in Hall after them—The Captured Bobby—The Head
Porter and the Barrister—By-and-By—The Common Room—
The Library—The Temple Church—The Management of the
Inn—Deficient in Firmness—The Third Row of Bottles—
Conclusion.

DOES anything ever really perish, in the sense of
utter destruction, so that in competent hands, and

with suitable appliances, no trace of its nature, form, or characteristics can ever be recovered?

The poets have said so; the Laureate, in a grand organ fugue of 'In Memoriam,' has told us :

> 'The hills are shadows, and they pass
> From shape to shape and nothing stands.'

The author of 'The Tempest' could make a simile—

> 'And like the baseless fabric of this vision,
> Leave not a wrack behind.'

But is it true either in Science or Society? Geology disproved it when a mutilated lower jaw in the Stonesfield Quarry revealed ancient marsupial existence in England, now confined to Australia; when conifer - stumps were found in 77° north, mangroves and turtles in Sheppey, and giant Wellingtonias with rhotang palms in Bovey Tracey lignite. Manuscripts and papyri, perhaps the most perishable of all muniments, contradict it also, and turn up legible in the queerest places. That strangely neglected but most precious document, 'The Teaching of the Twelve Apostles,' the fragmentary Primal Gospel, found by an Austrian Archduke in a Nitrian convent dust-bin, the treasures of Tel-el-Amarna and Tel-el-Jehudi, all attest that nothing, however frail, is wholly lost; while, in more solid materials, Assyriology has practically been recreated by this present generation.

Nor is this confined to records alone. The genius of Sir Henry Maine detected a strange persistence of Social Institutions in village communities; and almost the last work of Dean Stanley identified Primitive Church practices in about the last place where they could be looked for—the gorgeous ceremonies over which the Pope himself presides in St. Peter's. Indeed, it goes deeper still, even into long-forgotten racial sympathies. The wailing and tears with which Thebes Fellaheen on Nile-bank watched the passage of the barges which bore the long-lost Pharaoh mummies from their happy hiding-place at Deir-el-bahari down to a more secure asylum, came 'from the depths of some Divine despair' lying deep in tribal instincts.

Tyrants and oppressors of thirty centuries past though they were, their very names forgotten, their language a mystery to the people, these hard-fisted sons of toil, whose only thought is daily bread and how to get enough of it, rose to the hidden and Divine pulse-beat of a memory, long overlaid, but as deep-seated and permanent as Conscience itself.

Just as their ancestors mourned for those dead princes when the sacred boat bore them to the stately tomb-house, so wailed they, as Syrian women weep now for Tammuz, and Mussulmans for Hosein and Ali.

As the Laureate has told us in one of his ' Juvenilia,' ' Nothing will die.'

It may be well, therefore, to examine lightly the present life of a great and famous Inn of Court, second to none in the hearts of those who know it, to see if traces of its original form yet exist, if only by way of bringing into more common appreciation the fascination and delight which attend on the rehabilitating embalmed, though long overlooked, records of the past.

Can we then recover any evidence of the Templar Secret Society which it succeeded in the outwardly prosaic every-day life of the Middle Temple?

It is a grand old Inn, with its hall, in which Elizabeth has dined and danced, which

Shakespeare visited repeatedly when superintending the first representation of 'Twelfth Night' held within its walls—lined round, too, with armour which shows how small in stature, though stout of heart, were our Middle Age ancestors who wore it.

Its ancient buildings also have a homely and habitable look, like some old university college dropped down in the heart of the Metropolis. It possesses the most beautiful town view in London, where from New Court Steps the visitor looks through Fountain Court—past the sparkling jet dear to Charles Dickens, who wrote 'Great Expectations' close by—between the old hall gable and the library, across the historic garden, where the choice of two roses gave name to the most internecine struggle which ever devastated England, over the Embankment planes, whose greenery conceals the squalid southern shore, on to the bright and wind-swept Surrey hills which bound the horizon.

But it is its Human Interest which makes itself most felt. Outwardly quiet, this oasis of peace and calm, into which a wanderer restfully turns out of the hurricane roar of Fleet Street, dear to

Dr. Johnson, teems with human passions, fears, cares, hopes and, above all, disappointments.

It is not the quiet, small college—the Queen's, or Pembroke—it appears; and the men who tread its courts daily realize that tremendous reality—

> ' It shall not be all bitter, nor all sweet to all :
> It shall be *Life*.'

With all its outward tranquillity, the fierce jealousies which, in a small society whose members are perpetually in contact, attend even moderate success, show up luridly the seamy side of life.

Far more censorious than any club, because the men are always on the spot, in the same occupation and in constant intercourse, every man's faults and failings are common property to the circle round him 'having interest,' as the Probate Court phrase has it.

How Roland muckers his cases ; how Oliver won't hold a losing brief, but passes it on to a twenty-fifth ' devil,' to whom his two dozen predecessors have handed it down, with the result that, when the case comes on, the unhappy juniorest has not read his papers, and could not use them if he had, to the consternation of the

Court ; and what that imposing personage looked, but did not give tongue to ; how that most conscientious and laborious individual was most unjustly while at the Bar called ' Settling Day,' and ' the Day that never comes ;' how Blathers took silk, and got ' worsted,' are common topics. Nay, even sadder subjects—how, in the prime of life and work, some rising advocate has been struck down by illness, to the destruction of a connection hardly ever regained ; how another of the same type has been seized with acute mania in open court, and led away shrieking to await a merciful release the next day ; perhaps, saddest of all, how an over-wrought brain, too engrossed in its work. has led its possessor to the fatal leap in front of a train ! These are Temple tales.

It must, however, be said that what little help is possible in such cases is frankly given by circuit and sessions messes — all the more commendable because the contributors are too frequently little better off themselves than the comrade who has fallen out of the ranks. But, as a rule, detraction has the innings ; rarely is the good word given. It could not, however, be withheld in the case of one brilliant advocate, now the head of his profession, whose father had died poor, and who from the outset directed his splendid intellect to the discharge of that father's obligations, with the unlooked-for but surely well-deserved result that in his case great industry, commanding talents, natural eloquence, and con-genital *bonhommie* for once found appreciation from solicitors; and after a career without an enemy, he stands for the reversion of one of the two highest posts open to an English barrister.

Nor when another great advocate, sometime holder of the same high office, and standing as prominent in the opinion of his brethren, refused the Marble Chair and saw his junior pass over his head rather than support a measure which to his mind imperilled the unity of the Empire, was there any open approval of the tremendous sacrifice offered at the shrines of honour and con-science. We were all proud of him before; we are prouder of him than ever now, for in his own words to the writer: 'If it were to be done over again, I would still do it.' But such really noble acts as these pass unnoticed among us, though the partialities for a peer or a pretty woman shown by the last but one of the Barons were always commented on with a smile of . pity and amusement.

No good is said of a man when living, and not much more of it when he is dead ; but some men have occupied neutral ground. Among them, perhaps the most favoured was the late Mr. Benjamin—a man who passed through terrible trials — the life and soul of the Confederate struggle, fighting the game to the last, and escaping in an open boat in the Gulf of Mexico, when all other outlets were closed against him, reaching England penniless, to find all he had saved from the wreck of his fortune for wife and daughter swallowed up in a mercantile failure ; starting afresh with nothing but indomitable industry and his splendid legal reputation to go on, rapidly climbing the steep which leads to fame, until, when making £27,000 a year, he could refuse a Lord Justiceship, and retire to Paris, as he told the writer, to 'see the sun.' No subtler yet more daring advocate has ever adorned the British Bar. On one occasion he said to me, in the robing-room, with his usual slight twang :

'Saw yew just now in the Appeal Court.'

'Yes ; I was wondering how much higher you were going to force the case of " Bonomi and Backhouse." '

'Ah, Ai see, yew think I was talking blanked nonsense ; all Ai can tell you is, Ai've talked three times as blanked nonsense to men not half as blanked fools as those three, and pulled it off, tew.'

Mr. Benjamin unconsciously illustrated one of those great ironies of life of which our Temple experiences are full, but which rarely come out into the open. His chambers in Lamb Building looked through the Cloisters and Pump Court into a room at its western end, tenanted by one Oppenheim, also a Jew. At the very time when Dives Benjamin, one of the kindest and most liberal, be it said, of his ancient race, was weary of wealth-making, careless of rank and honour, seeking only the sunny warmth in which he was cradled, and abandoning all for that, Lazarus Oppenheim—genial, charitable, and a pillar of his People's institutions—was ending life by his own hand, in despair at his own non-appreciation by solicitors. The men were of the same nation, the same faith, and they both occupied opposite chambers when this ghastly antithesis worked itself out, as it were, in full sight of each.

To Benjamin we owe our only well-authenticated Temple ghost. He had left for sunny France, had pensioned his clerk, and transferred his chambers and library. The barrister who literally sat in his seat was returning from court at the lunch-hour in company of that most unimpeachable of all witnesses—an eminent solicitor. Rounding the Temple Church, and in view of Lamb Building door, the solicitor said :

' Why, there's Benjamin !'

The unmistakable figure and waddle, the clean-shaven face, the keen glance, drew forth the answer :

' Why, so it is !'

But the Shape passed on through the Cloisters, and was seen no more. The door of chambers was opened as they came to it by an awe-struck inmate, who held up the telegram from Paris—' Benjamin is dead.'

We cannot pause to inquire if the Persian belief that the soul lingers for three days around the mansion it has so long tenanted be well founded or not, but there is some evidence in its favour worth glancing at.   There is the Psychical Society's one undeniable success—the proved appearance of the Crimean officer to his sister and brother-in-law on the morning when he met his death before the Redan ; and the voice of George Smith, the Assyriologist, heard by his patron, Dr. Delitzsch, on an autumn evening in Great Russell Street, 'Ach, theuer Herr Doctor Delitzsch!' at the time when the spirit of the poor boy, originally a paper-seller in the street, whom he had befriended and brought forward, was attaining at Aleppo what Mussulman theology calls 'the mercy of God.'

Such neutral records as Benjamin's and genial Serjeant Parry's are, however, rare.

The writer has personally known the two advocates who have received the highest and smallest fees ever earned by an English barrister. The still living Mr. Petersen, when in Calcutta, received with his brief the enormous honorarium of Rs. 100,000, and Rs. 10,000 refresher for seven days, equivalent at the exchange of the time to £24,000, for the defence and cleverly gained acquittal of Jotee Persaud, the great Indian contractor, who during the Mutiny had found food for

Havelock's starving columns, and was afterwards criminally prosecuted by the Government he had saved. The late Sir John Holker accepted the other fee for showing a countryman over the House of Commons Library. The visitor's 'member,' an Irishman, was on his legs, and safe there for an hour to come, so the kindly giant, not in the least offended by the supposition that he also was up for the Cattle-show—which he undoubtedly looked like—whiled away the time as has been said, finally depositing his charge in the Speaker's Gallery, whence the horror-struck spectator, enlightened by his 'member,' to whom he had praised the civility of the servants, saw the Attorney-General go up to the Treasury Bench and address one of its occupants :

'I say, Smith, I've earned a fee while I've been away, and here it is—sixpence.'

Human nature is hard to satisfy, and though Sir John could describe himself once as having walked on the mountain-tops in the sunshine of prosperity, he told the writer a very different tale.

It was in the old robing-room in Guildhall, and the washing arrangements were so bad that the writer secreted a private towel. The Attorney-General expressed himself strongly—as was his wont—but when offered the private towel in his capacity of head of the Bar, simply answered :

' I suppose you think it a blanked fine thing to be head of the Bar ; but if you only knew how they humbug me, and play the fool with me, you would wish yourself where you are.'

A mild suggestion of what the child said about royalty when the same was said of that, ' I should like to try it just once, only for a little, to see what it was like,' met with no reply. Few men have lived more liked, have died more regretted, than the burly member for Preston, at a time, too, when a Government of the opposite party had gracefully recognised the merits of a quondam adversary by appointing him a Lord Justice of Appeal. Of the shadow, the fatal mistake which darkened his private life, nothing need here be said ; it is one to which his profession, at all events in the past, has been peculiarly and unaccountably subject, although it is terribly human, and therefore common.

Sir John Holker's strongest point was his slow, impressive way of speaking, with just a touch of 'burr' in it, an artifice employed with great effect by the late Mr. John Bright, whose expression in the Burials Bill debate, in a speech said to have been one of the finest specimens of modern oratory, is still remembered by those who heard it : 'As for me and mine, we shall be buried like dogues.'

Solicitors fancied him much as the 'heaviest' speaker at the Bar, and he did good public service for all time by his Crossed Cheques Act, which enacts that the simple words 'Not negotiable' written thereon shall cause the property in them to remain vested in their true owner. Stolen cheques thus marked are therefore no longer freely cashed over the counter by sporting publicans.

The late Chief Baron Kelly was a self-made man. Nor was he ashamed of his humble parentage, for when Sir William Ferguson recommended him the then vaunted panacea of native air, he inquired : ' Really, doctor, would you advise Bethnal Green?' Of his losses in the old Agra Bank, of his providing for his young family of daughters by heavy and costly life insurances, which necessitated, in order to pay the premium thereon, his continuing on the Bench till physical infirmities made his holding judicial functions almost a public scandal, nothing need here be said, except for a happy retort of Mr. Cole, Q.C., whose iron constitution was to break pitiably down under the combined strain of all day work in court and all night work in the House of Commons, when that august body took to sitting forty-one hours at a stretch over the Transvaal Bill. The failing old man piped out:

'You have told us that three times already, Mr. Cole.'

The old King replied:

'Yes, my lord; and it was *necessary* I *should* do so.'

One more personal anecdote of a great man in his day. Over thirty years ago the writer was staying at Lynton in showery autumn weather. But one other person was stopping in the hotel, and in the damp evenings the two inmates forgathered, in very despair, just as the people blown ashore on Saugor Island in a cyclone did not shrink from the society of an equally-cowed creature in the shape of a royal Bengal tiger. At Lynton in the evening it was impossible to go out, and the

writer, for a whole week, had the privilege of the
stores of learning, fun and anecdote which, in
most genial vein, were poured out to an apprecia-
tive listener by Dr. Doran, editor of *Notes and
Queries*, and author of heaps of good books
besides.   But one sunny noon, going up to
Watersmeet, the writer encountered a very old
man, very weak on his pins.   One chance word
led to another, one shuttlecock joke quickly hit
back led to another, English to French, and the
narrator was wondering to whom on earth he
was talking, when down came the '*deus ex
machina*.'   A country cart laden with fern for
bedding came sharply down upon us at right
angles from the hillside ; its conductor, a slip of a
girl about fourteen, was riding 'Miss - Bird '-
fashion.   In those days the young girls did
carters' work, and bestrode the animal man-wise.
The sudden apparition and its peculiar pose sent
us both into roars of laughter, to the discomposure
of the damsel, who bestowed upon us some strong
epithets of disdain, especially upon the senior,
thus :

'You bain't no better than a old oosbird.'

The vision faded, but when the old gentleman

could speak, he asked between recurrent spasms of laughter :

' Pray, sir, what is an " oosbird " ?   I thought I had been called everything they could lay their tongues to.   Denman did a lot that way in the Queen's trial.   Brougham had a good idea of slanging, and Campbell has gone in for me ; but really now, I was never called an " oosbird " before.   Whatever can she mean ?'

The writer took off his hat to the giant-of-old, John Singleton Copley, Lord Lyndhurst, but the cat had been let out.   The walk back was dull, in spite of the efforts on both sides to put the ball again into play : there was no life in the game, nor did another meeting occur.   But some of those inimitable French stories could be told over again to Dr. Doran, for even to him they were new, and he heartily enjoyed my contribution. He planned, indeed, a waylay of the old statesman to get some more, on his own account, but it did not succeed.   Faint echoes of them seem to have been told on circuit grand nights by Chief Justice Cockburn, but the ' gros sel ' which tickled that judge's palate appears to have got uppermost, no longer concealed by the subtle delicacy in which it was enveloped in the mind of the accomplished scholar and mathematician who had preceded him. Of Cockburn himself, the stories, countless as they are, and good of their kind, too, are not to this generation's taste.

Chief Justice Bovill gave rise to one of Lord Westbury's savagest sneers. The peer had looked in at the first Tichborne trial, and jingling his watch-chain, as was his wont when excited, re-marked : ' Ah, poor Bovill ! if he only knew a little law he'd be the very worst judge on the bench.' Bovill further managed to drive a Guild-hall special jury, of which I formed one, into downright rebellion. An action for cotton differ-ences tried there was arranged to be taken up to the Court above, with power to draw inferences from the evidence. Bovill directed the jury to find technically for the defendant, but the unanimous verdict was for the plaintiff. An ill-mannered sneer, ' It does not matter which way you find,' elicited the dignified reply, ' We are on our oaths, my lord, just as you are on yours !'

The late Chief Justice Jervis, a far kindlier man, is credited with the following circuit story, another form of the old *Tu quoque*.

A hospitable peer had invited Judge and Bar to dinner, in the days before water was the usual beverage at that meal. All dined freely, and the conversation after dinner got a little mixed. As a consequence, a somewhat priggish leader the next morning got the chance of taking to task a fellow silk-gownsman, whose exceptional talents were not accompanied by sufficient self-control in such matters—who, indeed, had to resign the ermine to which he brought rare judicial faculties, dying from broken health soon afterwards.

'I say, Honyman, do you know what you did last night ?'

'No, my dear fellow ; what was it ?'

'You called the judge a blanked fool, and must, of course, apologize.'

'Not a doubt about that ; here goes !'

'DEAR CHIEF JUSTICE,

'I have just heard with great concern that last night, after dinner, I spoke to your Lordship in a way which I never intended, and I am sure you will overlook.'

And the letter went to the Bench straight.

It was an interesting ‘breach’ case, and the lady was in the box under torment, but Jervis stopped the screw-turning to write thus :

‘ MY DEAR HONYMAN,

‘Your letter has removed a great weight from my mind. Until I got it I held the idea that I had applied the term to you, and was considering how to ask *your* indulgence.’

Fuimus Troes! Is there a two-bottle man left at the Bar ?

To glance at the Chancery Division, the late Mr. Glasse, Q.C., who led the Court by the nose, *tempore* Malins the much-appealed-from, was once in consultation, and said with great glee : ‘My dear sir, we shall *win:* there is but one case against us ; the only report of it is in our library, and I *am sitting on it.*’ This used to be told by cheery Mr. Ince, on whose decease there was but one feeling.

An amusing confession was made by a recently appointed judge to a friend of his own size (they are both among the highest authorities at the Bar).

There is a book called, shortly, 'The White Book'; longly, 'The Annual Practice'—comprising all the orders of Court, with the changes which indifferent administration of justice and its cat-jumps cause therein, written up yearly. The newly-ermined said 'he had just read it through, and it really contained a great deal of very interesting matter.'

The late Charles Warren, who wrote the once-famous novel, 'Ten Thousand a Year,' and died a Lunacy Commissioner, was gifted with veracity in an inverse ratio to pomposity, and stuck at no statement which would, even for the moment, increase his own importance. This was well known, and amusingly taken advantage of by the late Mr. Adolphus, Q.C. Rising from his seat in Court, Warren said :

' I must leave now ; I am going to dine with the Lord Chief Baron.'

The answer was :

' Well, I'll go too, for I am also dining with him.'

There was an awkward pause, and Warren, getting frightened, said :

' Ah ! by the way, that was a mistake of mine about dining to-day with the Chief Baron.'

The rejoinder was :

' And oddly enough, my dear fellow, I made the same mistake. I'm no more going to dine with him than you are.'

But more good stories circulated about Serjeant Ballantine than perhaps any other man. My first acquaintance with him commenced in a Guildhall jury-box, where I had the privilege of serving five days. It was the first of the cases wherein it has been sought by share and debenture holders to recover damages for misrepresentation.

The plaintiff, one of the carpet-making Crossleys, had been induced to sink £36,000 in debentures, and £14,000 in shares in a brewery company, on the strength of the profits said to be made by exporting beer, and he sued the managing director for deceiving him as to such profits. Ballantine was for the plaintiff, opposed by Sir John Karslake, Solicitor-General. The judge was Chief Baron Kelly, who soon announced that he knew nothing about accounts, nor did he suppose counsel did, and suggested that the jury, who knew all about such things, should go through the figures. So that when the accountant was in the box, I and two or three more went through some of the shipments from invoice to account sale. Ballantine hugely enjoyed this process, which took perhaps a day in all, careful never to say a word, and leaving it to Karslake to cross-examine nominally the witness, but really *me*. Now the thing counsel most fear is putting a juryman's back up, and Karslake not only did this with me but with some of my colleagues as well, one of whom at last told him not to ask questions concerning things he knew nothing about.

Ballantine *beamed* upon us, and especially upon me, and we got in time a nodding and speaking acquaintance. We of the jury had made up our minds during the second day, but we had to go on sitting wearily while the fees were being earned according to the rules of the game, with but one sensation, and that a startler. There being but ten specials, two common jurymen had been added to make the dozen, and at lunch on the third day I discovered one of them was DEAF.

A hurried consultation was held on the front bench. We might be there till doomsday. The deaf man was removed next to me in the front row, and the evidence instilled into him by those on each side of him. Karslake, upon whom was creeping the blindness which afterwards became total, did not notice it; but Ballantine did. If the case had to be tried over again, he would never again have the luck to get eight jurors out of twelve who knew this kind of accounts.

At last they let us retire, and our deaf man, duly escorted, was placed next me at the top of the table. Now, the practice is to take a show of hands on first sitting down, and ten were for plaintiff, the other two being the common jurors, and my friend the deaf man, the worse of the two. He didn't understand! ' Was we a-going to give £50,000 damages? He never heerd of no such thing, and he wouldn't do it nohow.'

There was but one argument possible. Would he go against so many? At this point the other objector wanted his tea, and was told he wouldn't get it till the next morning, as things stood, so he gave way; and then our deaf colleague agreed to a verdict for £36,000. But, as too often happens, it did Mr. Crossley no good. It was the first case of the kind, hence subsequent appeals; and the tenacity of the trustees, who held defendant's property in settlement, prolonged matters indefinitely, so the unhappy plaintiff died very poor.

But the Serjeant and the juryman knew each other thenceforth.

He was a wit from boyhood. One of his masters at school was very hard upon him, and finally said:

'Well, Ballantine, it comes to this: one of us two must leave the school.'

One can see the pupil's eye twinkle when he replied:

'You've got the chance to, and I haven't.'

Much has been written about the charm of a smile. Ballantine had it to perfection. His face at rest, was as ugly as Jack Wilkes'—oddly enough, a man equally successful with women—but with the first ripple of a smile the harsh lineaments softened, the unmistakable nose was brightened out of notice, and a light of almost feminine beauty broke out on the wooden moulding of the features, while the sparkle of a genius almost unexampled for quickness shone out in the eye, where, indeed, it was never quite hidden, even in the fits of depression which came over him towards the last. And the smile, too, was a kindly one, while the voice was simple euphony, marred only by that slight hesitation which seems inherent in

English eloquence, though our Irish brethren contrive to escape it.

His foibles must be buried with him, but facts relating to so remarkable a man are worth chronicling. His skill in cross-examination was something wonderful, and held in corresponding fear. But as the Yankee said: 'Double the tale of bricks, and then comes Moses.' Some of the tortured ones were able to devise expedients which enabled them to stand their ground against such a demon bowler. Thus, in a gun-patent case, a witness who held him in the direst fear was told to take the article in his hands while counsel applied the rack. Witness received it at the level, and unintentionally held the muzzle pointed straight at the Serjeant's wig, to the immediate perturbation of its wearer.

'Put that gun down, sir!' Witness complied. 'No, I don't mean that; take it up, but don't cover me with it; point it at somebody else.'

The witness held Lord Chief Justice Cockburn in almost as much fear as his torturer, and sloped the weapon in the direction of the Court itself.

'Not at me, sir, please!' was the bellow which came from the Bench.

So the much-worried man, warned off on both right and left, held it midway. Fear then seized upon the jury, and the four middle ones sprang to their feet.

' My lord, we've wives and families, and our lives are not insured !'

Where was the gun to go? If behind, the bothering-the-witness-blind could not come off, for the lock action would be out of focus, and the points could not be made ; moreover, for perhaps the first and last time (save, it may be, his excursion into the Chancery Division, and encounter with Mr. Justice Kay, who liked to be chief in his own Court, and told the new-comer that he knew even less of practice in equity than he did of common law), the Serjeant was nonplussed, and the Court, with a red gleam in its eye, and its sardonic mixture of roar and squeak which did duty for a laugh, interposed :

' Really, Brother Ballantine, is it any use going on with this ?'

' No, my lord ; in view of the utter and crass stupidity of the witness, it is not.'

And the witness, overjoyed, left at once, not stopping, like Sam Weller, who was dismissed for the same reason, to ask if any other gen'l'man wanted to ask him any more. Unlike Sam Weller again, for the Serjeant lost his case, everything having turned on the expert breaking down in cross-examination.

Ballantine's wit was something wonderful, even in its tersest form, the contrasting two incongruous ideas in the one focus of a conundrum. The more's the pity that, for the greatest part, they were only suited to the grosser ears of a pre-Victorian generation. Still, some were printable, and in the hope of his preserving some of these the writer asked the Serjeant if his book, then about to appear, left out all the riddles? When the answer was, ' My dear sir, it might be read in a Sunday-school,' one could only say, 'Ah! Serjeant, you've spoiled it.'

Personalities, again, and not of the kind which tickle in place of scratching, were a strong point of his. One day, in Guildhall robing-room, there were present only the late genial Mr. MacIntyre, another silk-gownsman, now an Indian Chief Justice, and the narrator.

' Billy,' his back to the fire, was keeping his audience in roars of laughter, when there entered to us an eminent Nonconformist, Q.C., M.P., much given, even when on circuit, to preaching. The appearance of this spiritually-minded person at once snuffed out all profane and worldly vanities ; so Ballantine, in desperation, changed his line :

'Ah, my dear fellow, there you are ! What a happy man you are ! If I'd only had your luck, I should have had twice as much of the kind of fun I like best as I have had !'

Now, the Serjeant's ideas of fun were popularly confined to the three W's — wine, whist, and women—-so the intruder shot round and fled, amid the screams of the auditors, one of whom, a very long man, had to sit down to laugh it off.

One of the W's, indeed—whist—was a bane of Ballantine's life. A shocking bad player in every one's opinion but his own, he rather fancied what were then called Blenheim stakes — 'fives and fifties, with the odds in ponies '—and intermediate bets to taste. He is credited with the House of Commons trick—of sitting six-and-thirty hours at a stretch ; but when, on the Monday morning, the Serjeant's sole remaining antagonist went to sleep over double dummy, his adversary, having pulled it down to £2,000, had a wash, went down quietly to chambers, looked into Sainsbury's for his usual 'pick-up,' and turned up in Court as fresh as a peony. When such a man, going out to India on his great case noted hereafter, landed at Bombay, he found any quantity of people ready to accommodate him at anything big he liked to play for. Not theirs, however, the late Duke of York's system—play every night from 8 p.m. to 2 a.m. with anybody, for anything or nothing; it did not matter to H.R.H., as he never paid when he lost. Fate did not smile on the brilliant advocate, and he is said to have left nearly all his magnificent fee of £10,000 within the hospitable walls of the Bombay club.

Good stories galore revolve round this magnificent honorarium, the largest ever received by any practitioner in English courts, though it practically cost more than it was worth; for Ballantine's practice was of a kind which perished unless continuously personally conducted, and on his return it was too far gone for recovery.

Thus one story goes: when the retaining solicitor attended to pay over the first moiety of

£10,000, counsel blandly smiled, took the notes, and, in his silveriest voice, counted, ' One, two, three, four, five,' and, rolling them up, trousered them, proceeding :

' Thank you. Now, my dear fellow, is there anything I can do to oblige you ?'

' Well, yes, Serjeant ; I was going to make one little suggestion.'

' Dear, dear ! and has my child-like simplicity led me into another hole, as on that one and only occasion when I wandered into what they call the Chancery Division ?'

' Well, Serjeant, it is not much, but I think you ought to know that pretty well all you do now will be watched and published in the native papers, so don't take too many Mrs. Ballantines with you.'

*   *   *   *   *

How that eminent solicitor, anxious to strengthen his counsel in Indian law, had pro-cured all the leading text-books thereon, and packed them in a box marked ' Cabin,' so that the advocate might fortify himself therewith *en route ;* how his laudable endeavour came to light when the baggage was examined in Paris ; how its contents were quietly taken out, and replaced by the newest studies in Zola-esque literature, is also truth-like, if not true.

The Serjeant did not prosper after his return from India. His magnificent fee—all expenses being paid in addition thereto—had been left behind ; his connection had dried up, and a new departure in legal practice had made his peculiar style of cross-examination less effective than of old. A lecturing trip to America was a failure, the points of his ' practice ' jokes were missed, and our cousins even caricatured the slight hesitation, which was the only blot on the euphony of his silvery voice, as ' er-er-ing.'

It was the writer's sorrow, in one sense, to see the final collapse of an advocate and a system once so great.

It was in the last days of the Westminster Hall sittings, before they were removed to the present grim Stone Jug, where you either shiver or stew, according to the season or the ventilators ; where you can neither hear, nor see, nor breathe, and where, after almost a dozen years, men habitually miss their way, and go down the wrong corkscrew stairs, even if they do not break their limbs in those dark descents, in the absence of even a hand-rail. This, by the way, is the only instance in which the building, as originally planned, is a failure, the idea of promoting juniors by crippling seniors who were to fall down them being a fiasco, like all the architect's other ideas.

To go back to Westminster Hall, of which Mr. Justice Grove took so pathetic a farewell, the scene of Ballantine's collapse was in the second Vice-Chancellor's Court, and the judge, not now on the Bench, had been trained mainly in India. He held strong views about evidence, on which he will ever be an authority.

The case was very simple, the establishment of a poor old woman's will, and the executor, a plain, elderly countryman, deposed in chief that testatrix was bed-ridden, and kept her snuff-box, money and will in a hole in the wall, on the left-hand side of her bed. All knew what was coming when the Serjeant with his sweetest smile and gentlest voice rose to cross-examine. For in ten minutes' time the witness had stated upon oath, of which he was continually reminded, as follows:

(1) That testatrix was not, and never had been, bed-ridden ; was good upon her pins, and

had even danced a jig the week before she died.

(2) That she never took snuff, but smoked cavendish out of a short black clay.

(3) That she kept her pipe, money, and will in a box on the right-hand side of her bed, ‘not in no hole at all, bekase there warn’t none in the wall nowhere.’

(4) And lastly, that she ‘nivver had no money, and nivver made no will.’

Thus was to close the brilliant sunset of a great career, in a last glow of colour and genius equal to any in its best days, but never to be repeated. For the witness lingered, and thus he spake :

‘ Zur, I doan’t quaite knaw whāāt Oi’ve been a-zaying to that there ginelm’n what is so pleasant laike, but all I cān saāy is :

(1) ‘ That she *wor* a bed-lier, and had been for two yeer.

(2) ‘ That she did taäk snooff, and nivver smoāked no cavendish, nor no black poipe.

(3) ‘ That she kep her mooney and her snooff-box, and her will, in a hōōl at t’ left haānd soide of her bed.

(4) ‘ And she nivver danced no jiggs in ’her

loife. 'Cos why ? she wor a Mooggletōnian, and didn't hold with no such things.'

Here broke in the deep bass voice of the Court from the depth of its capacious chest. Long may the voice of Sir James Stephen be heard in England! His Evidence Act will keep his name green in India :

'Gentlemen of the jury, you have witnessed a very brilliant and not-often-seen-nowadays specimen of a style of cross-examination which in its time was thought much of, and which has worked terrible injustice. Now, after what that poor man has just said, however, you can have no doubt he is the witness of truth.'

The jury *had* no doubt on the point, and said so at once ; the Serjeant's last bolt was shot, his occupation gone.

One is glad to think that the last year or two of so brilliant yet stormy a life closed in careful tending in the repose of a home perhaps understood for the first time, and certainly unknown since the days of early boyhood.

*   *   *   *   *

Though possessing Sheridan's eloquence, Hook's wit and power for mischief, Fox's love for high play and concomitant bad luck, for want of self-control, the brightest light of the English Bar set in shadow.   'His name is writ in water.'

But little foundation now exists for the still-abiding popular belief in the immorality of some, if not all, lawyers' lives, though one of Miss Braddon's latest novels, 'The Time Will Come,' all turns on a Lord Chancellor harbouring his cast-off mistress at his gate-lodge, and her terrible revenge on his family.

A well-known and comic instance of this belief is the remonstrance of his landlady to the then Sir John Campbell :

'All my gentlemen, Sir John, brings ladies ; and I takes no notice whether they're tall ladies, short ladies, stout ladies or thin ladies, fair ladies or dark ladies, which they always mostly is different every time ; but, Sir John, they gives them the protection of their names.   Now, I shouldn't have minded if you'd called the lady as come with you Lady Campbell ; but she calls herself Lady Stratheden, and my house ain't no longer respectable with such goings on as that.'

But, among ourselves, at all events, domestic relations are looked upon as ticklish questions ;

and some little interest is still taken in members' female belongings when they show up at church, or in the very few functions which come off in Hall, such, for instance, as when the late Mr. Milward, Q.C., marked his treasurership with a white stone by inducing Mr. Brandram to recite 'Twelfth Night' in the very hall where it received its first welcome and approval.

Could not, by the way, Lord Coleridge, who bears a classic name that English-speaking races will never willingly let die, arrange for us to hear 'Christabel,' the 'Ancient Mariner,' and 'Sir Arthur O'Kellyn' in the place which a poet but little greater than his illustrious relative first consecrated ?

This interest in 'Bar women' is, of course, but a shadow ; but it is based on a real ground, occurring in the lives of some distinguished lawyers, not long deceased, though, happily, no longer a scandal on the Judicial Bench, or among the most prominent of us. The real ground, of course, was that busy and anxious men, working from half-past nine to seven openly, and sitting up half the night as well to get up their cases, sought female company of a less exacting kind than society wives were in those days. Not common to lawyers only this feeling. Did not Robert Hall court his maid-servant this wise?

'Betty, do you love' (a name neither to be lightly written nor spoken). The natural answer to her minister and master was affirmative.

'Then will you be my wife?'

And a very good wife she made him during those paroxysms of agony so bravely borne which we read of in 'The Caxtons.'

But this desire for unbending after long hours of heavy strain led to some curious domestic results.

One judge at least within living memory married his cook—let us hope with better success than Alboni, who married her *chef* to retain his services, and never more was served with a dinner prepared by his hands! Another, also deceased within the last decade, did not even marry an honest woman, but made dreadful shipwreck as well of a magnificent constitution as of high position.

And there are cases in which this step has been taken under peculiar circumstances, as in that of the Indian judge who, being told he was on his death-bed, went through the marriage ceremony with the person whom he had lived with for many years, without that same. It did him more good than the doctors, for he absolutely *recovered.*

All this we have said is of the past, but if the easily intelligible taste for low company has come so near to our own days, which boast of a coster-monger Marquis, it was thought little of in the days of Gorgeous George and his Sailor brother, men openly tarred with the same brush.

A good story is told of the late Mr. Secondary James. One day at a Corporation banquet a friend congratulated him on the marriage of his son, Edwin James, Q.C., M.P., adding : ' I am glad to hear it.'

The old man looked down and sighed.

' I wish to Jove, sir, it *was* true !'

But the fashion of those days was not to say ' Jove.'

One distinguished barrister I knew whose domestic status was very mysterious. Outwardly a gay dog of a bachelor, leading a life ' free ' in its most expanded sense, he could at his zenith have married either rank, wealth, or beauty, as he might elect. But he took no steps in this direction.

Could there be some truth in a story told to the writer some quarter of a century ago by a still living beneficed London clergyman, who at all events himself gave it credence ? When a curate in the East-End, he was called to the death-bed of a poor outcast, evidently once a lady, and of great personal attractions, who had drifted down from the brilliant West to near that Old Gravel Lane Bridge which stood to those about there, sunk to the lowest depths, in the place of Hood's ' Bridge of Sighs.'

We must preface that some very few years previously a tragedy had occurred in Northumberland Street, Strand, to which the parties were a retired Indian officer and a shady money-lender resident there. Whatever the cause of the struggle, it was unprepared for, and silent. Both men fought with grim fury, and with the weapons nearest at hand. The people of the house heard nothing, and the first intimation of the conflict was the descent of the officer into the area from the second-floor *via* the rain-water pipe, terribly mauled by a poker. Upstairs they found the financial agent dying, brained by a recently-opened champagne-bottle. They took the officer to Charing Cross Hospital, whence after weeks of dumb suffering he was discharged. He said he knew nothing about it; the dead man told no tales, so the inquest brought nothing out. But the clergyman told the writer that the poor creature recalled this ghastly business to his memory, adding : ' It was all about me, and you must have heard of my husband : he is a great · lawyer, and his name is ——'

An old bad custom, happily seldom put in practice, has also died out—the ' set ' of particular judges against particular men, which used to be sympathized with, and carried on *con amore*, by their judicial brethren elsewhere. Its last known victim was a singularly ripe scholar and student, the late Mr. Purton Cooper, Q.C. He accidentally offended one of the two first appointed Lord Justices ; the other twin took the matter up quite as warmly. Poor Cooper not only lost the ear of the Court, but came in for its tongue, and even returned a hasty answer ! ! !

The solicitors, in the interest of their clients, gave him no more briefs. An attempt to start afresh in another Court met an almost savage reception from the judge there; the end was Boulogne and death. Only on the sale of his library was it known how ripe a scholar had perished, and all for one slight fault of temper!

The judges of the Chancery Division, pursuing the even tenor of their way, and with no gallery for advocates to play to, do not afford the same opening for mirth as the Common Law side, still less that division which deals with the pruriency of divorce cases, where a laugh is often a relief.

Perhaps Vice-Chancellor Malins, the always-successfully-appealed-from, though usually right in the matter of pure justice, has the best record. When the usual humdrum, dreary routine was varied by a successor of Miss Flite throwing an egg at the judge, whom it just missed, the Court calmly observed, 'That must have been meant for my brother Bacon,' which last venerable survival had his own idea of fun in a dry, usually acted, sarcasm. Thus, when a copy of his notes was called for in the Court above, it proved to consist solely of a clever but unflattering sketch of the learned but heavy Senior Wrangler, who had been boring him blind for the previous hour. Wit, in fact, in the Chancery Division is out of place ; and when, as a stranger there, I hazarded a couple of Latin epigrams at Mr. Justice Kay, promptly caught and returned ' hot' by that accomplished ex-Fellow of Trinity, the indigenous Bar stared aghast. None there now like Sir George Rose, who could write a sparkling epigram in Lord Eldon's awful presence. It is an old one, but so good as to bear repeating here, as a high-water mark for his successors :

> ' Mr. Leach made a speech,
>   Witty, neat, and strong ;
> Mr. Hart, on the other part,
>   Was heavy, dull, and long.
> Mr. Parker made the case darker,
>   Which dark enough, sure, was without,
> And on his close the Court up rose,
>   And the Chancellor said, "I doubt." '

Injunctions, when applied for in Court, are always dull going, save when, as recently happened, a chemical test is exhibited in evidence, and so mismanaged as to cause a blow-up in the Judge's private room. Those applied for outside its limits have more public interest.

It is an almost forgotten tale now how the then Duke of Newcastle (the one who would 'do as he liked with his own,' and got Nottingham

Castle burned about his ears in consequence) took to cutting down timber at Clumber, settlement restrictions thereagainst notwithstanding ; how the next tenant, Lord Lincoln, his eldest son, having demurred to no purpose, sought an injunction from the Court, then the only Vice-Chancellor, Sir Lancelot Shadwell. It was long vacation, but there was no time to be lost, for the historic oaks of Sherwood Forest were falling fast. So in those pre-railway days the local solicitor posted up to town, saw his agents, and had the affidavits drawn and engrossed during the night. At break of day the slumbering echoes of Barnes Elm, then a pleasant house embowered in trees on the banks of the Thames, were aroused by two coachfuls of people demanding access to his Honour. The sleepy domestics denied their master, for the odd reason that he was never ' in ' at that time, till the argument successfully pressed by Mr. Perker upon Sam Weller worked the revelation that, every morning at daybreak, Sir Lancelot took a half-mile swim against the stream, turned, and came down with it. Time was so precious that the boat-house was unlocked, and the party embarked, pulling wearily against the current, which they hoped the judge was coming down with. At length a man's head appeared; the boat made for it, and counsel (for they had roused one up to settle the form of order) opened :

' If your Honour pleases——' cut short by the interlocutor :

' Who the prince of darkness are you ?'

While the facts were being shortly put, the judge trod water—in order, however, to see the matter on both sides, diving under the boat with a splash that wetted the suitors to the skin.

The injunction formally applied for, the Court briefly said :

' Take it and be blanked to you !' turning on its back and floating down home.

Since the practice has been extended to the Common Law side, injunctions have been granted in almost as curious places. Mr. Justice Stephen has given one in a cab at Piccadilly Circus, being accidentally 'spotted,' and cabby hailed to stop. Mr. Justice Hawkins has done the same on Brighton Pier.

The last learned judge has the regrettable distinction of being the victim of a successful practical joke of the old Theodore Hook type, and if anything good can be said of such a nuisance, this was at least cleverly managed. At the very last moment at which advertisements could be delivered for insertion in the *Era*, one was handed in, postal-order attached, name and address — everything, in fact, outwardly correct. In it went, with its invitation to 200 ladies of the ballet desiring permanent appointments with good salaries to apply the following Monday, at 9 a.m., at Number 11, situate in the narrow gut in which Cleveland Row terminates at its Park End. As a matter of fact, not 200, but 2,000, damsels put in an appearance, backing outwards till they reached the Duchess of Cambridge's windows. Meantime the scene was lively all over ; the word was quickly passed that it was a ' something ' sell, and though only the front ranks could put the decorous butler in bodily fear by threats of doing for him and the house too, the rest could and did vent their disappointment in corresponding language, until police interference could clear away the crowd.

Sir Henry Hawkins is not a man to be trifled with, but investigation of all kinds failed to find out the perpetrator, so his very just and proper indignation was useless. It was, no doubt, the work of a single man, to whom the paradox of the learned judge's character suggested the joke, just as when Sheridan, reeling down the steps of the Thatched House, was pulled out of the gutter into which he had rolled by a watchman.

'What's your name, you drunken beast, eh ?'

Poor Sherry was never too far gone for a joke.

'Wi—Wi—Wilberforce.'

Many good stories centre round the late Mr. Baker Greene. A man of splendid abilities, he became soured in early life, and the acid then generated in his composition was ever afterwards freely given off to those around him, especially at 'The Savages ;' and when there entered there a very self-asserting personage who had worked his way up to the top by pure persistent push— we will call him ' Rose '—who thus addressed the ' Tabagie ' :

'You fellows will be glad to hear that I have at last got back our old family place in Kent, and when it has been done up I hope to see you all down there '—-

Then Baker Greene growled out :

' *What* do you call the place ?'

The smirking answer was :

'Oh! Rose Court !'

And the deep voice rejoined :

' *What number ?*'

He was for some years surgeon in a cavalry regiment, and when it went to India was continuously dunned by his long-suffering tailor, who in despair at last begged his debtor to take care of his health, otherwise 'what *will* become of me ?'

The reply was characteristic :

' I have received the hypocritical letter hoping that I will take care of my health in order that I may live to pay your bill !

' Hear, then, what your chances have been so far. I attend assiduously every cholera case in the cantonments, and make small-pox a special study. I swim every morning in a lake swarming with alligators. At the recent attack upon the hill-fort of Baghpore, I went with the forlorn hope, and was one of the three who returned unwounded. To-morrow morning, unaccompanied, and on foot, I shall go into the jungle, and wait for the man-eating tigress as she returns at dawn to her cave and her cubs. If it be she who falls, I shall spend my leave in the fever-haunted jungles of the Terai, following up big game, and if I survive that I shall cool myself after its heat by joining a party to ascend the peak of Dhàwàlagiri, whose snow slopes and glaciers are as stiff as your prices.'

However, the regiment came back with its doctor safe, and the tailor's anxieties and bill were both settled. But there was a kindly heart in him, as well as a rough and scathing tongue, and it was not heard without regret that, after correcting the proofs of his leader in the *Post*, Baker Greene had gone back to his chambers in Clement's Inn, and that there the enemy he had defied in its most appalling forms had overcome him in the guise of sleep.

A memorable example of what can be done by pure push in spite of natural drawbacks of speech, temper, and manner was the late Mr. Bottomley Firth. With most men the 'art of booing' has been the path to success. But Mr. Firth was not like that eminent statesman of whom an equally eminent philosopher remarked, 'The only thing I can't stand about him is his "blanked humility." ' He was congenitally afflicted with 'Ayrtonism' of the strongest kind. Speech being defined as consisting of words, accent, and manner, this special astigmatism consists in a civil dis-courtesy, a discourteous civility to which it is difficult to take positive objection at the time, but which nevertheless makes the person addressed even more uncomfortable than pure and simple contempt, though that, as the Hindoos say, will pierce the shell of a tortoise.

The name by which it is most easily diagnosed is somewhat unfairly taken from a sometime Commissioner of Public Works. The masquerade of courtesy existed before his time, and will never die out ; in fact, towards the close of his own life it had almost wholly departed from him, leaving behind only that amusing imitation which blossomed out in the reply of his footman to a caller, just after his master had been made a Privy Councillor, ' No, sir! the rite 'onorable gent has gone hout for a stroll in the grounds.'

But Mr. Firth was staunch, and even when pulled up before the Surrey Sessions Mess for employing six clerks to tout for business at as many Police Courts, could reply in his nastiest manner, 'I only do openly what you would all like to do, only you're afraid.'

How, with this unhappy manner, he got on at all is a mystery. As it was, it cost him heavily, bringing about the loss of his seat for Chelsea, and the Home Secretaryship, which would have followed re-election.

Many will remember the caricature of 'Bottomley's Bliss,' which came out when at last, after much opposition, he had achieved the long-worked-for goal—the Vice-chair of the London County Council, a salary of £2,000 a year, and an apparently free hand at his pet abomination the City Corporation.

But the dread irony of life was to appear again. The first vacation holiday was to see him, apparently full of health and vigour, breast the steep mountain path—stretched upon which, with up-turned face, the midnight searchers were to find his body, to be laid to rest, in a few days' time, in a quiet Swiss churchyard.

Such was the end. One more strong, self-confident, self-asserting man whose name is 'writ in water,' unless indeed it be remembered by the abolition of the London Coal Duty, carried out solely to weaken the Corporation of London's funds, but which, so far from cheapening coal, raised the price some twenty per cent. to consumers.

The Tichborne case has faded out of memory ; but all the mysteries about it were not cleared up, and one especially has always puzzled me : the Claimant's accurate local knowledge of the neighbourhood. During the trial, or trials, I was visiting Tichborne Church with a friend living some few miles off, and on quitting it met a labourer, who was hailed by my companion :

' So, Giles, you've turned round, and want to rob Sir Alfred ?'

The old man said :

' Zur, he be the man ; he comed up to me on Abbotstone Downs, and said, " Don't you know me, Giles ?" I said, " Zur, who might you be ?" " Roger Tichborne." " You baint Roger, though you're the height of him." " Ah," he said, " you forgot that time we had in Stratton Wood with that brindle bitch of yourn, and how we cleared out Sir Francis's game, and he wanted to transport the men who did it." Now, zur, this wur true. Roger and I and the bitch did it, but not a soul beside us knowed it; we were afeard. So I thought to catch 'im, and asked him what might be the name of that theer brindle bitch, dead years agone. He thought a bit and said, "WHYNOT." And so it wur. Yer see, they told me I should never rear the pup. I said, "Why not?" and the bitch pricked up her ears, and got the name.'

Endless stories of this kind were current in Alresford.

Another curious story was afloat about Jean Luie, to the effect that an eminent leading lawyer (not in the case) wrote down a few lines and said, 'That is what you've got to prove, now get a man to swear it.'

One of our stock perennial jokes is to assure each other that in the event of a scrape the speaker will defend the accused. The reply, of course, is quick:

'Non tali auxilio, nec defensoribus istis.' (Never with such help or such an advocate).

For the defence is not always easy work. One of Lefroy's counsel told me that in consultation the leader put their great difficulty. 'What we have

got to meet is the fact that the prisoner pledged
the pistol with which the deed was done, and
redeemed it the day before.'

I had occasion once to apply to the late Lord
Redesdale in reference to a private Bill then
before the House of Lords. I obtained an introduction from another peer, and having a heavy
life insurance, as well as one for personal injuries
in view of the chance of being bodily eaten alive,
boldly sent in my card.

There came out to me a waiter-like person in
very shabby dress clothes, with a tumbled white
tie resembling a broken halter.

'Now then, what do you want ?'

'To see Lord Redesdale.'

'Yes, I know ; but what's it all about ?'

'That I'll tell his lordship.'

'Stuff and nonsense ! tell it me.' I stared.
'Now then, *are* you going to tell me, or *are* you
not, for I shan't stop here ?'

He had my letter of introduction in his hand ;
it seemed impossible, but I hazarded the question :

'Do I address his lordship ?'

'Of course you do. Come, be quick !'

Then we got to business; but the burst of temper continued, and but for continually glancing at my letter of introduction, I should have had my nose snapped off. Poor Lord Redesdale! he was once bitten by a ferocious dog, and the result was that of Goldsmith's epigram:

> 'The man recovered of the bite;
> The dog it was that died.'

I could not make use with him of the quietus which worked like a charm on a late Alderman, whom I had to approach on a charitable errand, and who conducted himself generally like a mad dog. He was a timber merchant, and after I had received in silence a most offensive remark, I saw his stock out of the window, and merely said:

'Well, if you won't help me here, give me a price for 1,000 square Riga boards.'

This soothed his savage breast. I got what I wanted directly, but he did not get the order.

Another rough speaker was the late Mr. Justice Maule, who set the Temple on fire, and made the Divorce Act imperative. For he addressed a hawker convicted of bigamy thus: 'You have broken the laws of your country. You had a drunken unfaithful wife, the curse of your existence and her own. You knew the remedy the law gave you, to bring an action against the seducer, re- cover damages from him, then go to the House of Lords and get a divorce. It would have cost you altogether £1,000. You may say you never had a tenth of that sum : that is no defence in law. Sitting here as an English judge, it is my duty to tell you that this is not a country in which there is one law for the rich and another for the poor. Your sentence is one day's imprisonment.'

Lord Palmerston is said to have 'blessed the fellow.' Now, of course, there must be a cheap 'Divorce Act at once.' And a Divorce Act there was.

The Good Lord Shaftesbury, though of legal extraction and a barrister, never practised the law ; but some circumstances connected with him were much commented upon in our Inn. First of all perhaps, that ghastly irony of fate which made the ' Shaftesbury Avenue,' so-called as a record of the father's virtues, the scene, almost as soon as opened, of the suicide of his son and successor in the title.

Brought up in the Navy, full of the traditional frankness and *abandon* of a sailor, he was in every way his father's opposite, and when presiding at a public dinner, had been known to sing a comic song in place of the serious address which would have come from his father. What could have led him to charter a hansom and select this street of all others, to which his ancestral name had just been given, for the terrible use to which he applied his revolver when driving in it?

Some jokes, too, hung about the self-devoting philanthropist, though necessarily of the mildest kind.

His zeal sometimes ran into extremes. An absolutely full train forced him to travel third class, or be left behind. He took it meekly, as his wont was, not demanding a special train all to himself, as did Bishop Wilberforce in a similar case, when he asked: 'Do you really expect me to travel with my own servant?' But the good Earl improved the time by serious talk to his fellow - passengers, whose appreciation was expressed by one of them thus:

'I tell yer what it is, sir, you're a dashed good sort of an old buffer, and tries to do a lot of good.

And I'll pay yer back as well as I can. I'm a journeyman 'atter. Now if so be as when you buys a new 'at you puts a piece o' blottin'-paper hinside the linin', you'll find it'll last as long as three without it.'

Religious people, like all others in earnest, have, when in contact, their negative poles, just as when Bishop Philpotts, after a warm discussion with Archbishop Howley, ended with, ' I shall pray for your grace.'

'Anything but that, my lord, anything but that !'

Few of our present judges are strong enough to stand up against a really great advocate. We have seen in our own days one of this rank repeatedly told to ' Sit down,' yet calmly proceed with his objection, eventually to meet with Nemesis, and, like Charles XII., to collapse and experience utter defeat at the hands of a mere Lunacy Commissioner (so far as judicial rank goes), but whose calibre would have well suited the High Court Judgeship for which he was at one time ' fancied.'

Mr. Baron Huddleston has died so recently that

merely facts repeatedly commented on in public can be alluded to. Originally a private tutor, the 'Buck of the Bar,' as ignorant of law as was Dickens' Hindoo of skates, was raised to the Bench after much personal importunity, as a compensation for the crushing losses he had sustained in repeatedly contesting Norwich in the Conservative interest. Like Sir William Bovill, he has given us one more argument against promotions from purely political motives. Did not a clever and by no means overdrawn sketch of 'Mr. Baron Muddlesome' appear in *Punch* during the Belt case? Did not that victim actually initiate steps to hale up for contempt of court a very tough customer in the shape of a hard-hitting M.P., who edits a society paper and had made similar but even more rasping comments? the Judge only being dissuaded therefrom by strong pressure applied at the last moment before the perilous step was taken.

On two points the penultimate baron, one of whose expressed wishes was that he might survive the estimable Sir Charles Pollock and become the last of the barons, was always to be fetched— a peer or a pretty woman.

In Mrs. Besant's libel case it was amusing to contrast the different feelings which conflicted in the judicial mind. On the one hand, admiration and sympathy for the graceful mother telling with choked-down sobs how her only child—a baby girl—was taken away and taught to hate her for her opinions ; and, on the other hand, unconcealed detestation of those opinions and the form in which they were published. He had, too, other aversions—cycles and cyclists. For a splendid pair of horses, given on her marriage to his wife (fated, as *Truth* put it, to be ' born Beauclerk and Die Huddleston ') were started off by them near Richmond, and had to be shot. Hence, when an injured cyclist brought action against his manufacturer for hurts sustained from alleged bad workmanship, the baron woke up from a light slumber after lunch (his malady had not then seized him), and took the plaintiff in hand. The wheelman did not in the least understand what was going on, and when jerkily asked where the accident occurred, and the pace he was travelling, replied perkily :

' Esher Common, and twenty miles an hour.'

Huddleston, in his grittiest voice :

' Do you call that a proper place for such a pace as that ? How about passengers and horses ?'

'Oh yes!' (*loftily*). 'Our vice-captain runs it at five-and-twenty. People must get out of our way or take the consequences.'

The Judge called for the pleadings, took a technical objection, ruled in his own favour, and non-suited that cyclist there and then, with a glare of retribution.

The Baron did a terrible lot of mischief in one particular way. The confidential, gentlemanly talk of an accomplished man of the world, which, at the close of a long case, he addressed to a fagged and worried jury, usually had the fatal effect of making them see with his eyes and follow the latest word, that common refuge of weak minds. So that in the law reports the name of Huddleston, B., is appended to many a miscarriage of justice, and to some terribly bad law.

One last word for his dauntless pluck. Eaten up with gout, tormented with the stone, for which he was operated on some six-and-thirty times, he would be carried on men's shoulders up those never-ending-still-beginning stairs, of which the

Palace of Justice mainly consists, to the Bench. His leg on a chair, with a spasm of agony often shooting over his face, he would sit through a long case, only betraying by an occasional glance at the clock how the stroke of four and its consequent release was longed for.

He died at his post, with his drawn salary in his hand. His cremation at Woking was attended by friends who mourned the genial host and *raconteur*, but who had never suffered under him in a position he ought never to have filled.

Of far different metal was the accomplished lawyer who preceded him to the grave, and, in fact, was struck down on the very Bench by grim paralysis. No such shortcomings can be attributed to Mr. Justice Manisty, whose shyness—a Moses' veil which too often accompanies real merit—kept him too much in the background. Perhaps he never was happier than when he could take off his ermine and be found at daybreak with his salmon-rod, waist-deep in that much-loved Tyne on whose banks he was cradled. And he certainly never looked more miserable than when a 'funny' counsel was addressing the jury. After a dry cough, and a peculiar shruggle (the word is new, but exactly expresses the movement), the Judge buried himself in his notes, only looking keenly up when there seemed a chance of correcting the speaker, which he usually found or made. Then he struck a powerful discord by a sharp high-pitched squeak, full of native Northumbrian ' burr.'

How is it that dry law courts develop no wit? In every other case, healing Nature automatically evolves a remedy at some point or other. She places the dock close to the nettle; to use a pun of Lord Palmerston's on the name of a whilom President of the Board in his day: 'The Poor Law of this country has its antidotes as well as its Baines, and a d——d good thing too.' Dreary politics possessed Lord Derby, who could eulogize the Order of the Garter as having 'no d——d merit in it;' but Justice is as dull nowadays as a missionary meeting, save for Sir Henry Hawkins.

This learned judge is almost the only wit left on the Bench. When applied to, with hand uplifted to ear, by a person seeking to be let off a jury on the ground of deafness, his lips moved in a whisper :

' You may go.'

'Thank your Lordship,' came out at once, but the quick return was :

'Go into that box, sir !'

And a very good and attentive juryman he proved to be.

But off the Bench Sir Henry is said to 'act' his stories, as well as tell them. One which drifted into Hall from the Benchers' sanctum, or 'Parliament Chamber,' relates an application to him by a Jew, whose son had just received a severe sentence for perjury.

'Ah ! sir, my son is the very best boy in the world for de trut'. He always spoke de trut', and sometimes he was so fond of it, that he would tell more than de trut'.'

That seemingly self-generated contradiction which waits upon humanity like its shadow is very prominent in lawyers' lives.

Not to speak of Ryder, first Baron Harrowby, who died in the night between the making out of his long-sought peerage and its receiving the Great Seal, for lack of which the creation became void—is it not written in Campbell's 'Justices'? —a curious incident occurred when it pleased

Government to cut blocks with a razor and make Appeal Judges go circuit.

There was a murder case, and it fell to the lot of a learned and amiable Lord Chief Justice of Quaker parentage to pass the death sentence. An equity man all his days, he had never seen a black cap, and did not know how to put it on—the fumbling of his clerk, while pinning it round his master's wig, causing a ghastly hush—such as happened at Palmer's trial, when that dread emblem rolled out from beneath the Judge's desk on to the Court floor, eliciting from Cockburn the grim whisper, ' Ten to one on the rope.'

One more of later date. Another Lord Justice told off to try civil cases without a jury, sensibly and soundly lectured the Jubilee Plunger on the enormities of ruining name, fame, and pocket by racing, betting, and gambling. His very proper remarks appeared in due course in the *Standard*, but the very next column contained on the same level a report of the affairs of that very Judge's nephew and namesake, who had run the Benzon Course with the same result !

Once more. Men at the Bar envy Neverdun-talk, who won't read his briefs unless a special fee

be paid, and who swears strongly and impartially
at juniors, solicitors, and even the client himself,
when that much-perturbed person ventures into a
conference with his advocate.

One of these aspirants, young and handsome,
sought the honeyed path to success which leads
through marrying the daughter of a powerful
solicitor. Briefs came in merrily as a marriage-
bell at first ; but after a time the handsome face
was not always to be seen in the big cases, and
eventually a brief bearing his name was found in
other hands, with even then a mistake in the
pleadings, on which a great deal eventually
turned.

Counsel's metaphors often go astray, but they
seldom stick to their makers. One, however, is
remembered of a genial and kindly leader, now an
Indian Chief Justice ; the fun being increased by
its author never having been able to see where
the joke lay, though he is usually quick enough
to see the points in others' slips. It was in one of
the countless and costly Plymouth Tram Cases,
and the counsel for some of the defendants went
on, ' Really, gentlemen, after all, what have my
clients done ? They found themselves in the

same boat with people they did not like; they did what you 'and I would have done—*got out and ran away !'*

A curious outcome of our judicial system arises from the large number of the junior Bar who frequent the courts, and make up for the want of active personal practice by the study of Justice sitting armed in her sanctuary. Every judge feels himself more or less on his own trial, and when he sees the wigs turn round and whispers pass, knows that his ruling is undergoing criticism from keen observers. This is intensified on circuit, where there are at the most but two judges to occupy many men of their own training; and even the fierce light which beats upon a throne has its parallel in that then striking upon the Bench.

A judge's 'peculiarities,' however harmless, are special game, and it is even noticed that when one especial judge goes to church he provides a half-sovereign and a sixpence to be put in a plate or a bag, according to whichever is presented him. That representative of Her Majesty prefers the latter receptacle—unlike the Devonshire farmer who, being remonstrated with for abstention from divine service, replied, 'Us likes the Church very well, but us doesn't hold with they there nose-bags as they is always shoving in front of us.'

Nemesis, however, lies in wait for the silent critics as they sit in censure. Did not the other day, in the Appeal Court, a poor demented barrister rise and address the Lords Justices apropos of nothing, and have to be forcibly removed ?—brain, as well as heart, sickened by hope deferred and unbroken silence.

Some judges have stories they are fond of repeating in court. Here is one of Sir James Stephen's. A witness stated that his evidence was corroborated by that of his servant, who had lived with him thirty years. This pleased every-one, and the judge remarked it said much for both master and man, and that they must get on comfortably together. But the witness fidgeted and replied, 'For the first ten years there never was a better servant ; in the second, he became a confidential but too inquisitive friend ; and since then he has been a not-quite-altogether-unbearable master.'

But the successes and failures of litigants, or the significant comment as to what the costs

will be, and how much will come to the victor
when he has reckoned with his solicitor, are not
the only matters discussed at table. There is a
third, though not often - occurring class, where
Themis, sitting armed in her throne of Justice,
gets fairly humbugged and rendered powerless.

Some years ago a case of this kind came before
an amiable and painstaking, though by no means
strong, judge. The issue was a simple one. A
contractor to the Local Board of Slopperton-cum-
Ditchingham had sold his business, and the purchaser rued his bargain to such an extent that he
sued the vendor for a return of his money and
swinging damages for wilful misrepresentation.
Evidence, chiefly of the carters themselves, was
adduced to prove that in the profitable part, the
road-watering contract, the supposed self-acting
telltales of the carts were altered by any one of
some half-dozen processes of the simplest kind,
and made to register, say, 23 for 13, 29 for 22, and
so on, which the guileless superintendent accepted
as genuine, and certified for payment accordingly.

The evidence was numerous, cumulative, fitted
well together, and was not touched by cross-

examination, even upon personal peccadilloes and suggestions of eye-opening gifts and beer ; and the jury at the close of the day got restless, and wanted to confer with the judge. That dignitary, however, much to his own subsequent disgust, repressed the feeling, but added, in his very sternest manner (it would not have fluttered a fly with the least presence of mind), that on the following morning he would get to the bottom of it all.

That morning came ; the court was crowded, and reporters sat with sharpened pencils ; but the plaintiff's counsel calmly informed the Judge that the case was settled. Plaintiff had apologized, withdrawn the charge, and would pay all costs.

The case was mysterious, and quite explicable if a strong organization with a common interest at stake, and a heavy purse to back it, had intervened to prevent awkward things coming out ; but no such body was in evidence, and odder still, no press report of the case appeared! Still, somebody lost some £2,000, and in ignorance where it came from, the wonder why local taxation everywhere continually increases in spite of attempts to disguise it by increased valuations, is easy to understand.

Court jokes, however, are few and far between, judges being wary of hitting up balls for counsel to catch.   Sometimes the story of carrying-guts-to-a-bear is warmed up again, as when Mr. Justice Witty sat upon a junior thus :

' Do you expect *me* to teach *you* manners, Mr. Boswell ?'

' Certainly not, my lord.'

The current talk is such as the story about Lord Stowell—a man who liked a good dinner at other people's expense, and of whom it was said, ' He could drink any *given* quantity of wine.'

Lord Westbury comes in for a lion's share, and with him these illustrations of Temple sneers must conclude.

In the north window of that cold-catching and rheumatic edifice, the library, which was built by his wife's brother, there appear the coats-of-arms of all the then benchers—among them a red boar, the crest of Mr. O'Malley, one amongst many of the Chancellor's special aversions.   When inspecting the window, Lord Westbury asked the librarian, with a malicious smile :

' Whose cognizance may that be ?'

' Master O'Malley's, my lord.'

' What might you call it now—a red pig ?'

' It looks so, my lord.'

' Dear me ! how very appropriate for a sanguinary bore !'

Pass we on to pleasanter topics.

Having about it so many traces of the old secret society in whose seat it sits, the Middle Temple has a greater sociality among its members than have its sister Inns, save perhaps Gray's from its smallness. Barristers and students dine together, selecting, if they please, their own associates ; so that a mess is, in some cases, practically made up of the same men term after term.

For the information of non-members, I may say that in the Inns of Court the diners in hall are grouped in messes of four, to each of which is allotted either soup or fish, a joint, pastry, cheese, one or two bottles of wine, with beer *ad libitum.* On grand nights and feasts a bottle of champagne is added, and the loving-cup passes round, one member known as ' Captain,' having a nominal presidency, and speaking as head of the mess.

Traces exist of the old common life, when the

carver cut off the portions on the great table, and any fancied unfairness could be rectified on the instant. Thus if a mess complains of the quality of the viands or of the wine, the Captain causes the dish or bottle objected to to be carried up at once to the high table with his private card, whereupon the Master Treasurer, or his representative, is bound to taste it, and, if the grounds be sufficient, to cause it to be replaced by a dish or bottle of proper quality. Nor can any student leave the hall without the president's permission first obtained ; the barrister, however, leaves at his own pleasure. Every man wears the gown of his rank, whether Queen's Counsel, barrister, or student, and in none of his many official dresses does the heir to the Throne look better than when he dons his silken robes to dine in the Inn which has the honour to own him as master of its Bench.

As we have said, barristers and students mess together ; in the other Inns they not only dine at separate tables, but sit in order of seniority—a system under which sociality and friends dining together, even for one day, is impossible. Under our Middle Temple rule friendships can be kept up, and made to continue, after hall is closed or student life at an end. Moreover, with an occasional lapse into dreary 'shop,' jokes, stories, and epigrams pass round, coupled with just that spice of personality which tickles without scratching—experiences from all parts of the world (for the Middle is the great Colonial Law School) interchange freely, so that in the hall of the dismal science itself there are heard peals of laughter, the best of all digestives.

Not, however, so much at the benchers' place of honour, still less at the dismal table where sit the ancients, eight in number, like the benchers in order of strict seniority, who receive a somewhat better dinner than the rest of us. A member who by chance got admission to it has left a record of his sufferings. Essaying to break the monotony by a joke in two syllables, he found his neighbour deaf; the man opposite wanted it repeated ; and, this treat over, the fourth asked it to be explained. He was not even a Scotchman, either!

That in the general hall sociality is congenital and continuous is in evidence by the discovery, when the old oak floor was taken up, of numbers of dice which had fallen through the chinks, most of them cogged, if scandal is to be credited. At that time, however, men lived in chambers, saw their clients there, whether solicitors or private persons, and dined and supped in hall, as we shall shortly see, the church serving as a kind of general meeting - room. The possession, too, by each bencher of a key to hall and garden, admitting therein both by night and day, carries us back to the far-off past when men slept there as well, on the rush-strewn floor, what time the great lantern was but a chimney for the great brazier in the hall, which last, indeed, survived in Westminster School sixty years since.

But the great centre of life, whether human or animal, around which everything turns, is the dinner, the social meal — sacramental in the original sense of the word, the Roman military oath of fellowship and obedience. Just as a herd of cattle give a new-comer the cold shoulder till use and wont—the French *tout casse, tout passe, tout lasse*—have broken the ice ; just as a party of Englishmen abroad look askance at a stranger who joins their party, unless he be especially well introduced, so the unwritten law that a meal taken in common implies something in the nature of a mutual connection has preserved some traces of the old Templar fellowship in the Term dinners or 'commons,' as they are technically called, now, as formerly, the only channel which leads to the Bar. They now are held for four Terms of about three weeks each, in place of the whole year as of old ; and during this period the parliaments are held, in which the society renews itself by the election of benchers, the admission of new members, and finally calls to the Bar.

In every other country save in this land of anomalies, the Judicial Bench reserves to itself the admission of those who are to plead before it. Here, however, admission has been committed by it to the four learned societies of the Middle and Inner Temples, Lincoln's and Gray's Inns, the only power reserved to the judges being the right of appeal to them, which any disbarred barrister can avail himself of, as against the benchers of his Inn, who have to appear and justify their conduct. This dates back to a time when lawyers were priests, and had a consecration as such.

The benchers have lately taken to 'screening,' *i.e.*, publicly posting up the names of barristers behind in their fees. as if this were an offence almost worthy of disbarral. The better plan would be, as in a club, to let the name drop off, unless a hint could be taken from the sister Inn— the Inner Temple. On the Jubilee, a member long in arrears applied for his seat in hall. He was kept amused until his bill could be made out, when he absolutely paid the £40 arrears claimed from him, in order to get his dinner-ticket.

Students have no status and no seniority, and can be expelled without appeal. This was amusingly brought out by accident one day after dinner. The reader of grace, a man not strong in health, had dined incautiously, and gone beyond the ' truly rural ' point. He made rather a hash of it, spoke thick, and caused a titter, resulting in the advent of the big head-porter to the table whence it came.

' The Bench desire to know who it was that laughed, as, if a barrister, they'll suspend him, and, if a student, they'll expel him.'

No candidates, however, appeared on these terms.

But so lately as two centuries back the Inn had a distinctly collegiate life. A barrister's ' diet ' cost him £6 10s. a year for dinner and supper, except on Tuesdays and Fridays, when the last meal for some cause was omitted. The meal was almost invariably loins of mutton—vegetables, even potatoes, being apparently absent—bread and beer, the last served in green earthen drinking-pots specially made for the society, and which survive in the memory of Mr. Hume, the venerable and cheery 'wash-pot' (may he long retain the ancient office he has held for some half-century). For cheese the members paid the butler weekly. Once in the year there was a breakfast of calves' heads, for which one shilling a head was paid ; but, as this was turned into a dinner in 11 James I., there could have been no connection with the fate of Charles I. suggested, as in the after-days of Fox and Sheridan.

The Inn found the provisions and certain other requisites—'table linnen,' 'coles,' pewter vessels, and wages for officers and musicians, including the panyer-man, who sounded his horn, and still sounds it, in all the courts as a summons to meals— a custom now only retained in the Black Prince's College, Queen's, Oxford. Trenchers and table cutlery are not mentioned. Could the members have provided their own? Wooden trenchers seem to have held their ground till about 1825, according to my informant, Mr. Hume aforesaid.

The butler, by the way, was also a 'censor,' having it in charge to report to the Bench all persons who incurred a fine of one shilling by coming into hall in a hat, or church without a round cap, or who outside those sacred places, instead of the said round cap (still to be seen in the portraits of the period, and which even now survives in the fatal judicial black cap), wore hats, as also swords, boots, long hair, or other frivolities. The chronicler dryly comments that the said butler was commonly out of the young gentlemen's favour.

As to the dinner itself, it was approached with as much ceremony and sacredness as, in Lord Brougham's days, the Bishops accorded to it in the House of Lords, quitting the House at dinner-time, whatever the subject under discussion, and receiving his sneer—'men whose gods are their bellies and whose bellies are their gods.'

We have spoken of the panyer-man, or bread-man—a most important personage ; indeed, as the waiters in the Inner Temple are called panyers to this day, it would appear as if no member helped himself to the staff of life, but had to call specially for it. The panyer-man's duty was to fetch the bread from Westminster, and then sound his horn in all the courts to call members to dinner from their respective chambers, each of which held two members, the benchers alone occupying a single one. Chambers apparently were used for sleeping purposes only, the hall, church, and library serving as common rooms, where clients could be seen and business done, as in the days of Old St. Paul's, by the general public, who make a lounge of its successor, varying sauntering, sandwich - eating, and sleep by an occasional suicide.

The library, however, seems not to have served much useful purpose ; it was open, but members stole the books ! No librarian's stipend is mentioned, and their care was probably everybody's business, with the to-be-expected result. The garden, too, was a pleasant lounge in fine weather, and perhaps as famed for its roses as Ely House in Hatton Garden for its strawberries. Anyhow, the gardener received £6 13s. 4d., or two-thirds of the pay of the lordly cook and butler, ' to dress the garden.' So somebody took pleasure in its looking nice, as we know the illustrious Bacon did in the Gray's Inn garden, where the trees he planted still remain.

To return to the maimed but still imposing ceremony of our present 'commons.' The horn has sounded, and passing strangers have heard what they may well take as

' the cry
Of dying porkers in their agony.'

The hall fills—it holds some 300—with barristers and students in their respective gowns. The Bench have assembled in their parliament chamber, and arranged themselves in the order of seniority—a rule to which until lately our genial Prince was subjected, as he has walked behind the Master of the Temple, Dean Vaughan, and the treasurer of the year. We may here note that a handsome parcel-gilt loving cup is the form in which H.R.H. refunded to the Inn the fees which accrued to him when he served the office of treasurer in the Jubilee year.

Preceded by the mace, the emblem of authority everywhere, replacing the consular fasces, the procession enters the hall by its lower end, and walks up it, in that double file, taken from the monastic Templars, of which the channels worn in the stone-paved entrance of their chapter-house by Westminster Benedictines attest the universality. Not for our benchers, however, to pass a door where, beneath the hammer-headed nails, can still be felt the skin of the fair-haired Dane who plundered the Confessor's treasury, and whose flayed-off epidermis still remains as a warning against sacrilege, or, rather, being caught in the act of committing it. All have risen in their places, the Benchers move up to the daïs, and, on a sign given, three strokes with a wooden mallet upon an oak table replace the three blows of a lance-butt used in Templar times. The grace itself is not like that of the Inner Temple— ' Benedictus benedicat,' with, for return thanks, ' Benedicite benedicto,' but a post-Reformation one adapted from Luther's ' Tischbot,' and printed in Day's black-letter Psalter, 1571, in the possession of the writer. A profane wag, however, questions this ; it cannot be Luther's, because it is *after Knox.*

The mace of authority then disappears ; all are brethren, and, with closed doors, the meal is eaten in peace. No longer, however, in silence, while the reader, still appointed as a matter of form every spring and autumn, replaces by legal syllogisms the Templars' patristic instruction. That also has passed away, and the friendly social intercourse already adverted to replaces it. But everything has an end, and so has dinner.

The mace is brought back into hall; the assembly rises. The three mystic knocks are again struck, and between the ranks of their fellow-members, but on the opposite side to which they entered, the Bench return to their parliament chamber, with more or less cheering. As this prevails on Grand Nights when distinguished persons are invited guests, and, with the bencher told off to each, have to elbow their way through a narrow passage of cheering men clapping their hands, strangers are sometimes puzzled, and the dignified look of a Spanish ambassador, who followed close upon H.R.H., did not indicate that sympathy with the fun which the Prince's smiling countenance displayed, at the time, too, when his elbow was gently pressing back the exuberant loyalty of a big and hearty ex-Navy man, in order to get past him.

One curious reminder of the sacramental nature

of the dinner has passed away within the last few years, and as Serjeant's Inn has perished also, and a new judge no longer has to resign his Inn on his appointment, it can never be restored.

When a bencher of the Middle Temple was raised to the Judicial Bench during term, he dined at the high table in the usual way ; but at the close of dinner he rose and passed down the hall between shouted 'Good-bye's!' The doors swung open, and, as he passed out of them, the bell tolled solemnly as for a parting soul. He had gone from among us !—he was no longer of us !

Sir George Honyman's was the last instance of this ancient form of 'send-off.'

Our Inn is the only one which 'calls to the Bar' in public before dinner, the others performing that ceremony in the benchers' private room, and at dessert. On the appointed day of term— the same in all the Inns, because Bar seniority depends upon it — the music gallery above the famous oak-screen, which one would like to believe made of real Armada oak, is filled with ladies and friends of the candidates. These candidates enter the hall following the benchal procession, stand in front of the daïs, and on their names being called, step forward and sign a small book. They afterwards dine in hall in the wigs and Bar-gowns they have donned for the first time, conspicuous among the rest, who dine as usual ' in their hair.'

Until the last few years, there then ensued a very fair revival of the ancient revels, in which, in the same old hall, Queen Elizabeth had danced with Sir Christopher Hatton.

The benchers gave up the hall to the newly-admitted, with permission to invite outside strangers to their respective call-parties. As no check existed even on the quantity of wine, or even whisky, the fun got sometimes fast and furious; in fact, a kind of small Saturnalia as well within as outside hall.

On one occasion, an unwise city policeman who ventured to interfere was captured by a sally from within, treated to his own 'frog's march' face downwards, and laid face upwards on a table till he had drunk a bottle of champagne (sitting up for the purpose) to the health of the Inn, after which he was restored to his inspector right side up, and the threatened storming the hall by that functionary to recover his man abandoned.

On another, an almost Don Juanic shudder fell on the noisy assembly when a former gigantic head-porter was seen to hale a barrister up the hall by the collar, and grimly say :

' By Jove, sir ' (only it wasn't Jove), ' I've a good mind to kill you !'

Interference promptly stopped that result. It turned out that both parties had taken quite enough, but the thing would not have happened if Anak's young and pretty wife had, as she really ought to have, absented herself, on such an uproarious night, from hall, and not tempted the kiss which the barrister thought he might snatch with impunity, not knowing, as the lady did, that the husband was round the corner, and on the look-out for what, however, only once came off.

Our Inn servants are both deaf and blind to a joke, so one made by the lady just referred to shall be given here. Mrs. Bye had presented her big husband with twin sons, and was asked by men in hall what their names were to be. The answer came pat :

' Don't bother me now ; I'll tell you—*Bye and Bye.*'

But the benchers' perfectly legitimate fear for the safety of the hall led to the prohibition of smoking. Members resented it, and although the Prince, when he honours us with his company, causes dessert to be served round, lights his own cigar, and all who smoke follow suit, the chain has been finally snapped, and Call Night is no longer a scene to be remembered, but has become one more of many memories.

Still, a revival of it was attempted in 1890, as a close to the treasurership of the deservedly-respected Mr. Justice Day. Dessert was served in hall, an extra bottle of wine issued, and the benchers remained to take dessert, while from a prettily-arranged bosquet of palms and flowers the Inns of Court Amateur Musical Society played some very excellent music for a meeting which, it is to be hoped, future treasurers will provide at their own retirement, even if it be not, as in the last, at the learned judge's sole expense, but at the cost of the Inn, which does practically nothing for the social comfort of its members, save, perhaps, in a lately-opened 'common room' below the library, where, for the nominal charge of half-a-guinea, members obtain club privileges, such as they are. But the rooms are small, wholly unsuited for the purpose, while numerously-signed petitions to the authorities for better and more accommodation have hitherto fallen on deaf ears. It is to be hoped that a remonstrance lately got up may be more favourably received—a hope that has borne a flattering tale so far.

An authority that very properly shows so much consideration for outsiders as to give up half of a very small garden for the poor little waifs of the Strand, can hardly disregard much longer the better-founded, because of right, request of its fellow-members, some of whom must hereafter sit in their own high places.

Owing doubtless to former members' weakness for abstracting them, noted by Dugdale, there are really no old nor valuable books in the Library— no first folio of Shakespeare or 'Paradise Lost,' nor any other of the silver medals of book-wormism. One pamphlet, found in a volume bound up with others, from the press of the Schoolmaster of St. Albans, alone represents in its way the day-dawn of English Typography, though Wynkyn de Worde dwelt in Fleet Street at the sign of the ' Sonne,' next Middle Temple Gate, and the site of his ' chapel ' is even now in the trade, and occupied by the evergreen Messrs. Butterworth.

Indeed, new books are almost as scarce as are the old. Not only is the supply starved, but the library committee have a short way with suggestions for additions, in this form :

' If the book be anything better than a hash-up of what is already in the library, it will run to a second edition, and then be better worth buying,' a snub which sends the applicant off to the British Museum Reading - room, or some other place where the new book, which should deal with the point on which he is engaged, may be looked at. It causes a little loss of time and temper, but the Inn is a corporation, and, like charity, is not easily provoked.

A little improvement has occurred of late, and it was time, too, as the National Reading-room authorities in Great Russell Street complain bitterly of the number and quality of the law students who crowd in there by reason of the defects of their own proper libraries. A few scraps of paper for notes have lately been placed on the tables, with a grave caution against using too many of them, and a new steel pen can be obtained by application to the courteous librarian in not more than five minutes at the outside ; but every precaution is taken against general paper-staining or literary composition, although some good books of reference exist, and Mr. Hutchinson and his assistant spare no pains to make them as useful as possible to readers. But a set of letter scales and weights have been often applied for, and so far in vain.

George III. is credited with the saying that lawyers know no more law than other folks ; they only know the books which contain it. Expanding this idea, one of our members gifted with subtle French wit hazarded the suggestion that the water-buckets in the library had an intimate connection with the library committee's heads, inasmuch as both were M. T., referring, of course, to the initials of the Inn, not to any other empty idea.

Hitherto no reference has been made to the Temple Church, for the ' snakes in Iceland ' reason, as few of the regular diners in hall, from whom these illustrations of ' Still Life ' have been drawn, ordinarily attend it.

Although the structurally oldest place of worship in London, and a rallying-point to Americans, with whom it ranks in interest second only to Bunyan's Chapel at Bedford, and the cottage from which sprang the Washingtons, there is but little, apart from its antiquarian interest and Jeffreys' organ, to comment upon.

It is the joint property of the two Temple Inns, and supported from their own funds. They have offered large sums to the Crown for the purchase of the advowson, so as to have the patronage of the ' mastership '; but the days are past when a minister to serve a dependant could barter away to a then Duke of Portland an enormous slice of Sherwood Forest for the living of St. Mary-le-bone. The value of the Temple incumbency is small, and a good house is the best part of it ; but its holder is styled ' Master of the Temple,' and on Grand Nights leads the procession up the hall, while princes of the blood, ambassadors, and dukes walk meekly behind this practical demonstration of Church before State. It must be said, however, that successive Lord Chancellors have rarely jobbed this piece of patronage, and have usually appointed men more or less worthy of the post ; always good preachers too — witness Dr. Benson, the port-drinker, whom Sydney Smith liked better ' in the bottle than in the wood.'

It requires a man of some tact to get on in it, as the control of all but purely spiritual matters vests in a joint committee of the ecclesiastically-minded benchers of both Inns. These have opinions of their own, so that friction may arise out of anything, or even nothing.

An instance of this occurred lately. The venerable scholar and liberal-minded theologian who now fills the pulpit gave out therefrom : ' It does not seem like a Sunday without a communion, and henceforth it will be administered weekly in place of fortnightly.' The musical voice had not reckoned with its church committee, and the old practice remains unchanged.

The preacher, too, has repeatedly bewailed that there is but one collection in the year, and this of late introduction—Hospital Sunday ; but the governing body spare the worshippers' purses for all that.

In a church where one of the Inns provides

Greek Testaments among the service-books, the present master wisely continues his old Harrow School practice of ' no dogma,' and the whisper goes that he is not quite deaf to the (anonymous or otherwise) post-cards, which are the sole refuge against tyranny of the oppressed and perfunctorily dumb members of his audience.

The joint committee, whom an Archdeacon's fifty minutes finally ' fetched,' have now ordered that the door shall be opened for egress during sermon-time if demanded, but fuller liberty than this is still required. The bidding prayer, or a minute or two before it, should be accepted as the moment when those who come to pray might not feel forced to remain to utter something quite the other way ; but withdraw without being the target of all eyes, while the preacher pauses in the midst of a mellifluous passage to look plaintively at his sheep making for the fence-door. Anyone can leave St. Paul's Cathedral at any time, the orator distinctly understanding that his sole hold upon his hearers is matter and manner, by some such sermon as Mrs. Caxton preached to her son, ' Why life was given, how life shall end, and how Heaven stands open to us every day.'

Even such an orator—are there any left, save perhaps that great Puritan* whose long-continued struggle against a fatal disease, now run its course, may suggest even to Professor Huxley that there is, after all, some power in an Avalanche of Prayer? —even such an orator may unwittingly come in for a repetition of what happened to a great preacher lately deceased. He had held forth with wonted fervour in St. Paul's on 'Bearing one another's burdens,' and the next day received a request from an auditor for the loan of a £5 note on the terms of his text. The ecclesiastic, who died unmarried, and worth some· £50,000, replied, with practical worldly wisdom, that his discourse was of general, not particular, application.

It may be added here, as not generally known, that for a few minutes after morning service the attendants at church can walk unaccompanied through the ancient Middle Temple Hall and the parliament chamber and corridors, these last reserved at all other times for the masters of the Bench alone. This of itself is one of the sights of London ; but on a Sunday, when nearly every-

* The great Puritan has, since this was written, passed away.

thing else of the kind is closed, but few avail themselves of the privilege.

In the extensive alterations made half-a-century ago, some of the bodies buried in the church were exhumed. They were sewn up in leather, and some of the skulls still retained their long fair hair, apparently worn unclipped when in life as Nazarites. More care was taken with these interments than with that of Sir William le Bachelier, Grand Preceptor of Ireland, who was starved to death in the penitential cell, a dreary place of solitary confinement formed within the thick wall of the Round Church, only four feet six inches long, and two feet six inches wide, so narrow and small that a person cannot stand up nor lie down within it. It looks into the church through two arrow-slits visible from below, facing the altars of the Round and Long Church respectively. In this narrow prison disobedient brethren were confined in chains and fetters, 'in order that their souls might escape from the eternal prison of hell.' The hinges and catch of a door firmly attached to the doorway of this dreary chamber still remain, and at the bottom of the stair is a stone recess or cupboard for the prisoners' bread and water.

On a charge of malversation the unhappy Sir William languished for eight weeks, until Heaven granted the mercy which its self-styled servants denied. When stripped of the habit of his order, because excommunicate, his naked body was carried at dawn of day to the Court of the House, now on the south side of the church, and there buried.

The Inn plate is scanty in quantity, poor in design, and insignificant in weight for so large and important a body. Few of either treasurers or benchers have kept their names green by memorials in silver, except, as has been said, the Prince of Wales.

One tradition is that the original pre-Commonwealth Inn plate was sent to Oxford to be melted down to swell Charles I.'s military chest. Another has it that it was secretly kept back and buried in the garden in a place whose locality has been forgotten. Both traditions are unvouched for and *primâ-facie* unlikely. Lawyers are equally bad at giving or losing anything of their own, and the fair presumption is that either there was no plate worth mentioning, or that it shared the fate of the books in the library.

But there are two little snuff-boxes belonging to the senior messes in hall, bestowed by former members, which have not shared the fate of that traditional bequest to provide oysters when in season for the general body during term time in hall, a bequest that, according to report, has been quietly diverted exclusively to the governing body.

One of these snuff-boxes, of silver, was given by the late Mr. Charles Beavan to the Ancients' Mess, where he constantly dined until raised to the Bench. A bequest of £500 for a stained-glass window in the church is also an evidence that he loved his Inn, as did an Athenian the City of the Violet Crown.

The second snuff-box, of round tortoiseshell, was the gift to the next senior messes by the late Mr. Hans Buck, of Volunteer Artists' Rifle Corps fame. It bears also some initials—IN to IB, 1677, and a legend has grown up that this signifies a gift by Sir Isaac Newton to Barrow; but the letters are of palpable Regency shape, and the epigram made upon it, 'If not exactly a fraud, it is, at all events, tortous,' is a joke not to be understanded of the laity.

From its nature as an unattached profession, the law is the only one open to the many educated men who, for whatever reason—dislike to or non-success in the occupation for which they were originally trained—desire a change. Comparatively few enter it from mercantile pursuits; the present Lord Bramwell and Mr. William Willis, Q.C., are perhaps the most conspicuous instances. Men from the services come to qualify themselves as judge advocates, medical men as coroners or public health officers. Consuls abroad, and the Indian Civil Services almost to a man, find the Bar degree an aid to advancement.

But it has always had an attraction for clergymen, and a special obstacle to their admission as students is provided; but still they come, from the married curate who has taken the ruinous step of 'verting,' to others who have resigned orders with a view to resuming lay life or entering Parliament.

One very genial ex-rector, with this last object in view, is among us. His fame, even when beneficed, was in bull-dogs and St. Bernards (will it be hereafter in Rotherhithe?), and to him the writer owes the correct text of the jingle relating to his former parish church :

> ' There was an old lady of Cheadle,
> Who, in church, sat down on a needle ;
> 'Twas deeply imbedded, but luckily threaded,
> And was promptly drawn out by the beadle.'

Much dissatisfaction is felt with the manner of electing the governing body. Though it consists of many very eminent men, they are mostly too busy to spare time to attend to its interests, which, indeed, from a commercial point of view, their peculiar education and habits of thought are not fitted to advance. Making three-halfpence into twopence for other people is a gift few eminent lawyers possess. Hence the direction of affairs is more or less in the hands of men who rarely attend two consecutive Bench meetings or ' Parliaments,' so that the direction of things is always changing.

The admission is by co-optation, and not unfrequently a gentleman is elected as being, let us say, the son of a former bencher, or for some other unknown reason, of whom not a soul in the Inn has ever heard. The ring is hard to break through, and it is said that it required a strong personal effort by Lord Coleridge and others to bring in an outsider, long and honourably known as the chief law-reporter for the leading journal.

And while there is no impeachment of the accounts, it is felt that the resources of the Inn are somewhat slovenly managed.

The Inn servants seem to be fairly, but not extravagantly, paid.

But the management is 'sleepy' to the last degree, and it is felt that the members generally ought to be admitted to some greater benefits from the income of the Inn, as well as a voice in the selection of those who administer it.

And there is a limpness, too, in their proceedings, due, doubtless, to the changing in personality of those who attend them. They cannot realize the American story of 'Emigrants requires firmness.'

The narrator is supposed to be a Yankee skipper hailing from Liverpool.

' No, sirree, emigrants requires firmness. The last time I hev' out o' Leverpool there kem aboord a cuss, and, says I to myself, " If Sam Skysail don't have to heave that beggar to, there ain't no sech things as Amŭrican institooshuns. Emigrants eats their rations whether they're sick or well, and they're death on the medicine chest." Afore we'd been out three days, he comes aft, and says he to me, " Cap'en, I feels bad." " Now," says I, " look here, my man, take a friend's advice, and get better right away, or you'll have to begin at the top left-hand corner of the med'cine chest, and go right away through to the bottom." " Cap'en," says he, " you'll never be that hard !" " Jerusalem," says I, " but I will. You've got to go through the whole of it, from Pelgrim Fathers to Benjamin Harrison, as a man may say." And sure enough he did, and it wasn't till he got to the third row of bottles that he caved in, and got better.'

There is but little more to add. We are one of the few unreformed lawyers' corporations, just like lawyers generally, who are always urging clients to make wills, yet not unfrequently die intestate, even if they don't have their wills buried with them, like Lord St. Leonards, or leave them to be caustically interpreted by a successor like Sir George Jessel, as did Lord Westbury. The Master of the Rolls loved him little, and would premise, ' It is a dictum of Lord Westbury's that every clause in a will can be interpreted. I wish he would show me how to do it with his own.' The Chancellor had kept the Master of the Rolls four years waiting for silk.

There are said to be no trust-deeds of our Inn ; the property is held by co-ownership, and the accounts are, like General Booth's, taken on trust. There is some advantage in this, as when the irregularities of a former official were left to be gone through by one of the benchers, the terrible treble muddle which resulted had to be dealt with, as Louis XIV. did with the bills for the building of Versailles—thrown in the fire.

The pen of one who knows and loves his Inn— there are many like him, he is glad to say—might adduce many other vestiges which go to prove that with the Templar's House—for which, only 200 years ago, they paid to St. John's, Clerken- well, £10 7s. 8d. as rent—the Middle Templars have kept, and even now keep up, much of the forms and even spirit of the Warrior Monks whose faults, whatever they were, were surely atoned for by the terrible tortures in which their last survivors bravely died protesting innocence. But enough has been said to show to the crowds of our Indian and Colonial fellow subjects who throng its doors the magnificent heritage they are admitted to share in, and to encourage them to prove themselves worthy successors of those who have gone before them in the dear old lovable Inn.

TEMPLUM QUAM DILECTUM,

FLOREAT IN SÆCULA.

INDEX

A

B

THE END.

BILLING AND SONS, PRINTERS, GUILDFORD.
J. D. & Co.